Rosemary in Bloom

Khristy Reibel

Open Books

Published by Open Books

Cover image © by Edoma /Shutterstock.com

ISBN-13: 978-1948598095

1942

Rosemary

As the first light crept through the open window, a subtle outline of the bedroom took shape. A cardinal began its morning call, bringing the world out of its slumber. Rosemary lay, staring at the ceiling, and wished she could fall back into her dream and drift into blissful unawareness. The mysterious dream man had just been about to kiss her when she awoke. But the sun was relentless. The room lightened in gradients. She looked over at her older sister, Virginia, her lips pursed in sleep, unaware of the dawning day.

Rosemary sighed. The sound of Virginia's breathing and the birds' chirping both lulled her to sleep and prodded her out of bed. A warm August breeze rustled the curtains, providing little relief from the heavy humidity that coated everything with a sticky film. A typical summer day in Illinois.

Rosemary tossed her arm over her head and willed herself back to sleep, if only for a few more minutes. She wanted to be kissed, to feel his lips on hers. She hoped he looked like Cary Grant when the dream haze cleared. As she nestled into her pillow, she heard the rhythmic clacking of steel wheels along a metal track. The morning coal train rumbled towards Rosemary's house, rolling to drop the coal off at Owen's Glass factory. It was a constant reminder of the work she needed to do.

Rosemary's white foot stuck out from under the light cotton sheet draped over her. She squeezed her eyes closed, concentrating on her dream. She felt a tickle on the bottom of her foot. Her eyes snapped open, and she jerked to a sitting position. Her brother stood at the end of her bed, grinning like a mischievous schoolboy, his blue eyes sparkling.

"Why do you do that, Junie?" she grumbled. Everyone called him Junie, short for Junior—William Junior. He acted like a child, rather than an eighteen year old.

"Ssshhh!" He held his finger to his lips, tilting his head toward Virginia. She had returned home from the night shift at Owen's, where they worked. Virginia was twenty-two and had moved home with her two small children to get away from an abusive husband. That was a year ago and she was still trying to get on her feet. All of the children worked except Jack, the youngest. He was still in school. Rosemary had quit school in March when she turned sixteen to help support the family. Money was scarce. Their father was in a sanatorium, recovering from tuberculosis. With the children to support and no income, their mother was forced to send them off to work, one by one.

Rosemary rolled her eyes and turned away from Junie, looking out at the pale clouds creeping across the sky. She didn't want to think about her father being sick, the responsibilities heaped on her shoulders. She just wanted to dream.

"Come on, you grouch. We've got to go get the coal before we go to work," Junie whispered and slapped at her legs.

Rosemary threw back the sheet and crawled out of bed. She pulled on denim dungarees and a button up white shirt. She looked in the mirror above the chest-of-drawers. Her ash blonde hair was mashed against her head on one side and curling in all directions on the other. She shook out her hair and wrapped a blue bandana around her head, tying it at the crown.

After lacing up a pair of work boots, she walked into the living room. Junie held out a wicker basket as she walked to the front door.

"I don't know why we need to do this today, it's going to be so hot," Rosemary said as she took the basket from her brother.

"Well, it gets cold in the winter, Rosie," Junie said, trying to coax her into a good mood. She rolled her eyes, her favorite expression of exasperation.

They crossed the gravel street and walked into the park. The tall grass swirled around Rosemary's ankles, the dew soaking the cuffs of her pants. The sun crept over the oak trees in the distance, burning off the humid haze. She glanced at the tennis courts to the right of their path, longing to be playing tennis rather than collecting coal. A single drop of sweat dripped down the back of her neck. It was going to be another scorching day.

She and Junie reached the tracks. The coal had fallen from the overflowing boxcars. Rosemary bent and picked up the fist-size pieces.

"Make sure you get as much as you can—not just the big chunks," Junie called.

Rosemary grimaced, mimicking her brother behind his back. She hated this chore. Her hands got dirty; the coal dust collected under her fingernails. Her mystery dream man would never kiss her if she had coal dirt under her fingernails. But then again, the man was only a dream; there was no guy in Rosemary's life right now.

She walked back and picked up the smaller pieces that she had passed up. She deftly separated the coal pieces from the rock gravel. Her mind wandered. Why didn't she have a guy? Rosemary snorted—with the war on, all the young men were itching to kill some Jerries and Japs. They were all leaving. She didn't want to take a chance of falling for someone and having him leave her and get killed. But that didn't stop the men from haunting her dreams.

She stood up and placed her hands on her back, stretching like a cat, tilting her face to the sun. Junie was a hundred feet down the tracks. She watched his blond head bobbing up and down as he picked up the coal lumps and dropped them into his basket. His white cotton undershirt was soaked already, clinging to his back.

She just knew that he was going to get it into his head to go and sign up for the war. He wanted to be a hero, to serve his country. *Stupid war*, Rosemary thought. Every day there was something else on the radio about the invasion of Africa, the battles in the Pacific, at Guadalcanal and the losses, the losses of American boys. The Jerries and the Japs—they were insatiable, bulldozing over smaller, weaker countries.

Rosemary shivered in spite of the heat. She couldn't bear the thought of her brother going over there—or any guy that she had feelings for. The killings, the suffering, the horrors. No one should have to see that!

She turned her attention back to the tracks, to the giant foxtails wilting in the thick summer air, their furry stamen flopped over. The tall leaves of the Orange Day lilies fanned out, supporting the delicate orange petals. A few volunteer corn plants popped through the gravel, their yellow tassels bursting from the top of the green leaves. Morning Glory ivy twisted its way around the volunteer corn and sprawled out, its white blossoms breaking the greenery. At the grass line, the point where the crabgrass threatened to overwhelm the gravel, Rosemary spotted tall, thin stalks of green with bushy tops.

"Junie!" she said. "Look, wild asparagus!" She ran over and broke off a shoot. She munched on it, savoring the sweetness of the starchy stalk. Junie shook his head, chuckling at her.

"That's not coal."

"Oh so what? We can get more coal tomorrow—asparagus we can eat today!" she said and crunched down on the stalk again.

"Come on, Asparagus Head, let's get back home so we can get ready for work," he hefted his basket onto his hip and turned towards the house. Rosemary threw a wistful look over her shoulder at the rising sun, the tall oak trees, the winding ivy. She longed to remain outdoors, to feel the sun cover her pale skin with brown freckles. But this was not her life. She hurried to catch up with Junie and return home.

Junie drove them to the factory. Rosemary watched the trees whiz by as they drove down Vermillion Street. They sped across Main Street. Rosemary barely had time to look down the street at the bank, the drug store, or the club they hung out at after work. The movie theater was a blur as her brother rolled through the stop sign. Rosemary shot him a look.

He grinned at her. "What? No one was coming."

"One of these days, someone will be."

"But they weren't today." He was incorrigible.

She sighed. Junie looked over at her.

"What's that sigh for?" he asked, laughing.

"It's going to be so hot in the factory," she said, cupping her chin in her hand as she leaned out the window. "I wish I still had my job at the bowling alley."

Her first job had been setting the pins at the bowling alley. She made a game to see how quickly she could set up all ten pins and get back up into her little cubbyhole before the next bowler launched the ball down the lane and the pins scattered in every direction.

"Yeah, but you didn't make any dough there!" Junie said. Rosemary scowled and folded her arms, pouting. She knew she should be grateful to Junie for getting her the job at the factory, but on days as hot as this, it was hard to have gratitude.

"How do you do it, Junie? How can you be so happy to go roast in that hot box?" she asked, knowing she sounded like a whining toddler.

"Because it's only temporary until I join up, that's how," he replied, looking at the road ahead.

"Junie…" Her voice trailed, cut off by fear.

"What? You asked."

Rosemary just shook her head; it did no good to try to talk to him about the war. She knew she could not change his mind—not now that he was eighteen. He would leave them; it was only a matter of when.

Junie made a left turn, and they almost lost their transmission barreling over a set of train tracks. The red brick factory, Owens-Illinois Glass, loomed like a predator. Smoke billowed from the two smoke stacks, blackening the air. The bottle making was continuous, the lines never stopped. It ate Rosemary's energy, her joy. Junie parked and Rosemary dragged her feet all the way to the women's locker room. With heavy arms, she pulled out her blue jump suit, her uniform. The fabric was stiff, constricting. She felt as if she were stepping into a strait jacket.

She walked to her place on the line. Surrounding her were steel girders and belts moving the bottles along to the next station. She pushed her bandana back a little further on her head. The coal-burning furnaces heated the factory, turning the entire building into a giant oven. Her skin prickled from the heat. A thread of sweat trickled down her back. The sound of the automated belts scrambled her mind, pushing out all thoughts of the outdoors, of playing tennis. All she could see was the endless line of bottles that she must inspect. She sighed and got to work.

She fell into her rhythm, pick up a bottle, examine, left belt if it was cracked or damaged, right if it was fine. Pick up next bottle, examine, left or right. Her mind soon wandered to a conversation she and Junie had had the week before.

———

They sat in the living room listening to the radio. *Your All Time Hit Parade*, guest-starring Judy Garland, had just finished. She sang, "Somewhere over the Rainbow." Her voice was liquid velvet, golden honey. Rosemary could listen to her sing all night. It took her outside of her everyday world, transported her to the mystical Land of Oz. The announcer began the evening's news report in a droning monotone. Rosemary tuned out and watched Virginia work a puzzle. Sandy, Virginia's toddler, played on the floor. Rosemary tossed kernels of popcorn at Skippy, their Chow-terrier mix. He jumped at each kernel, catching them in his mouth.

"Goddamned Japs!" Junie exclaimed.

"William!" their mother said. "Watch your mouth." She stopped crocheting, shooting Junie a look. Rosemary glanced at Virginia to see if she had been paying attention, but she was absorbed with the puzzle.

"I'm sorry, Ma," Junie said, jumping to his feet. "But the boys are taking a beating in the Pacific. The Japs are wiping the floor with 'em." His eyes flashed. Rosemary's heart sank. She knew what that look meant.

"I just want to go over there and lick 'em!" he said. Virginia looked up from her puzzle. No one wanted Junie to put himself in harm's way, not knowing if he would come back.

"William," her mother said, "You are too young to go and fight."

"But Ma, I turned eighteen last month!"

It was the same argument they had had since he turned eighteen at the end of June. Their mother had purposely forgotten that Junie had turned eighteen. An uncomfortable silence fell on the room.

The announcer described the fighting. "On August 7, American troops landed on the island of Guadalcanal and succeeded in taking the strategic airport. The Japanese attacked today and the American Marines lost an entire platoon, but held their ground and the airport."

"I'll bet they are using the Tokyo Express to bring troops down," Junie said, using a term he heard on the radio for the night transports of Japanese troops down through the Solomon Islands.

"See, they are still holding their ground," Rosemary said, hoping to take her brother's attention from the radio.

"Yeah, but I could lick them," he muttered.

Rosemary's head snapped back to the belt. The bottles rolled by, clinking as the belt moved. A few bottles went by unchecked. She reached for them, but it was too late. Hopefully, they didn't have cracks. She would have to stop daydreaming and pay attention. She couldn't afford to lose her job.

Albert

Albert awoke to the clambering of breakfast being served outside his bedroom door. He rubbed his head, trying to shake off his sleep. The shades were drawn to keep the cool night air in, but it was no use. The heat radiated through the thin material. Albert slung his legs over the bed and stood up, stretched his arms overhead and then swung them in circles like the baseball players did. The beds next to his were neatly made; his brothers were up before him again. He pulled on a pair of twill pants and hiked the suspenders over his undershirt. He smoothed his dark hair away from his face.

Albert opened his bedroom door and stepped into the cacophony of the house. His mother was at the stove, frying eggs. "*Dobré ráns, zlatko,*" she said in Slovak. *Good morning, sweetie.* She had been in America for almost twenty-five years and still did not like to speak English. She and Albert's father had come to America from Slovakia after the first Great War.

She balanced the spatula on the edge of the pan and put her hands on his face, kissing him roughly. Her hands were thick, strong and calloused from cleaning all day. With nine children to take care of, his mother never had a moment's rest. He studied his mother, a stout, sturdy Eastern European woman with a round, full face and dark, wavy hair. Her family was her life and taking care of them was her sole purpose.

Albert walked through the French doors with yellow and red flowered curtains and into the dining room where his brothers and sisters crowded around the table in mismatched chairs, eating their breakfast before heading off for the day. Albert was the second oldest. His older brother, Ed, was engrossed in his eggs, shoveling them into his mouth with a piece of toast. His remaining siblings, two sisters and five brothers, were either waiting for their eggs or shoveling them into their mouths like Ed was. Albert shook his head. *You'd think they'd never eaten!*

He walked over to the radio perched on a side table, a dome-shaped relic, and cranked up the volume. The announcer's voice boomed, drowning out the chatter of the children.

Albert's mother jumped. "*Preboha*! Turn that down!" She rushed over, pushed Albert out of the way, and turned the volume down.

"Ma, the Cubs are playing a double header today!" Albert protested.

She held up her hand. "Not so loud, Albert. You make the children not hear." Albert put his hands together and pretended to swing a baseball bat at her. His mother clucked and doffed him on the shoulder before heading back to the kitchen to save the eggs from burning.

Albert pulled a chair up to the radio to hear anything related to the Cubs. He longed to be a baseball player like Bill "Swish" Nicholson. Man! Could he hit! Of course, he missed a lot, too, hence his nickname "Swish." Albert had sat glued to the radio a month earlier. Nicholson had hit four home runs in a row and then was walked intentionally with the bases loaded. The Cubs lost the game, but it was still a great effort by Swish. And today they had a double-header against the Brooklyn Dodgers.

"We interrupt this program to bring the latest news from the European front. The Germans have taken Sevastopol, the Russian port on the Black Sea. I repeat, the Germans have taken Sevastopol."

Albert leapt up; his brother Ed let out a frustrated cry. Albert's brother Steve, who was one year younger than Albert, said, "We've got to join up and go fight those Jerries!"

Albert and Ed nodded, forgetting their promise to their mother that they would not join until the younger kids were back in school. Their father strode into the dining room. A high widow's peak dominated his forehead, a strong nose and jaw line, a cleft in the center of his chin. Albert felt like he was looking into a mirror when he looked at his father.

"Da, the Germans have taken Sevastopol! They are marching towards Stalingrad now! It looks like they're going to lick the Ruskies," Steve said, bursting out with anger. Steve was clean-cut, with dark hair cropped short to his head. He had an eager smile and bushy eyebrows which accentuated his deep set brown eyes. People mistook Steve and Albert for twins.

Their father snorted. "Justice won't be done until that Hitler pays for enslaving the Slovak people!" George, Albert's father, was a staunch Slovak national. When the English and French signed the Munich Accord, annexing Czechoslovakia to Germany, he exploded, "Sudetenland! *Do riti!* Hitler wants the whole country, and the British lie down like dogs and do nothing to stop him. *Skopová hlava.*" *Meat head.* It wasn't clear if he was talking about Hitler or the British.

"That's why we need to go and fight, Da," Ed said, always the calm voice of reason.

"Psh! Tiso needs to be shot, acting for Germany's puppet, giving over our people," his father muttered. Josef Tiso was the Prime Minister of the Slovak Republic, which was created after Hitler invaded the western part of Czechoslovakia, called the Sudetenland.

"And the one with no brain," his father continued, using his favorite euphemism for Hitler, "killing all the innocent people in Lidice." Hitler ordered the Czech village of Lidice massacred after a rebel killed his prized soldier, Heyden.

Mary Lou, Albert's youngest sister, and his favorite, climbed onto his lap. "Al, please don't go and join the war," she said, her eyes wide with fear.

Albert ruffled her brown curls and said, "Don't you worry about me, Mare. I'll come back and still tickle you to death!" He tickled her below her ribs, and she contorted in a fit of giggles and bounded off his lap.

He had to go to war; he had to do his part. It wasn't right, him staying here while boys were dying over there. He knew he would join; it was just a few more weeks until the kids went back to school.

"*Dost*! Enough!" Ma pushed her way in between the boys. "Albert, go! Go to work." She shoved Albert towards his room with an effort that he could not resist. The conversation of war was over for now. She wanted the boys to serve their country, but the reality of it frightened her and she changed the subject whenever it came up.

Albert walked to the factory, Owens-Illinois Glass. His mind wandered to the war. He couldn't stand by and watch everyone else do the fighting. He had to contribute, to do what he could to help win the war. Maybe he could be the one to break through the German lines. Maybe he could become a sergeant or a lieutenant and lead men, brave men, and be brave himself. He could lead a secret mission behind enemy lines, deep into Nazi country and take Hitler out himself.

Albert was lost in his thoughts as he walked along the tar and gravel street, lined with oak and elm trees, providing shade from the glaring sun. Sweat dripped down his neck, soaking the collar of his shirt, but he was too self-absorbed to notice. A car horn blared from behind him. He jumped to the side of the road.

"Watch where you're going!" a gravelly voiced barked. Albert growled and snapped his head around. A young man with wavy brown hair leaned out from a convertible. Albert relaxed when he recognized the driver.

"Hey, Merle, where you off to?" Albert asked. He and Merle were acquaintances from the factory and the Paddock Club, a local watering hole. The club had great bands on the weekends, swing bands that got the toes tapping. Not that Albert ever danced himself; he just watched from the sidelines.

"Oh, I've got a date later today with my lady, so I'm heading to the barber to get spruced up," Merle smoothed his hair back with his hand, his lips pulling back in a toothy grin. His voice was harsh from the constant chain of cigarettes.

"Yeah?" Albert grinned back, wishing he were going on a date. "Who's the lucky gal?"

"She's my wife, name's Norma Ruhrmann, well, Norma Graff now," Merle replied, puffing his chest out.

"Never met her, but have a good time," Albert said and turned back to be on his way. He needed to hurry to get to work on time.

"You should meet her sister," Merle called after him. "She's a looker. We're all going to the Paddock Club this weekend. They're having a big shindig for the War Bond drive."

"Maybe I'll go," Albert called over his shoulder, picking up the pace. He was conscious of the sun climbing higher in the sky. No time to fantasize about being a war hero or Merle's sister-in-law.

He crossed the railroad tracks that brought the coal into the factory and walked around to the front of the building. The lines went straight up the front of the building, taking his eye to the sky. Albert hurried through the doorway, to his locker and out to his station.

He walked toward the mold shop, to make the casts into which the hot glass was poured to shape the bottles. The heat was going to be insufferable, but he liked to work hard. He liked the feeling of accomplishment at the end of the day, when he was tired and sweaty. He rolled up his sleeves and walked through the lines back to the mold shop. All along the line today, he noticed women working. Various women with bandanas on their heads, baseball hats or hard hats invaded the factory. He realized that women had come into the factory to take the place of the boys who had gone off to war, but he hadn't realized how many. One more reason to join up, so he wasn't the *last* man in the factory working!

Rosemary

"Rosie, you up?" her sister Norma asked, pushing the bedroom door open. Rosemary groaned and rolled over, which Norma interpreted as a yes. She came in and sat in the edge of the bed. Norma was a year older than Junie. She lived around the block with her husband, Merle, and baby. Rosemary wondered what Norma could possibly want as she dragged herself out of bed. It was Sunday morning, and she had to get ready for church. She pulled on a navy dress with puffed short sleeves, buttoned the pearly buttons, and fastened the belt at her waist. The dress hit just below the knees and with nylon being rationed, there were no stockings. *Oh well,* Rosemary thought, *it's too hot for them anyway.*

"Merle said he's got a guy he wants you to meet," Norma said, her doe-like blue eyes searching Rosemary's face for a glimmer of interest.

"Norm, I'm not interested in dating. I told you that a million times," Rosemary said, fiddling with her hair. She desperately wanted to meet him and fall in love, but the world was too unsure right now. A boy who was here and interested today might be in the war tomorrow, dying on the battle field. *No thank you,* Rosemary thought. *I don't want to open myself up, only to be broken-hearted.*

"Well, his name is Al Jedoga and he works at Owens. I think you two would hit it off," she said. Rosemary blocked Norma out and focused on getting her hair just right. It twisted in every direction, so she swept the sides back, securing them with a barrette. She turned her head from side to side to critique herself. Her reflection was striking—high cheek bones, a small, straight nose, deep set blue eyes, small mouth.

"Rosie!" Junie called. "Quit preening and get out here! We're going to be late to church!" Rosemary sighed with relief, her conversation interrupted. She wouldn't have to make excuses to her sister. Or worse—tell Norma the truth and expose her fears.

She and Norma walked through the living room and into the kitchen where Junie, Jack and her nieces were finishing breakfast. Her mother and Virginia rinsed dishes at the sink. Rosemary took a piece of dry toast from the serving plate in the center of the kitchen table.

"I want to tell you all before we go to church," Junie said after Virginia had wiped the children's hands. "I enlisted yesterday." He thrust his shoulders back, his chin jutting forward.

"No, Junie!" his mother exclaimed.

Rosemary went faint, her head spinning. *Junie going to war? He can't be!* "Junie, why?" she asked, leaning against the wall to stop herself from falling.

"I have to. I have to go and fight for our country," he said in a manner that exuded confidence, almost arrogance.

"When are you going?" Jack asked, his eyes shining. Rosemary was afraid he wanted go to war too. He wanted to do everything that Junie did. She was glad Jack was too young to enlist.

"I leave for Fort Mead next week."

Rosemary closed her eyes, the weight sank onto her chest, and she struggled to get air. The room was stifling; the air heavy, pressing against her. She felt her knees buckle. Jack took hold of her arm and guided her to a chair. Junie had really done it, he was going to war. He was leaving her, just like her father had left them.

Junie patted her hand. "Don't worry, Rosie, nothing's going to happen to me!"

Rosemary wasn't reassured.

After Junie's announcement, they squeezed into the car to go to church— Rosemary, her mother, Jack, Norma, her baby, and Virginia with her two children perched on laps, and Junie in the driver's seat. They elbowed and pushed each other for room, but they all had to go to church. That was one of the commandments—*remember the Sabbath, to keep it holy*. And to break a commandment was a sin.

St. Anthony's twin steeples soared 125 feet above the earth. They could be seen for miles outside of the Streator town limits. When they returned from a long trip, Junie and Rosemary would have a contest to see who could spot the steeples first. The church was built with bleached limestone. Between the twin spires hung a large round stained glass window through which the afternoon sun shone, making it glow incandescent—true God-light. The heavy cast iron bells tolled, calling everyone to mass. It was a deep, sorrowful sound, pitching Rosemary deeper into her gloominess.

They walked into the vestibule and took their seats; each family had their own pew. The Ruhrmann's was on the right side of the church, halfway down the aisle. The wooden pews were hard, with no cushioning to make it more comfortable. One needed to be uncomfortable, a sacrifice for Jesus, who gave his life for mankind. Rosemary looked around the church to take her mind off her discomfort. Lining both sides of the wide church were stained glass windows. The sunlight streamed through the southern windows, illuminating Jesus with the little children, St. Agnes, and several other scenes of Jesus and the saints. Above Rosemary's head were statues of each of the twelve disciples. She let her eye travel all the way to the vaulted ceiling, with its gilded beams.

Rosemary had a possessive connection to the church. It was built in 1897 after a fire destroyed a previous building. Her grandfather was one of the craftsmen who worked on carving the main altar. He had designed it himself. She swelled with pride as she studied her grandfather's craftsmanship. The altar rose majestically from the floor of the church to the top of the dome. The main centerpiece of the altar was the crucifixion—Jesus on the cross, his crown of thorns cutting into his head, adorned in only a white loincloth, his expression serene despite his agony. To the left was his mother, Mary, clad in her blue robe and white head dress. Mary of Magdalene knelt in front of the cross, her face contorted with grief. The apostle John stood to the right, looking at Jesus' face, beseeching him not to leave. Rosemary knew that look well. She wore it when her father was taken to the sanatorium, and she was sure it crossed her face again this morning.

Rosemary loved the pageantry of mass. The pipe organ blasted from the balcony at the rear of the church, a signal the congregation to rise, and the priest to make his way down the aisle. The melody of *Te Deum Laudamus,* Holy God, we Praise Thy Name, echoed through the cavernous church. Rosemary sang the meaningless Latin words.

The priest stood behind the altar, raised his arm and began. "In nomine Patris, et Filii, et Spiritus Sancti, Amen," he said, making the sign of the cross. Rosemary repeated the sign of the cross, whispering, *In the name of the Father, the Son and the Holy Spirit.*

The priest conducted the mass in Latin. It was a mystical, lyric language that made God seem remote, that the priest was the only gateway to God. She thought about becoming a nun, then she could pray and be in the church all of the time, but there was no money to send her to a convent. Plus she wasn't sure that she could be pious all the time. So that plan went the way of other plans in her life; it slid by with little notice from anyone but Rosemary. Sometimes she felt little control over her life, sliding along through circumstance and expectations from others. To quit school, to work, to get married. No one asked her what she wanted. Had she asked herself?

She stole a glance over at her brother's blond head bowed in prayer. Feeling the weight of her stare, he turned his head a slight bit and winked at her. Rosemary frowned back, trying to look annoyed. He was leaving her, her heart fluttered, seizing at the thought of losing him. Junie kept Rosemary balanced, kept her grounded so she didn't float off into her daydreams.

She crossed her hands, closed her eyes and prayed, "Please, God, please, please keep Junie safe in the war. Please don't let anything bad happen to him." It was said that God heard all prayers, but Rosemary was doubtful.

After Junie left for basic training, Virginia claimed the car, declaring that she needed it for the kids. With gasoline rationed, Virginia feared they would run out of gas if there were an emergency. So Rosemary rode her bike to work. She didn't mind the ride or the wind whipping through her hair as she flew down the hill behind her house. But she missed Junie. She thought of him as she rode past the stop sign by the Majestic Theater, and remembered him skidding through it and grinning like the Cheshire cat. Would she ever see that grin again?

Her skin rose in hot goose bumps. *Stop it! Stop it!* He would be fine. Maybe the war would be over soon, maybe he wouldn't even go overseas. But she knew, deep in her heart, that he was destined to be in the war, that he would not feel complete if he did not see some fighting. She pedaled faster—as if she could outrun her thoughts. But the sense of abandonment and dread always caught back up to her.

There was a fund-raiser at the Paddock Club on Saturday night, to sell war bonds for the troops. Her friend Betty had gotten Rosemary to commit to going with her, but now

Rosemary wasn't so sure she was up to a night out, her mind consumed with Junie's well-being. They had not heard from him yet. Could something have happened already? Surely, they would have notified the family. He probably hadn't even left the States yet.

"Come on, Rosie," Betty said, "You're not going to help him by sitting at home and worrying." Her brown hair was in Victory rolls—parted in the center and rolled back to meet in a V. She grinned at Rosemary, her teeth jutting forward.

"I know that. It's just that I won't be much fun," Rosemary said, her arms hanging like dead weights.

"Well, it is a fundraiser for war bonds, so the money will be going to help him." Betty pulled on her jumpsuit. "And besides, my fiancé is over in the Pacific too. You're not the only one who has someone you love overseas."

Rosemary looked into Betty's face. She saw the tell-tale circles of worry under her eyes, her wan face. A lump of guilt blocked her throat. She knew Betty was afraid, but Betty was willing to do something about it, not wallow. Rosemary gave in. She needed a night of dancing and some fun and wanted Betty to have that too.

The Paddock Club was packed. It seemed as if the whole town had come out for the war bond drive. Rosemary wore a simple light pink dress with an embroidered boat-neck. The embroidery repeated at the waist, giving way to a full skirt which swished around her calves. Her light brown t-strap heels were comfortable to dance in. She puckered her lips and fiddled with her ashen curls as she scanned the bar. She saw Norma and her husband, Merle. Norma waved her and Betty over to their table at the far end of the bar.

"Any word from Junie?" Norma asked, her eyes full of concern. Rosemary shook her head. Norma knew what it was like to be anxious for news. Merle had been in the Navy before the war broke out. He went out to sea for months at a time, leaving Norma alone with her baby.

"I'm sure he's fine," Merle said in his gruff sailor voice. He always sounded like an angry bulldog, no matter his mood. "He'll be in basic training for a while anyway and probably miss the fight. I wish I could join up."

"Merle!" Norma said.

"I would! I'd go shoot some Japs. I've got the experience too. They just won't let me because I've got the ol' ball and chain." He hitched his thumb towards Norma, a smile pulling at the corners of his mouth. She frowned at him, her eyes narrowing. He threw his arms around her.

"You know I love ya, Norm!" He kissed her loudly on the cheek. She pushed him away, but smiled.

Rosemary watched them, her stomach tightened with envy. They had such an easy relationship. Merle was so obviously in love with Norma, even though he joked that he wasn't. And Norma loved Merle too. Rosemary wanted that kind of relationship. She wanted to find a guy who would look adoringly at her, make her feel as if she were the only woman in the world. But she was also afraid of being vulnerable, afraid of finding that feeling and losing it.

She looked onto the dance floor. The band was already in full swing, clarinets and horns blaring. Behind the band were draped red, white and blue banners. There were a few couples out on the floor, doing the jitterbug. Rosemary tapped her toes under the table in time with the beat. She was eager to get out there and dance, to get lost in the music and forget that she was alone, that she didn't have someone special in her life.

"Come on, Betty, let's dance!" She pulled Betty to her feet and onto the floor. The beat was infectious, hard and driving. Rosemary's knees moved in and out, back and forth and she shook her shoulders, moving her arms to the rhythm. Betty took her hand and twirled her around, her skirt fanning out like a flag in the wind, and then wrapping itself around her legs. She laughed and gave Betty a spin of her own. Rosemary lost herself in the music, the bass rumbling in her chest and the horns vibrating her eardrums. Betty did the Charleston and Rosemary copied her, stepping forward and swinging her arms right, stepping back and swinging left. She shook her head as the trumpet blared, and then sprung back into action as the rest of the band kicked in.

Albert

Albert and Ed walked into the Paddock Club, following two guys in uniform. *Probably on leave,* Albert thought. *They've probably had grand adventures while I've been making bottles.* He stared at the tailored olive jackets, colorful square patches and stripes on the arm which told where they had been, where they were going. They were Army guys, Albert knew, but he wished he knew what unit the insignia patch stood for.

He slapped Ed on the back and said, "That's going to be us in a few weeks!"

"Yeah," Ed said, nodding. Albert licked his lips as he watched them disappear into the crowd, wishing he were an army private on leave. Instead, he followed his brother to the bar.

Albert scanned the crowd, seeing familiar faces through the thick, smoky haze that hung in the air and stung his eyes. The chatter and laughter floated above the horns. The lead singer crooned a favorite, Irving Berlin's "Cheek to Cheek," and couples danced closely, twirling like cogs of a wheel.

Ed handed Albert a Schlitz beer and Albert took a long pull, the bitter liquid cooling his insides as it slid down his throat, providing little relief from the heat building in the club. Red, white and blue streamers sagged from the ceiling, patriotic reminders of why they were all there—to raise money for war bonds, to keep giving to the war effort. War bond posters covered the walls. The silhouetted soldier holding his rifle stared at Al. *Why aren't you fighting?* It taunted. Albert took another swallow from his beer, wanting to forget his promise to his mother.

"Makes you want to join up tonight, huh?" he said as he elbowed Ed in the side.

"Yeah, seems like there are a lot of boys home on leave tonight. Aren't they supposed to be overseas?" Ed asked.

"I won't be taking leave when we join up. I'll be too busy killing Jerries!"

The band finished "Cheek to Cheek." The band leader cradled the microphone and said, "Well boys and girls, we all know why we're here, to raise money for the war effort, to support our boys over there fighting for us." Hoots and cat-calling erupted from the servicemen in the corner. "So tip your hats and give all that you can to help our boys! Here's one to put you in the mood!" He turned to the band and they fired into "Anchors Aweigh." A great whoop drowned out the band for a moment and everyone sang—

Anchors aweigh, my boys, anchors aweigh.
Farewell to college joys,
We sail at break of day day day day!

Arms linked and people swayed, undulating like ocean waves. Albert and Ed sang as loud as they could; Al couldn't even hear the band over the din. As he sang the song, he pretended that he was sailing off tomorrow and the crowd was singing to him. He glanced over at the Army fellows. Their faces beamed, eyes shining. One of the service men grabbed a pretty little red head and planted a big kiss on her, tipping her backward. Her face flushed and she gave him a playful slap.

The song ended. Albert turned his back to the crowd, signaling the bartender for two more Schlitz. The glass felt cool under his hands, not glowing molten glass that burned his eyes all day.

The band launched into a swing number, the tempo faster and upbeat.

"Say, look at this," Ed said, his eyes riveted on something.

"What?" Albert turned, leaning against the bar. He handed his brother one of the beers.

He saw her before Ed could answer him. Two ladies occupied the dance floor, jitterbugging. Albert's eyes locked on one with sandy hair. Her eyes were deep-set and shining, her small mouth stretched into a concentrated grin, her cheeks glowing. She twirled around her friend's outstretched hand, the skirt of her dress fanning around her like a pink halo. Her legs were slender, sinewy and pale. She moved like a jackrabbit, puffing her cheeks.

Albert's heart pounded in time with her footfalls, beat, beat, beat, pause, beat, beat, beat. She twisted her hips, her bottom half seeming to move independent of her upper body. Only her blonde curls, swishing in time with the music, revealed the connection between the two. She spun her friend around, throwing her head back and laughing, showing her small, pearly teeth.

He nodded towards the ashen beauty.

"Who's she?" he asked in a manner he hoped was calm. Ed shrugged.

Albert followed her with his eyes as she and her friend left the dance floor. They settled at a table in the corner. She lit a cigarette and took a long drag, exhaling the smoke. It ringed around her face, giving her an ethereal glow. He longed to be the smoke around her face. Her fingers cradled the cigarette, wrist bent with the grace of a ballerina. She dabbed at her face with a napkin, absorbing the perspiration from her forehead. Every movement was mesmerizing. An empty bottle of beer stood before her.

"I'm going to buy her a drink," Albert turned and ordered a beer in one motion. He took the neck of the bottle in his hand and weaved through the crowd. The girl laughed again, her face beaming. Albert's heart thumped against his chest. He almost lost his grip on the bottle. He pushed his way through the crowd, keeping his eye on her.

And then he was in front of her. Her eyes were steely blue, almost gray. They pierced his throat, taking away his ability to speak. Her mouth was set in a scowl, which Albert hoped to remove. He wanted to see her beautiful teeth again. The entire table stopped their conversation. Albert was aware of all eyes on him, but he could not think of any words to say.

"Say, Albert!" A hand thumped him on the back. Albert turned to find Merle pointing to a pretty girl seated next to him. "This is my girl, Norma."

Then he motioned towards her, the one he had come to meet. "And this is her sister Rosemary, the one I was telling you about."

Rosemary. Her name rolled around his brain. It felt fragrant and delicious. She raised her perfectly shaped eyebrows, the apples of her cheeks flushing pink, matching her dress. Albert felt like someone had hit him in the solar plexus. He struggled to take a breath, forced himself to swallow.

"I noticed your beer was empty," he said, hoping he did not sound as nervous as he felt.

She—Rosemary—smirked and said, "You noticed from all the way across the club?"

Albert felt like he had been caught doing something wrong. Had she felt him watching her? He pushed his insecurity down and said, "I've got a good eye."

He handed her the beer. Her fingers touched his. Electricity shot up Albert's arm and into his head, scrambling his thoughts.

"You must have." Rosemary raised her eyebrows. Her voice was light and melodic, joking and sardonic. An interesting mix of qualities.

"Have a seat," Merle said, pulling out an empty chair. Albert sat down but kept his eyes on Rosemary. She flushed under his gaze and giggled with her girlfriend. That was an encouraging sign. He took a large swig from his beer, wanting to talk to Rosemary, but having no idea what to say.

Merle broke the ice. "Albert works at Owens too, Rosie."

Rosemary looked up at Albert. "Oh? What shift are you on?"

His heart hammered against his chest when she looked at him. "A-shift."

"Me too. What do you do?"

"I work in the mold room." Albert felt stiff, unable to relax. He took another swig of beer. Rosemary nodded and an awkward silence fell over the table. The low roar of background noise told Albert that no one else was having difficulties making conversation. Only him. Rosemary fidgeted with the label on her beer.

Merle cleared his throat, breaking the bubble of silence surrounding the table. "So how about them Cubbies?" His eyes crinkled as he smiled.

"Yeah, they look good this year," Albert said. "They may actually win the pennant." Albert was grateful for a neutral topic, to take his thoughts off this beautiful, mysterious creature in front of him.

"Yeah, maybe even the series!" Merle yelled out. They talked about Swish and his four home runs in one game, the schedule ahead. Albert kept looking at Rosemary out of the corner of his eye. She was engrossed in conversation with her sister and friend, not paying any attention to Albert and Merle. As he looked, she glanced up at him, meeting his eyes. A shy smile played at her lips as her head snapped down. Albert's heart stopped. He wanted to talk to her, but didn't know what to say; she was beautiful, so unapproachable.

Rosemary

She was so mad at Norma for arranging this set-up. She never would have agreed to come if she knew this was a set-up. He was just going to leave her, join up like Junie did. But this man, Albert, was handsome. He had a cleft in his chin which deepened when he smiled. She listened as he talked to Merle.

"You hear about Mikey Poo-tie?" Albert asked. "He got it in his head to jump off the viaduct." The viaduct was the bridge spanning the railroad tracks that led into Owens. At the apex, it was almost thirty feet high.

"So I says, 'I dunno Mikey, that's pretty high,'" Albert said.

"He says, 'Yeah, but if I use an umbrella, it'll break my fall,'" Al mimicked Mikey, using a slow, obtuse voice. Merle burst into laughter. Rosemary stifled her own giggle, not wanting to be drawn into his story.

"He goes up on the viaduct. I think he's going to chicken out. There's no way I would jump from the viaduct—it's a hundred feet tall!" Albert exaggerated. "But, there's Mikey, holding his friggin' umbrella, his knees knocking as he is standing at the railing. 'Do it if yer gonna do it,' my brother Steve says. So what does Mikey do?"

Albert looked over at Rosemary. She flushed, not wanting him to know she was listening. She didn't like him, didn't want to like him. But her body betrayed her. As Albert caught her eye, her heart quickened, a fluttering erupting deep in her abdomen. She watched his thick hands move as he pretended to hold an umbrella over his head. He shrugged and said, "He jumped."

A peel of laughter broke out. Rosemary laughed, keeping her eyes on his hands. She wondered if they were rough. How would they feel against her bare skin? She shook her head to clear her thoughts. Merle wiped his tears away, still chuckling, and swigged his beer.

"So what happened to him?" he asked.

Albert shrugged. "I guess he broke his leg. Stupid kid! Who would'a thought you could jump off the viaduct with an umbrella!"

He and Merle started talking about the Cubs again. Rosemary wished she knew something, anything about baseball so she could join the conversation. She wanted to get his attention, to feel the fluttering inside of her, the vibrating.

Betty clinked her bottle against Rosemary's. "You're staring," she whispered into Rosemary's ear.

"Am not." Rosemary flushed, not wanting to get caught.

"Looks like Cupid's struck tonight," Betty said, taking a swig of beer.

"Stop, Betty!" Rosemary elbowed her, feeling punch-drunk all of a sudden.

"What are you two giggling about?" Norma asked, leaning into their private circle.

"Rosie's been struck," Betty said, a smug grin pulling at the corners of her mouth.

"Am *not*." Rosemary tried to keep her cool. She didn't want Albert to think she was a silly, immature school girl. "Norm, is this the guy Merle wanted me to meet?"

"I told you that you would like him!" she said. "Why don't you talk to him?"

"I don't like him. Besides, what would I say? They're talking baseball," Rosemary said, looking once again at Albert. He met her glance, his deep brown eyes connecting. Her head felt light, as if she were floating above herself. She smiled against her will. Could this be the mystery man she dreamt about? His thick lips stretched into a smile. She looked away, overwhelmed by the feelings.

"Oh who cares what they're talking about? Just interrupt and ask a question. Fellas like it when you ask about them," Betty said.

Rosemary looked at Albert, her mind spinning for a way to cut in. She cleared her throat as the band ended their song. Albert and Merle looked at her, waiting for her to speak. She froze, mortified, all thoughts chased out of her head. It felt like an eternity of empty silence.

"Cat got your tongue, Rosie?" Merle said. "Well, that's a first! She usually talks a blue streak."

Betty, Norma and Albert laughed. Rosemary blushed, embarrassed that Merle was telling this stranger her secrets. She wanted to seem mysterious, not like a childish chatterbox. Albert's eyes connected with Rosemary's, and the left side of his mouth curled upward. Rosemary relaxed, comforted by the small gesture.

"I don't talk *all* the time, Merle," Rosemary said. She turned to Albert, summoning the courage to speak to him. "So you like baseball?" she asked and immediately regretted her question. Of course he liked baseball, isn't that what he and Merle were talking about?

"Yeah, it's the best sport. Every pitch is like a new game. You never know what's going to happen next," he said, his voice full of passion. Rosemary smiled in spite of herself. She didn't know much about baseball, but his enthusiasm made her want to go home and listen to a game and learn more about the sport.

"How about you?" he asked. "Do you like baseball?"

"Me? Oh no! I don't know anything about baseball!" she exclaimed and tittered. She shook her head to regain her composure and try again to appear sophisticated and cool.

"What do you like to do?" he asked, his eyes locked onto hers. The fluttering erupted in Rosemary's insides, she squeezed her cigarette with her fingers to stop the vibration from moving into her hands.

Rosemary shrugged, "I like all kinds of things." She took a drag off her cigarette and hoped her hand didn't tremble. "Like horseback riding."

"Really?" Albert seemed surprised by her answer. "I've never been horseback riding."

"You've never been?" Rosemary asked, her voice rising, nervousness forgotten. How could he never have ridden a horse? "It's amazing, like flying. I feel like I am a part of the horse when I ride, you just glide over the ground, the wind blowing over your face, its muscles flexing…" She let the sentence trail off and looked around the table. All eyes were on her. Her cheeks burned with shame. She had said too much, talked too glibly. How was she ever going to attract a man if she acted like a little girl all the time? She needed to act cool, so she snapped her mouth shut and looked away in a manner she hoped was indifferent.

"Maybe I'll have to try it some time," Albert said, his left lip curled into a smile once again. All was not lost. Rosemary relaxed.

"Yes, you definitely should, but it's not as easy as it looks," Rosemary said, falling back into sarcasm to shield her feelings.

"Oh yeah? I think I can handle it," he replied, his eyes sparkling at the challenge. Her pulse thundered in her ears. She took a swig from her beer to wet her mouth which had become as dry as a desert.

Rosemary wasn't sure what was said the rest of the night. She was riding the feelings Albert had awakened in her. Before she knew it, the band played "The Star Spangled Banner," signaling the end of the evening. They all stood, placed their right hands over their hearts and sang, most off key, the words to the national anthem. When the song ended, Albert took Rosemary's hand.

"It was very nice to meet you, Rosemary," he said. "And I hope to see you again soon."

"That would be nice," she said, her voice shaking. She hoped it would be sooner than later.

Merle whacked Albert on the back and escorted his wife, Rosemary, and Betty out of the bar. Rosemary glanced back and met Albert's eyes. The fluttering carried her as she exited the bar.

———————

She gushed about him at her horseback riding lesson with Betty. As she saddled up Yankee Clover, she lamented, "Why didn't I just talk to him?"

Betty rolled her eyes and led her horse, a black quarter horse with white hind feet, out of the barn. "Rosie, you are too hard on yourself!"

Rosemary pulled the reins over Yankee Clover's neck. She rubbed his russet mane, smelling his essence, the smell of hay, dirt and sweat mixed together. "But what if I don't ever see him again?" she asked.

Betty stopped Lady Leaton and turned around. "If it is meant to be, you'll see him again." That didn't comfort Rosemary.

They mounted the horses and rode along a wooded trail. The sun was still low in the sky; they wanted to get their ride in before it got too hot. Rosemary rolled the legs of her dungarees up over her knees to keep herself cool. Yankee Clover snorted, chomping on his bit; he was restless and ready to run. Rosemary put her doubts and questions about Albert aside. She clucked Yankee into action. He broke into a canter, tossing his head back. The trees flew by, blurring into green streaks. Rosemary's hair blew back from her face. She felt alive when she rode, one with the horse, an extension of his strong, muscular body, his legs working as her legs. Yankee Clover's haunches flexed as he pulled his back legs under himself, shoulders pulled the soil past him as they sailed over the ground. This was the feeling that she tried to communicate to Albert. The world melted away when she was on horseback—dissolved and dropped into oblivion. There was no future, no worries, no abandonment. All the worries were left in the dust; she outran them if only for a few moments.

She came out of the woods into an open field, a field of oats, waving in the breeze, all the individual blades moving as one unit. She pulled Yankee Clover up, the oats parting as they walked through. The sky was brilliant blue, azure as an uncut sapphire, interrupted by wispy clouds. A pheasant flew up out of the oats, his brown and cream feathers fluttering, tail feathers fanned out. Yankee Clover's ears perked up, but the pheasant was far enough away not to spook him. The bird disappeared into the adjacent cornfield.

The sun climbed higher into the sky, the heat rising. The sweat beaded at the back of her neck and ran down in a single drop. She patted Yankee's neck, heat radiating off him. Her freedom was going to have to end for today. She turned Yankee Clover back towards the barn and prepared herself to enter the real world again. Her only consolation was that she may get to see Albert at the factory.

Rosemary's whole body was drenched as she inspected the bottles. She ran her arm across her forehead, pushing back a strand of hair that escaped from her bandana. The bottles clinked along and she picked them up—no cracks, to the left, cracks, to the right. Her thoughts turned from Albert and the hope of seeing him to Junie and wondering where he was.

She wanted to punch him and scream at him. She wanted to break his leg so he wouldn't be able to be in this stupid war. Most of all, she was scared. She was afraid she was going to lose her big brother, her friend, the one who knew her best, who could make her laugh. It had already happened with her dad—struck down by illness, the light and laughter sucked from him. Even at the sanatorium, with the healthy fresh air, he was not getting better. She felt as if she'd already lost him, would never feel his strong, wiry arms embrace her, never take her fishing again. And now, Junie could be next, she

33

could lose him too. Her heart cramped from the pain.

The bell sounded, jolting Rosemary from her morbid thoughts. She headed into the locker room, stripped off her uniform and ran out. She needed to ride her bicycle home, to try to outrun her fears.

She rounded the corner and ran smack into someone. Strong hands held her up. She opened her eyes—it was Albert. He smiled at her.

"Hi," she said. Her skin tingled from his hands, her heart thundered, blood rushing in her ears; here he was, standing in front of her.

"I was hoping to see you again," he said, his eyes boring into her.

"I… I, I'm sorry. I wasn't watching where I was going," she talked over him. "What did you say?"

"I said I was hoping to see you."

"Me? Why were you hoping to see me?" Rosemary felt her cheeks flushing. She hoped he didn't notice. She shook her curls, trying to look collected.

"Well, I was wondering if you would like to go to the Majestic this weekend to see *And the Angels Sing.*" His smile slipped a little, nervousness creeping into his voice. The Majestic Movie Theater was having a special screening of the movie to raise money for war bonds.

"Of course!" she blurted out before she had a chance to think about being aloof. She was rewarded with a large grin from Albert, his smile lighting up his face.

"Great, I'll pick you up at six o'clock," he said.

"I'll be waiting," Rosemary replied. She turned before she burst out. Her feet felt like they were not touching the ground. The fears she felt for Junie evaporated, replaced by the fluttering Albert kicked up. She pedaled her bicycle, weaving back and forth, thinking of her date with Albert, until a car honked at her, interrupting her reverie.

Albert

The late afternoon sun filtered through the sheer bathroom curtains, basking the room in warm, orange light. Albert hoisted his suspenders onto his shoulders with a snap. His skin radiated heat, the coolness of his bath dissipated. He smoothed his wet hair back with a fine toothed comb, accentuating his widow's peak. He felt refreshed, even though he had worked eight hours in the oppressive heat. His mind was on Rosemary and the evening ahead. He whistled to himself as he shaved. He finished and walked to the back door.

"Da, can I borrow your car tonight?" Albert called his father, who was picking tomatoes from the garden. The family had always had a garden behind the house, but since the government implemented the Victory Gardens, planting of vegetables, fruits and herbs by families, Albert's father had expanded the garden and added vegetables like lettuce, carrots and squash.

"Ack! You waste my gas. I have one ration coupon this month," his father complained. Albert rolled his eyes. His father never drove anywhere and was in no danger of running out of his gas ration.

"It's only to the movies and back," Albert said.

His father waved him off, "*Dobre*, but when I run out of gas, you can carry me where I go!"

"Fine!" Albert said and was out the door.

The blue Nash's headlights protruded from either side of the narrow metal grill, making the car look alive, as if it had eyes. The wheel-wells rounded high and rolled into the rubber running board that ran the length of the auto. The car was sleek, every line rounded and aerodynamic. Albert slid behind the wheel, inhaling. The car smelled like oil, dust, and leather. He ran his hands over the steering wheel and adjusted the rear view mirror. He looked at himself, winked and started the car.

He drove to Rosemary's house and parked in front. The lights in the front room glowed. Albert swallowed hard and rang the bell. He heard rustling inside of the house and Rosemary's voice calling goodbye. The door swung open and Rosemary appeared in silhouette, the light hitting her narrow waist, her curling hair. She stepped out and closed the door. They were nose to nose. Albert's heart pounded against his chest, his breathing labored. Rosemary's eyes glistened as her chest rose and fell with her breath. She smelled like rose water, sweet and sensual. There was a quiver at the base of his abdomen.

"Well, shall we go to the movie?" she asked with a nervous laugh.

Her voice jerked him out of his trance. "Yes, of course," he said and placed his hand on the small of her back, the cotton of her dress soft and smooth under his palm. He led her to the passenger side and opened the door for her, for which he was rewarded with another smile. He closed the door and hurried around to the driver's side.

They saw the line for the movie as they rounded the block. The crowd swarmed the front of the theater and wrapped around the corner. It seemed the whole town had turned out for the movie, to show their support for the war. They walked around to the end of the line, both fidgeting. Rosemary walked ahead of Albert so he had a chance to observe her. She had a navy dress on, with cap sleeves that showed her slender arms. The dress had a wide belt cinching her waist and flared over her hips. As she walked, the skirt swirled around her calves, causing Albert's heart to pound. She had a slight bounce to her step, bobbing her curls up and down.

Albert cleared his throat, to break his ogling of Rosemary. "Did you have to work today?" he asked.

She shook her head, "No, I had today off. Did you work?"

"Yeah," Albert could not think of anything witty to say and the conversation faltered, stuttered and failed. He tipped his head back to see the last remnants of light streak the sky purple and rose. *Like her*, he thought. *Rosie*.

"What church do you go to? I've never seen you at St. Anthony's," Rosemary stared at him with her steely blue eyes.

"No, we go to St. Stephen's," Albert replied, glad that she had started a conversation.

"Oh, you're Slovak?" Rosemary asked. St. Stephen's was the Slovak church in Streator; St. Anthony's was the German church.

"Yes, my parents came here after the war," Albert said. "My father is still Slovak at heart. When Hitler invaded Czechoslovakia, I thought my father was going to enlist!" Albert laughed, but Rosemary remained silent. "Did I say something wrong?" Albert asked.

Rosemary shook her head and forced a smile, "No, not at all. It's just..." She took a shaking breath. "My brother just enlisted. I'm so afraid something bad is going to happen to him."

Albert felt pangs of guilt—guilt that yet another person was joining up, reminding him of his lack of commitment.

"I'm sure he'll be fine," Albert said, a little too quickly to cover his uneasiness. She plastered a smile on her face and nodded, but Albert didn't want to see a fake Rosemary, he wanted to see the real person. He wanted to put his arms around her narrow shoulders, to put his hands in her hair and pull her to him.

They walked under the bare white bulbs that lit the marquee of the theater and passed into the lobby.

"Popcorn?" Albert asked. Rosemary nodded, a real smile easing onto her face. They took a seat in the center of the theater, tripping over people already seated. The seats quickly filled and the lights dimmed, the red velvet curtains opened, revealing the white screen.

Albert reached into the popcorn at the same time as Rosemary. Their fingers connected and Albert felt the shock of electricity again—it shot up his arm, stopped his heart. She jerked her hand back. Albert wanted to remain connected, to feel the pounding of his insides.

Rosemary

When Rosemary's fingers touched Albert's, she felt the flurry of tiny hummingbird wings inside her abdomen. She pulled her hand back, afraid of the feeling. It washed over her like a wave crashing the shore, stirring up emotions inside of her—feelings she had no control over. They pulled at her like a hidden eddy, dragging her under. She was drowning—and yet, she didn't want to stop these feelings, she wanted them to keep rolling over her. This lack of control was intoxicating.

She glanced at him out of the corner of her eye. He sat rigid, eyes fixed on the screen. A newsreel played—showing the awfulness of the war. Oh sure, they showed the troops advancing on the Nazis and the Japs, blasting them to bits. But Rosemary knew that for every one of the Nazis and Japs that died, an American died in the cross fire. They never showed that side of war in their film, but she knew that some Germans were sitting in a movie theater just like they were and seeing a film of our boys being blown apart. She pushed it out of her mind and watched Albert.

His profile was strong, nose straight and long, chin protruding in an authoritarian way. She wanted to lose herself with him, to forget about the war and the world—to have that sense of freedom that she felt when she was riding Yankee Clover. Is it a sin to be attracted to a young man? Yes, one of the deadly sins—Lust.

Finally, the movie started and Rosemary shifted her thoughts from Albert to the film. It was a musical. Dorothy Lamour played Nancy Angel, the main character. She led a struggling, Andrews Sisters–like singing act. The sisters did not want to sing together, but accepted an offer to sing at a night club after their father bought a soy bean farm. The band they played with was led by Happy Marshall. A love triangle ensued—one of the sisters, Bobby, pursued Happy, Happy pursued Nancy. And of course, it all turned out happy at the end. Rosemary sighed, disappointed that her life was not like a movie, all tied together with a neat ribbon.

They filed out of the theater as the credits rolled, swept up in the throng of exiting bodies. Albert reached out for Rosemary's hand so he didn't lose her in the crowd. As his rough hand surrounded hers, she felt her face flush and dared not look at him. She wanted to be aloof, like her sisters had taught her.

They separated themselves from the crowd. Albert let her hand drop. She was surprised at the strength of her disappointment.

"What did you think of the movie?" Albert asked.

"It was okay," she replied, her voice rising, betraying her lie.

Albert smiled a little sideways. "So you didn't like it."

Rosemary sighed, "It's just that movies like that are so neat and tidy. Everything works out in the end."

"What's wrong with that?" Albert asked, laughing.

"It's just not realistic. Things are never that easy."

Albert looked at her. Rosemary flushed. Had she said too much? Why couldn't she be one of those girls who didn't speak every thought that came to her mind? She walked faster to escape Albert's gaze.

"But can't life be that easy?" Albert said, quickening his step, "At least if you let it be."

She shrugged her shoulders, and they fell into silence. How

could she explain to him that her life had not been that neat, that people she loved abandoned her?

"Maybe it can be easy for you," she said to break the awkward silence.

"Me?" he chuckled, "you think my life is easy? I just choose to keep my head up, that's all."

Rosemary raised her head, "That's fine. All I'm saying is that I'd like to see a little more realistic movie."

"So what is your favorite movie then?"

"Oh, a movie like *Gone With the Wind*," she said. She both loved and hated Scarlet O'Hara. When Scarlet made some of her despicable choices, like marrying her sister's fiancé to save Tara, Rosemary understood Scarlet's need for security. Albert tried to stifle a laugh.

"What? Why are you laughing?" Rosemary said, slightly irritated.

"That you think *Gone with the Wind* is realistic."

"Well, the love story is more realistic anyway. It isn't just a happy ending," she said and crossed her arms.

"I prefer a story with a happy ending though. Gives me hope that it could happen in real life. Call me a hopeless romantic," he smiled and slowed his pace. Rosemary slowed too.

"Hopeless romantic," she said and grinned at him. She was rewarded with a soft laugh, a belly laugh from Albert. She sauntered ahead, quite pleased with herself.

They arrived at Albert's car. He opened the door and Rosemary slipped into the car, passing close enough to smell Albert's aftershave—a clean smell with a hint of something else beneath. He smelled like a man.

Albert drove through town, down Vermillion Street. Rosemary felt the leather creak underneath her. The car rode as if it were sliding along smooth ice.

"I like your car," Rosemary said.

"Thanks," Albert said, "But it's my father's car, not mine."

"We share a car too. It was Junie's... before he left," her voice drifted off.

"Yeah, my dad is pretty strict about taking the car," Albert said, dropping his tone to imitate his father, "He says, 'Albert, you no take my car! One scratch and you clean pig pen for a month!'"

Rosemary laughed, "You have a pig pen?"

"Yeah, and chickens. And a garden. I have six brothers and three sisters."

"Wait… how many brothers and sisters?" Rosemary thought growing up with six children had been crowded.

"Six brothers and three sisters," Albert laughed. "There is always something going on at our house. My youngest sister, Mare—well, her name is Mary Lou—she's only eight, and she really looks up to her big brother." His eyes crinkled as he thought of his siblings. Rosemary relaxed, comforted to know that he was close to his family. He wouldn't abandon them!

"Gosh, I thought my house was crowded. I have three sisters and two brothers, but my oldest two sisters are married. My third sister is married too, but she had some issues and moved back home with her two little girls," she said and immediately regretted it. What would Albert think of her gossiping? She gulped and twisted her hands.

"I heard about that. My brother knows your sister's husband, Ernie. Works at the Parkway, right?"

Rosemary nodded, embarrassed that her family's problems were known all over town.

"My oldest sister doesn't live at home either. She had to move out," Albert continued, his knuckles glowing white as he gripped the steering wheel. "My dad made her go to a convent."

"She's at a convent?" Rosemary heard the envy laced in the comment.

"Yeah, she… well, she and my dad," he paused, clenching his throat, "didn't get along."

Rosemary wanted to tell him that she understood; families were complicated. She wanted to reach out and pat his hand. But she couldn't, so she changed the subject to a more neutral topic.

"I love having my nieces at home. They are younger than your sister, Mare, but still a lot of fun. My niece Sandy is three and always asking questions. Why, why, why… that's her favorite word now," she said. Rosemary wanted children, of course she did, but she could not imagine having a child now, with the war going on and so much uncertainty. She was not going to be her mother, raising a houseful of kids alone. Intellectually, she knew her father hadn't chosen to get sick and leave them, but emotionally she couldn't accept that and it made her wary of all men.

"Yeah, kids are great. I remember that age. Mare was into everything and drove my ma nuts, always in her hair while she tried to cook. I got used to taking them outside to play so my ma could have a break," Albert said.

"She must have appreciated that."

Albert shrugged, "It was nothing. I got to practice baseball with my brothers and Mare would just run around in the field. You gotta do what you gotta do, right?"

Albert cocked his head and grinned. She nodded, warmth spread through her body. She wanted to forget about families, Junie leaving and just curl up under his crooked smile.

———

He turned on Sterling Street, pulled up in front of her house and cut the engine.

"Well," Albert said, looking at Rosemary. The fluttering kicked up against her abdomen. She reached her hand to her hair, trying to smooth it and calm her insides.

Albert got out of the car, came around and opened her door. They walked side by side up the sidewalk to the porch, electricity jumping from Rosemary to Albert. Rosemary felt tense and wound up, like a cat getting ready to pounce. A big, fat, orange, tabby cat getting ready to pounce on a little, defenseless mouse. She giggled at her own thoughts.

"What's so funny?" Albert grinned at her. His smile was so

big, stretching across his face, pulling at the cleft in his chin, crinkling the corners of his eyes. It was stunning.

Rosemary shook her head and said, "Nothing. It's just... well, I was just picturing you as a mouse." She burst into giggles again.

"A mouse? Huh..." Albert looked down at his barrel chest and stocky arms. "I don't look like much of a mouse, more like a bull." They both laughed.

"It was silly," she said, feeling like an immature girl.

"I like silly."

They stood at the front door. Albert was the perfect height. She could rest her head on his shoulder without bending her legs or stretching on her toes. He gazed at her with his intense dark eyes, devouring her with his glance. Her heart leapt into her throat, choking off her breathing. He leaned in and Rosemary could feel the warmth radiating off his body, his muscles tensing, holding himself back. She felt his breath on her face, could almost feel the stubble of his chin when a light flooded the porch in brightness. No cover of darkness in which to steal a kiss.

Rosemary saw Virginia's disapproving face in the window. She sighed, always the little sister being spied on.

"Well, I had a great night," she said, reaching for the door handle.

"Yeah, me too. We'll have to do this again," Albert said, his eyes full of hope.

Rosemary nodded, "Definitely." She flashed a big smile and dove into the house.

She closed the door behind her and turned to find Virginia standing, tapping her foot, with her arms folded. Her eyes looked drawn, tired. Rosemary could feel a lecture coming on and she wanted none of it. She tried to walk past her sister.

"You're going to get yourself in trouble, Rosemary," Virginia said.

She snapped, "I can take care of myself, Ginny. I'm not a child." She didn't want Virginia projecting her men problems onto her.

Virginia snickered. "You don't know anything about men.

You think you do, but you don't know anything." Rosemary had heard this story before. She glanced over at the coffee table and saw a half empty glass. She knew it had whisky in it without even smelling it.

"Look at me," Virginia continued, "I thought I had met the man of my dreams. Ernie was good looking and funny. He said he'd protect me. I gave him children. And what did he do? He knocked me around, blacked my eyes, busted my lip. Made me lie about it too. Told me to tell people I ran into a door jam. Like I am that clumsy! Ha!"

Virginia's words were slow and slurred. She drank a lot, especially late at night when the kids were asleep. Rosemary guessed it was how she dealt with a husband who had treated her worse than a dog. She didn't blame or judge Virginia for drinking. She would probably do the same in her shoes. But Rosemary told herself that she would never, ever get herself into a situation like Virginia. She would never marry a man who beat her and made her feel insignificant.

"Ginny, let's go to bed," Rosemary said, putting her arm around Virginia and leading her into their bedroom. Rosemary knew better than to try to reason with Virginia when she was in this state. Sometimes she fought Rosemary, but tonight she followed like an obedient child.

Albert

Mary Lou pulled at Albert's arm, urging him to walk faster. She was afraid they were going to miss the beginning of the parade down Main Street, miss the fire truck sirens. Albert held back, smiling at her irritation.

She turned and said, "Come on, Al!" She punched her glasses up the bridge of her nose with her index finger and scowled at him. He chuckled at her enthusiasm. He had agreed to take her to the parade since he had the day off from the factory. His youngest brothers, Jim and Ray, loped behind them, pushing and punching each other.

The sidewalks were crowded—children, the elderly, everyone coming out, enjoying the summer day, supporting the town's scrap metal drive. The parade raised support and donations for scrap metal, just one of the many items that were needed for the war.

Mary Lou pushed her way up to the curb and stepped onto the red brick road, plunking herself down, her skirt flying up over her knees, showing her spindly legs. She yanked it down. Ray and Jim came barreling up behind Albert, banging into Mary Lou and thrusting her forward. She screamed holy murder. Albert pulled the boys back.

"Hey you two, watch out for your sister!" he said. Mary Lou gazed up at him, her own personal hero.

The fire engine sounded—a long, loud wail that vibrated Albert's eardrums. Everyone craned their neck to see the fire truck rounding the corner onto Main Street. The engine was bright red, shining under the midday sun. One of the firemen reached out and rang the brass bell hanging from the driver's side. The firemen were standing on the running boards, waving to everyone in the crowd.

The boys pushed for a better view, Ray pointing to the ladder extending from the back of the truck upward. They both gaped in awe. The fire engine passed in noisy fanfare. Albert was glad it had passed, his ears ringing.

Next came the Streator High School marching band. The band leader walked backward, waving his hands, his tall white hat firmly secured under his chin. The majorettes were next in their short red dresses with white braiding across the front. They wore calf-high white boots, which accentuated their muscular legs. The band passed by next, playing "You're a Grand Old Flag." Mary Lou clapped in time with the music.

Albert looked across the street. His eyes were drawn to Rosemary. She was laughing and singing, holding hands with a blonde toddler. The toddler giggled as Rosemary swung her arms back and forth. She wore a simple blouse and twill pants, her hair fastened at both sides with red barrettes. Her cheeks flushed as she entertained the child. She looked up. Albert waved, hoping to catch her attention, but she turned back to the band again.

"Al, I want a soda!" Mary Lou whined. Albert wrenched his gaze from Rosemary. The parade was over and the crowd was dispersing.

"You want a soda?" he asked. The boys shouted in agreement. Albert gave a mock-skeptical look. "Do you have money?" he asked them.

Mary Lou slapped Albert in the stomach. "No, Al! You do!" she exclaimed.

"I do!" He pretended to be shocked, making Mary Lou giggle.

She looked expectantly up at him. He saw Rosemary heading up Main Street, towards Hill Brothers, the soda shop.

"Okay, let's go!" he said. The children whooped with glee. Albert crossed the street, pulling Mary Lou's arm, trying to catch Rosemary.

"Owwww!" she cried. But Albert was focused on Rosemary. She was right in front of him.

"Hi there," he called out. She spun around, her hair spiraling in a golden arc. A smile lit up her face.

"Hello yourself," she said, still clutching the toddler's hand. The little girl squirmed to get away, to go off and explore on her own. Rosemary was oblivious, staring in Albert's eyes.

"Is this your niece?" Albert motioned towards the child.

"Yes," she said, "This is Sandy. She thinks we should get a soda."

"We're going to get a soda. We should go together," he said in a way he hoped was nonchalant. Her niece whimpered, her knees buckling. Rosemary picked her up, but the child started wailing.

"I want shake! I want shake!" she screamed.

Mary Lou pulled on his arm, "Al, let's get a soda!"

Rosemary looked from her niece to Mary Lou to Albert. "Well, I guess they've decided for us," she said, a smile lighting her face.

They walked to Hill Brother's together. Albert found an empty table.

"So, what'll it be?" he asked. Ray, Jim and Mary Lou yelled out their orders—chocolate shakes.

"A chocolate shake would be great for my niece," Rosemary said, wiping off her niece's hands.

"And what about for you?" Albert asked. He saw her cheeks flush.

"Oh, I don't need anything," she said, a nervous giggle erupting from her.

"Everyone likes shakes," Albert said, trying to coax her into getting something. Rosemary relaxed.

"Oh, well, I'll have a vanilla malt," she said, looking pleased.

Albert couldn't hide his grin. He felt like he'd won a fight, a knock out. And Rosemary's smile was his prize.

He hurried to place their order and returned with the shakes on a tray. He held it out as if he were a waiter.

"Bon Appétit," he said, trying a French accent. It came out sounding more like Slovak than French. Rosemary smiled and he guessed he hadn't made a fool of himself.

The kids dug into their shakes, slurping loudly. Rosemary tilted her straw towards her and took a drink. Her neck flexed like a swan dipping towards water. Albert stared, mesmerized by her every movement. He felt tongue-tied again, not knowing what to say. His brothers and Mary Lou were arguing loudly and Rosemary's niece had wiggled out of her high chair and was running between the tables.

"So I had…"Albert started to say.

"I'm finished, Al. I wanna go home," Mary Lou whined, hanging on his arm. The boys were slurping the last of their shakes. Rosemary chased down her niece and came back to the table, the toddler wriggling like a feral cat. No time to talk here. Albert ushered everyone outside into the sunlight. He turned to say something, anything to Rosemary to keep her attention.

"I guess I should be going," she said. Albert nodded, Mary Lou pulling him away. But he didn't want to leave her like this. He spun around.

"Wait!" he called. Rosemary stopped and looked back at him. "Do you want to go out again this weekend?"

She smiled and nodded, struggling with her slippery toddler.

"That would be nice," she responded. Albert's heart soared. He was going to see her again. A large grin spread across his face.

"Great, I'll pick you up at eight on Saturday?"

She nodded before turning and rushing towards her vehicle.

"Can we go now?" Mary Lou whined again. He picked her up and swung her around, her knobby knees dangling like doll legs. She grabbed his arms in fear, but then relaxed and laughed.

"Mare, we can go where ever you want!" he said.

Rosemary

Rosemary collapsed, exhausted, onto the sofa in the front room. Her shoulders hurt from the repetitive motion of checking the bottles. She rolled them back, trying to relieve the tension. She pulled the bandana off her head and shook out her curls.

"Don't sit on that sofa until you've taken a bath!" Rosemary's mother called from the kitchen. Rosemary rolled her eyes; her mother must be able to see through walls to know she was on the sofa.

She lumbered into the bathroom and turned on the faucets, testing to see if the water was too warm. Rosemary wanted a cool bath, barely luke-warm. The water rose as Rosemary shed her clothes and eased herself into the water. She leaned back and closed her eyes. The bathroom was dim, lit only by the late afternoon sun that clung to the horizon. It was silent in the bathroom, only the sound of the water rippling when she moved. She could sense the rest of the house, her baby niece crying, Virginia soothing her, her mother clanging in the kitchen, but none of the sounds penetrated through the thick oak door.

She swirled the water under her palm, feeling the coolness as her hand glided back and forth. She was alone with her thoughts and wasn't sure if that was a good thing. Her mind drifted to the factory and the clear, greenish bottles. She imagined Albert, waving as she sauntered past him on her way to her station. She wanted to look seductive and enticing. Then she tripped over her shoe as she turned. She hoped Albert hadn't seen her.

Junie floated into her consciousness. Where was he? What was he doing? Horrible images crossed her mind—of him lying in a pit of mud bleeding, of his leg blown off by a German cannon, of him being run through by a bayonet. Did they still use bayonets? She didn't know. She splashed at the water to dissolve the images.

She climbed out of the bathtub, wrapping a large towel around herself. Tonight was her second date with Albert. Where would they go? She wondered as she walked to her room. She wanted to borrow Virginia's dress, the one that made her eyes look cobalt blue instead of gray. It hung in the closet. Rosemary pulled it over her head, smoothing it into place.

The dress was blue, with checks of green and white in vertical stripes. It had a thin blue belt that accentuated her narrow waist, short cap sleeves and a plunging neckline. She pulled her hair back and sucked in her cheeks. The dress made her feel confident, feminine. She applied black mascara to her pale lashes to make her eyes more striking and drew a cupid's bow on her lips with coral lipstick. The face staring back from the mirror looked fresh, yet intriguing. Just how Rosemary wanted to look. She was ready for her date.

———

Albert picked her up at eight o'clock sharp. Rosemary bounded out the door before her mother could ask her any questions. She was too tired to answer questions about Albert's background, not yet wanting anyone to know he was from the other side of the tracks or see the anticipation that this might lead to marriage. Her mother was always trying to marry her off. She was only sixteen, for Heaven's sake! And even though it was something she herself desperately wanted, she wasn't sure how much she could open her heart with the war going on. Albert led her to the car.

"Where are we going tonight?" Rosemary asked.

"Impatient, aren't we?" Albert said, a smile creeping on his face. Rosemary opened her mouth to protest, but laughed instead.

"Well, I'll tell you anyway. There's a swing band playing at the Paddock Club tonight. I thought we might go and listen to them," he said.

"And dance too?" she asked, clasping her hands.

Albert laughed. "I suppose we could dance too. Although you may reconsider that once you see me dance." Rosemary beamed as she slid past him and into the car.

———

They walked into the Paddock Club, which was already in full swing. On the stage was the sixteen piece band, consisting of five saxophones, four horns, and four clarinets, plus a stand-up bass, drummer, and a pianist on an upright piano. All sixteen squished onto the stage, with a female singer in a red dress at the microphone at the front center stage, crooning "Chattanooga Choo Choo." Men twirled women in time to the music.

Rosemary bounced to the beat.

"Would you like something to drink?" Albert asked.

"A beer would be great," she said. She wished she could be one of those dainty women who liked gin, but it tasted like a pinecone to her. She liked the hopsy taste of beer, the bitter coolness that she felt as it eased down her throat. Albert handed her a beer and waved hello to a few friends across the bar. He brought his attention back to Rosemary.

"Do you want a cigarette?" Albert asked, pulling one from a crushed pack. Rosemary nodded, a cigarette sounded good. She was so nervous, she hoped the cigarette would calm her down. She put the cigarette to her lips and Albert struck a match, cupping her hand. Her heart pounded, knees weakened at his nearness. He looked so handsome, in his white starched button-up shirt, the wide collar extending over the lapel of his black gabardine jacket. His shoulders filled out the jacket, broad and sturdy. There was a mischievous sparkle in his eyes that reminded her of Junie—he usually got that look when he was up to no good.

"What's that look for?" Rosemary asked, exhaling smoke sideways.

Albert grinned and shook his head.

Rosemary narrowed her eyes in mock-suspicion. "You look like you are up to no good," she said.

He laughed, throwing his head back. "I swear I'm not!" He held up his hands as if to surrender.

She took a big drink from her beer, finishing it in one swig. She wanted the alcohol to help her unwind, ease her tension. Her hand shook as she placed the bottle down. Albert had the strangest effect on her.

He was already ordering another drink for her, leaning over the bar. His neck was thick, widening into his shoulders, and then tapering to his narrow waist. She felt the quivering at the base of her abdomen, flushing her in warmth. She took a long drag off her cigarette to stop the vibrating inside her.

He handed her another beer, his fingers brushing hers, setting off fireworks of emotion inside of her. If he could see her insides, she would look like the Fourth of July, all red, blue and green exploding. He observed her, just looked at her face. His eyes were so intense, as if he could see into her soul, reading her inner desires.

"You look nice tonight," he said.

"Thanks. You do too." Her pulse beat wildly, her head spinning.

The band started their next song, the clarinets weaving a slow melody, filling the air with a sweet sound as the tenor saxophone wavered notes over the top. "Moonlight Serenade." Rosemary loved this song, the unhurried rhythm, every note deliberate and purposeful. She swayed, the clarinets hypnotizing her.

"I suppose you want to dance to this song," Albert said. Rosemary nodded, her heart leaping. She wanted to dance, wanted an innocent excuse to put her arms around him.

He led her into the center of the dance floor and placed his hands on her hips. Her skin vibrated where his hands were, up her torso into her hands. They swayed in time to the horns, clarinets. Rosemary felt light-headed. Was it being so close to Albert or drinking the beer too quickly? She didn't know, but she felt like she was flying.

He smelled like soap and musk. His leg brushed against her thigh and the hummingbirds returned to her stomach, fluttering. She thought she would explode, her pulse raced, heart pounded, brain whirled. Albert spun her around, in slow circles, to the left, swaying. He took her hands and pushed her out, spinning her around with his right hand outstretched. She spun, dizzying herself. Albert deftly caught her at her hip and began swaying again in time with the music. Rosemary could do nothing but follow his lead and feel the whirling all over her body.

The song ended and they walked back to the bar. Rosemary wanted it to go on forever, to keep spinning with him, revolving in an endless dance.

Before Rosemary knew it, the evening was ending, the band finishing with a huge crescendo, all of the horns sounding together in a loud, final note. She clapped, regretting that the evening was ending, that they soon would be going home and her magical evening with Albert would be finished.

Albert

They walked out of the Paddock Club after the band played one encore, Albert placing his hand at the small of her back. It was damp from dancing, warmth radiating from her body. They stopped at Albert's car. She seemed to glow under the yellow street lights. Albert could see the fair, down hair on her cheeks. Her hair looked golden, gilded and surreal. She looked at Albert, her eyes wide and questioning. He just wanted to remain with her, to not take her home.

"It's such a nice night," Albert said, coming up with an idea to extend the evening.

She nodded, not taking her eyes off him.

"I was thinking we could take a drive and look at the stars," he said. He held his breath, hoping that his strategy worked.

She smiled and said, "That would be nice. I love the stars." Albert celebrated inside, while maintaining his cool exterior. He hoped.

They headed toward Main Street. Albert drove to Airport Road, two miles out of town and stopped the car at the top of a slight rise. The airport was to the left of the gravel road. The lights from Streator shone in the distance, a faint white light. The black sky was full of twinkling stars, wisps of star dust. A sharp contrast of black and white. The runway was a barely discernible shade of gray, surrounded by shadows of corn standing tall, breathing in the coolness of the evening, releasing the heat accumulated during the day. The crickets serenaded them, their symphony filling the darkness.

"There's the Big Dipper," Albert said, pointed towards the western sky.

"Where?" she asked, leaning over him. He inhaled, taking in the smell of her, the rose water still clinging to her. He took her hand in his and pointed to the four stars marking the corners of the bucket and then arched her arm to show the handle. His hand vibrated from touching her. Her skin was soft and warm, the bones in her hand solid, letting him know that she was real.

She lit up. "I see it!" she exclaimed. She leaned back, satisfied. "So that's the Big Dipper?" Albert nodded, his skin prickling.

Rosemary sighed, closing her eyes. "I wish we could just stay out here forever." She looked angelic, like a small child. The weight of her thoughts and worries lifted and her face relaxed, released the tension she carried. Her lips parted and she looked so peaceful. Albert wanted to stay out there forever too, to watch Rosemary breath, sigh, smile, sleep. He wanted to feel her lips. Were they soft like her hands?

Her hair escaped the barrette and waved over her forehead. Albert reached out and brushed her hair aside. Her forehead was smooth and warm. She radiated warmth as if she had a fever.

Rosemary

The stars sparkled in a black sea like diamonds. Some of the stars blinked different colors—pink, orange, purple. It was so quiet; none of the town noises invaded the solitude out here, only the crickets chirping in their steady cadences. As Albert took her hand and showed her the big dipper, her heart hammered against her breastbone so hard she thought Albert could see it beating. She leaned back and closed her eyes to prevent herself from fainting. Her head was whirling, emotions rolling around her like a tornado.

He was only a few feet away from her, sitting there in his unconscious masculinity. Every time he shifted in his seat and the leather creaked, her heart hammered, the quivering erupting from the base of her abdomen. *Should I even be here?* Rosemary thought. Her breath caught as she thought of kissing him, his lips touching hers. She squeezed her eyes shut to block out these feelings, this sense of hysteria rising inside of her. As she was trying to gain her composure, she felt Albert brush her forehead.

Her eyes snapped open, heart pounding anew. Was he reading her thoughts?

"So your brother joined up, huh?" Albert asked. Rosemary shot him a look. "I mean, I think we all have a duty to serve our country," he continued.

"So you think my brother should be sent to die?" Rosemary asked, the passion mixing with anger, burning her up. She knew they all had a duty. Duty, duty, duty. She was sick to death of hearing about everyone's duties. Her duty was to ration her gas, sugar, meat, butter, everything good in her life! But her duty was small compared to the boys' duty—to lay down their lives to protect their country. She knew, she knew that it was her brother's duty, but that didn't make her any less fearful.

"No," Albert sputtered, "I, I only was saying, well, every able bodied man should want to kill the Jerries and the Japs for what they are doing, what they have done. Hitler wants to make the whole world German!"

"What's wrong with being German?" Rosemary snapped. Had he forgotten that *she* was German?

"Nothing is wrong with being German! But Hitler wants to rule the world and kill everyone who doesn't agree with his principles," Albert covered. "You don't agree with the persecution of the Jews or him invading Czechoslovakia, do you?"

Rosemary crossed her arms, feeling guilty that she should be patriotic and support the troops, but her fear was crushing. "No, I don't agree with either of those. But I don't know any Jews. I know and love my brother and I'm just afraid for him. Am I not allowed to be afraid?" She thought of the newsreel they had seen before the movie. Her stomach churned. She swallowed hard, wanting to escape the fear that overwhelmed her.

Albert

Albert hadn't wanted to upset her. He just wanted to tell her how she made him feel. How she made all thoughts go out of his head the second he saw her. And now, he had gone and blown his chance. He wanted to say that he understood why she was afraid and that he was afraid too—but that he had to fight through his fear. This evening with Rosemary solidified his resolve to go and fight. He was afraid, but he knew that the cause was worth the risk. He felt like a coward, knowing her brother had joined up. What must she think of him?

He could not put his thoughts into words. Once again, they fell into an uncomfortable silence.

There was that fear behind her eyes that Albert had seen at the Paddock Club, the fear of losing someone you love. Albert had never had that experience, never been in danger of losing someone he loved.

"I'm sorry," Albert said, knowing that the words were totally inadequate. She shrugged. Albert chewed on his lower lip. "Of course you have every right to be afraid. I've never been in a situation to lose a brother or sister," he said.

"It seems to be all that is on anyone's mind these days. The war. I know you're right. Hitler has to be stopped, and it isn't fair what he's done to the Slovaks or Poles," she said.

"Well, let's just try to forget about all of that and just enjoy the evening," Albert said. Rosemary smiled and looked out at the stars.

"Can you show me any other constellations?" she asked.

Albert nodded as he focused on her face. Her lower lip was open and he could see her pearly teeth, pink tongue. Her heart was racing, a vein pulsing at the base of her neck, in the depression between her collarbones. He watched it pulse; it made her look vulnerable. Instead of answering her, he leaned forward, as if she were a magnet. She turned her face towards his, and he moved closer. Rosemary's breath held as he came in contact with her lips, his lips on hers. And they were soft, so soft.

Rosemary

Rosemary sat, mesmerized by Albert's eyes. In the dim star light, they looked like solid black ink pools, cool and inviting. He leaned into her and kissed her. His lips were strong and she found herself kissing him back, felt her heart throbbing. He wrapped his hand around the back of her neck and into her hair. She placed her hand on his arm, stout and muscular. He tasted like peppermint and beer. Rosemary didn't remember him eating a peppermint, but it was delicious. His tongue flickered into her mouth, setting off the fluttering in the base of her abdomen. She had never been kissed like this, with passion and craving. But she liked it, wanted more. She wanted to be devoured by him, to forget the world.

His left hand crept from her neck down to her collarbone and lower. Rosemary felt the light pressure of his hand gliding across her bare skin. His hand drifted lower. He clutched her breast as he kissed her deeply. Her sense of morality bounced back into her mind. What was she doing? She was petting with a man on a dark country road! What would her mother think?

She pushed Albert away roughly. "What do you think you're doing?" Rosemary yelled. "Is this the only reason you asked me to come out here? I thought you were a gentleman! I'm not that kind of girl!"

She was angry, more so with herself that she could have let herself go with him. But instead of recognizing who she really was angry with, she directed her rage at Albert. With one motion, she reached over and snatched the keys from the ignition. She opened her car door and jumped out. "Cool off while you look for your keys!"

She cocked her right arm back and launched the keys into the cornfield on the opposite side of the street. Albert looked at her like she was crazy. Deep down, she knew it was irrational and that she wanted it as much as he had. The Catholic conditioning kicked in and overrode her emotions. *Some gentleman he is!* She huffed. She watched him scurrying in the dirt, looking for the keys, indignation replacing her guilt.

She turned on her heel. Seeing him roll around in the dirt just solidified that she couldn't trust him—he would only hurt and leave her. She pushed her shoulders back and raised her chin. She was not going to be hurt again. She was not going to put herself in this position to be swept away with her emotions. She stamped down the road, looking back to see Albert still on his hands and knees in the star light.

Albert

Albert groped in the dirt for his father's keys. He had to find them; he could not go home without the car. He thought about Rosemary as he searched. What had happened? His passion had overwhelmed him. Her lips felt so good, and her cheek was like a baby's newborn skin—untarnished and smooth.

His hand had a mind of its own, sliding down towards her breast. He had just wanted to feel her cheek and the next thing he knew, his hand was on her breast and she threw his keys into the cornfield. He chuckled to himself. She had spunk. The second Albert crossed the line, she went into action like a cornered bobcat, clawing its way to freedom. All he could do was sit back and watch her in awe. Even as she hurled his keys, she looked gorgeous. The arch of her arm, the determined look on her face all endeared her to Albert. He had to find the keys and pick her up, explain what had happened.

He pushed the dirt around, kicking up a swirling cloud. The earth tasted metallic and dry. He looked up at the stars, the Big Dipper. Only a moment earlier, he had been tracing the stars with Rosemary's willowy wrist. He had no idea what came over him. But oh, she had felt lovely. He chuckled again under his breath.

To his left, he saw a glint of metal. He dove into the dirt and connected with his keys. The keys! He rejoiced. He hurried back to the car, he had to catch Rosemary and explain to her. He floored the Nash, the engine roared in response, kicking up gravel behind it. He was almost at the end of Airport Road when he saw her, limping along.

Albert pulled up alongside of her and saw she had broken the heel off her left shoe. Rosemary did not look over at Albert, but kept tottering along.

"Ro-sie," Albert sang to her. She shot him an angry look and tried to walk faster, stumbling on the loose gravel. He laughed, angering her more.

"Come on, Rosie," Albert sang again, leaning into the passenger side of the car as he coasted down the road. "Are you going to walk all the way home?"

"Yes!" she snapped, setting her face in stony determination.

"It's a long way," Albert retorted. She walked on in silence, the crunching of the gravel drowning out the crickets and the cicadas. The exertion of walking with one broken shoe showed on her face. She huffed, her face crimson, sweat beading around her forehead, soaking the back of her dress. She was beautiful.

"Roooo-sie," Albert sang again after a few moments. He was rewarded with a stifled smile. She tried not to laugh, although she had to see the ridiculousness of the situation. They were still two miles outside of town. With her broken shoe, it would be a long walk indeed.

"I'll keep my hands to myself," Albert said, one final plea. Rosemary stopped short, her breathing labored. She wiped the sweat off her brow, placed her hands on her hips and turned towards Albert. Her chest heaved as she tried to catch her breath.

"Come on, I promise," Albert said, opening the door for her. She hesitated and glanced at the city lights in the distance.

"You so much as make one move towards me and finding your keys will be the least of your problems!" she said as she plopped into the passenger seat and slammed the door.

"Oh I don't doubt that," Albert laughed. She sat, arms crossed, staring straight ahead.

"Can I say I'm sorry?" Albert asked.

"You can, but I don't think it will do any good," Rosemary said through tight lips. Her eyes flashed a hot rage.

"Well, for what it's worth, I'm sorry," he laughed. The corner of her mouth turned up into a smile, but she fought it off.

"I don't know what came over me, Rosie," Albert said, "I wanted to tell you how I felt about you and then I don't know what happened."

"And how do you feel about me? Do you think I'm some cheap bar girl who you can have your way with?" Rosemary shot back.

"No, not at all. I... I love you," Albert blurted out, not intending to say that. His heart paused as he realized that was what he felt for her. He loved her. He wanted to spend his life with her—and he knew in that moment that he would.

Rosemary

He loved her. All of her anger about his getting fresh with her went out of her head. Her heart started again, hammering and jumping. She felt like she could love him too, may love him already.

"You're crazy, trying something like that," she said coolly, but her voice had lost its edge. All the anger had dissipated from her body.

"How about you?" Albert laughed. "You threw those keys farther than Swish!"

"Who?" she looked perplexed.

"Swish Nickolson, from the Cubs," he said. "Anyway, it doesn't matter. The only thing that matters is that I'm sorry and I... I don't really know what came over me. You make me act all different," Albert said. "I... I just want to be with you. I feel like we could have a happy ending, like the movie."

He reached over and put his hand between them, palm up. His look pleaded with her to give him a sign that she felt the same. She placed her hand in his, her small hand engulfed in his broad, rough palm. His fingers closed around hers, warming her hand, sending waves of emotion from his fingers into hers, up her arm and into her head. They drove back into town, hands entwined.

"You know I don't believe in happy endings," Rosemary said.

"But wouldn't it be neat if we could be the happy ending?"

As they pulled up to Rosemary's house, she didn't want the evening to end. Albert loved her. She wanted to bask in those feelings, feel his love. He cut the engine and there was silence. No lights illuminated Rosemary's house, no one waiting up for her. Her hand was still in Albert's. She felt shy. There were so many things she wanted to say, that she wanted to have the happy ending, the security. She felt as if she were in a spell and a word would break it.

Albert turned to her, his serious eyes pleading. "Rosie, I know this is going to sound crazy. Maybe it is crazy…" He drifted off, lost in his own thoughts. Rosemary leaned forward in anticipation. What was he going to say? Had he changed his mind already? She hoped he hadn't, he couldn't.

He clutched her hands, pulling her towards him. "Rosemary," he said, "Will you marry me?"

Rosemary's heart paused, waiting to see if she had heard correctly. Time seemed to stop, the air thick with anticipation. She cocked her head, joy, surprise and fear creeping over her, enveloping her in a thick blanket. She opened her mouth to speak, but what would she say? This was so sudden. She had barely time to process her feelings and realize what they were. And now… it was all too fast.

Before she could answer, Albert continued, "I'm going to enlist. But before I go, I want you to marry me. I want you to be my wife."

Rosemary sat, stunned. He wanted to marry her, but he was leaving to get killed? No, no, this was not happening. He was going to say he was only joking, that he would be at work tomorrow and they would go out again and again and eventually get married. She could not believe that he said he was enlisting. He just couldn't!

"Rosie, say something. I love you, I want you to be my wife," he pleaded.

"You're enlisting?" she whispered.

He nodded, "Yes. I've felt like it was something I needed to do for some time, but I promised my mother I wouldn't until the younger ones started school. But I can't wait any longer. And, well, I wouldn't want you to think that I'm shirking my responsibilities since your brother is fighting."

Rosemary's head spun in confusion. Just as she was beginning to feel she could open herself and give herself to Albert, she was losing him. Every man in her life left her in some way or another. She couldn't take it. Her heart felt as if it were shattering. She placed her hand between her breasts to hold her heart together.

"Rosie, we will have a good life," Albert started. Rosemary's temper flared.

"Good life? Good life? What kind of a good life can we have if you're overseas getting killed? How dare you ask me to marry you and tell me that you're leaving in the same breath! How dare you!" she raged. "I can't marry you, Albert. I can't, knowing that you are going to war and might not come back."

"I will come back. I promise," Albert grabbed both of her hands in his and clutched them to his chest.

"Don't make promises you can't keep," Rosemary cried. Tears threatened to spill from her eyes. One slid down her cheek. She pulled her hands out from his and ran into her house as the tears came flooding from her. She shut the door and leaned against it, crying for the life Albert had offered and ripped away in one stroke.

Albert

Albert awoke the next morning with an awful feeling in his stomach. He had laid his heart out there, put himself on the line and Rosemary had denied him. He pulled his clothes on and smoothed back his hair. She was in shock, she must be. Her brother had enlisted, and then he had told her that he was enlisting. She was afraid that he wouldn't come back. But if he promised that he would come back, maybe she would marry him when he returned. If he could just get a guarantee that she would wait for him, that she would give him a chance to prove that he would come back in one piece, then she would marry him. He cheered himself with his logic. She would be his wife.

His father drove him and his brother, Ed, to the enlistment office in Ottawa the following Monday. He was so proud of his sons for volunteering, serving their country. His mother prayed to God that He keep them safe and made the sign of the cross over and over. She remained stoic as they pulled out of the gravel driveway. Albert put her out of his mind, focused on the task at hand, enlisting and getting Rosemary back.

The enlistment office was in the LaSalle County Courthouse. It was an imposing white limestone building, tall pillars at the top of a steep staircase holding up the pointed roof. He climbed the stairs behind his father and Ed. His heart was beginning to feel heavy.

What if the war wasn't all that he thought it would be? What if he did, God forbid, get killed? He began sweating and looked over at Ed. Ed looked calm, collected and not the nervous wreck that Albert felt he must look like. Albert pushed those thoughts down and reminded himself that he was going to be a hero, save thousands of lives… then come back to Rosemary with honor.

They were directed to the enlistment office, to the left, down the hall. The green and black linoleum tiles were newly waxed and reflected the sunlight. Albert's shoes squeaked as he walked, the sound filling the empty hallway. The hallway narrowed in on him. His breath was shallow and rapid. His legs felt wobbly and he had to concentrate to keep putting one foot in front of the other. His father clamped him on his shoulder and gave him what he thought was a reassuring shake.

They stood at the door—Army Enlistment. Albert could see outlines of people scurrying behind the beveled glass pane. They opened the door and a man dressed smartly in his army uniform was seated at a desk in front of them.

"Are you here to join up, boys?" the man in an olive uniform asked Ed and Albert. Ed's head bobbed up and down. Albert nodded in a way that he hoped was as convincing as Ed's. The man in the uniform gave them some paperwork to fill out. Bars, stars, and patches covered the jacket. Soon, soon Albert would have this too, the symbol of fighting for his country.

It was a blur to Albert—paperwork filled, exams given. The only thing Albert clearly remembered was raising his right hand, taking the oath, "I, Albert Jedoga, do solemnly swear to bear true allegiance to the United States of America, and to serve them honestly and faithfully, against all their enemies or opposers whatsoever, and to observe and obey the orders of the President of the United States of America, and the orders of the officers appointed over me."

And with that oath, he was an official enlistee in the United States Army. He was heading into the war. There was no turning back now.

Rosemary

Rosemary sat on her porch, her face turned up to catch the autumn sunlight. It warmed her skin. Skippy barked sharply, his sharp ears pointed forward. Rosemary threw a stick to the dog. He retrieved it and waited for Rosemary to toss it again, his back end wiggling in excitement. *That dog never tires of this game,* Rosemary thought. Why wasn't her life simple, like Skippy's? Skippy didn't have to worry about falling in love and then having that person put himself in the middle of a war, possibly never coming back. Rosemary's chest hurt, her heart constricted to stop it from breaking into a million pieces. Sandy chased Skippy as he fetched the stick, kicking up the multi-colored leaves which had fallen in the late September air. Sandy giggled as she ran after the dog with outstretched arms, blond curls bouncing. She heard her mother and sister in the kitchen, canning more tomatoes for the winter, complaining about the shortage of sugar, how there was not enough for all of the canning they needed to do. Rosemary was tired of shortages, tired of the war, tired of uncertainty.

Thinking of uncertainty, she hadn't heard from Albert in weeks, over a month. Her heart leapt every time she thought she saw him at work, but she hadn't seen him. She prayed that he'd changed his mind about joining up, that he'd come to his senses and that he was staying here, working at the factory, out of harm's way. She had tried to numb her feelings, but the fear shadowed her, lurking like a burglar, stealing her happiness. Where could he be? What could he be doing? Had he left for the war and not even let her know? She wavered in her feelings—not for him. No, those feelings seemed to strengthen in his absence. Her wavering was regret over not agreeing to marry him, not grabbing the chance for happiness that he promised. Would she get the chance again? If she said yes, maybe she could change his mind about going overseas to fight. That sounded terribly unpatriotic, even to her own selfish ears, but she just wanted a chance at happiness with someone who wouldn't leave her like her father and Junie had done.

She heard a car coming up the street. Albert's blue Nash motored down the road. She patted her hair as Albert alighted from the car. He had not changed his mind. His cap was pulled low, the brim just revealing his dark eyes. The green jacket hugged the edges of his broad shoulders, two stripes on his left arm. The buttons down the front of the jacket were unnaturally shiny, as if they had their own energy source. His green pants were neatly pressed, a crease running the length of his legs to his shiny black shoes. Rosemary's hand flew to her throat, fear choking her breath.

He smiled and walked towards her. She sat down hard on the porch step, jolting her tailbone, pain shooting up her back. But the physical pain could not dull the ache in her heart. He had done it. He really had enlisted. *Idiot!* He had not returned to offer her security, only to break her heart all over again. Her body trembled.

"Rosie, I'm here one last time before I ship off to basic training," he said and knelt in front of her. He took out a single silver band, held it with an outstretched hand. Rosemary could not get enough air. The world faded into a twinkling background of white stars. He was leaving her. Just like her father, just like Junie. Everyone left her.

Albert was on his knee, devotion in his eyes. "I've said it before and I'll say it again. I love you, Rosie, and I want you to be my wife, but I know that you are afraid I won't come home. I'm not asking you to marry me right now. All I'm asking is for you to take this ring and make a promise that you will wait for me, that you'll wait and marry me when I come home from the war."

Rosemary was frozen, could not move. She hoped that if she stayed still, time might stop and Albert would not leave, would not have joined the army. If she could only have made him understand the futility of joining! What good would it do? Her eyes welled with tears, her bottom lip trembled.

Albert mistook this emotion as happiness, as consent from Rosemary. He reached for her, trying to place the ring on her left ring finger. Rosemary sprang into action, slapping his hand away, kicking at him.

"No! Let go of me!" she screamed. "I can't believe you did this! I can't believe you! You won't come back, you won't!" She sobbed, tears running down her face. She wanted to make a life with him, and he was leaving and ripping that life away from her.

"Come on, Rosie! I'll be back. You gotta believe me. This is my promise to you. That's why I want you to have this ring, as a reminder that I will come back. Because I will. I'll be back and when I come home, then we'll get married," he said. She shook her head slowly.

"Albert, please. Don't make promises you can't keep," she cried, her body shaking. He put his arms around her, squeezing her. Her face was crushed against his gabardine jacket, smelling the industrial detergent. It burned her nostrils. She clutched his jacket, not wanting him to go, not wanting to let him go.

"I will come back," Albert pulled Rosemary away, forcing her to look him in the eyes. "Rosie, I will come back and I will marry you. We can meet at George Hasckak's and get married at St. Stephen's."

Rosemary threw him a look at the mention of St. Stephen's.

Albert laughed and said, "Alright, or St. Anthony's. I don't care as long as you say you'll marry me when I return." He was so sincere, his eyes full of determination.

"Say you'll wait for me, Rosie," he pleaded, "Say you'll wait and marry me." He was so confident; she wanted to believe him when he said he would come back. She could almost see the house, the children, feel the happiness and completeness. But the fear was so much stronger, overpowering her heart and showering her in raw pain.

"I… I don't think I can take that risk," she whispered into his jacket and untangled herself from his warm embrace. Her chest squeezed around her heart, wringing it like a wet sheet. Her hands grasped at air, opening and closing, feeling the heat evaporate as she looked at Albert.

"I can't, Al. You're leaving me! Leaving me! I can't sit here and hope you will come back. Why? Why did you go and join up? Why are you leaving me?" Rosemary's voice rose from calm and level to shrill, screaming at Albert in her hurt frustration.

Albert's lip tightened, the hurt flashing across his eyes. "I have to go, Rosie. I wish you understood why this is important to me. I will come back. You'll see. I will come back for you."

He stepped back from her, his arms stiff at his sides. For a moment, he looked as if he were going to pull Rosemary back into his arms, to put his lips on hers. Rosemary held her breath, alternately wanting him to kiss her and just wanting him to go away. He turned toward his car and threw his shoulders back.

Doubt seized her. She wanted to run after him, throw her arms around him and tell him that she would wait for him, that she would marry him. But she was petrified. What if he were wrong? What if he didn't come back? What if this was the last time she would feel his strong arms around her? These thoughts kept her frozen as she watched his car roll around the corner and out of her life.

1945

Albert

Albert took a drag off his cigarette, pulling the collar of his jacket up to protect against the biting winter wind. He was somewhere in Luxembourg. After he went through endless training, he was sent to Camp McCoy in Wisconsin. He learned how to use his rifle, was taught maneuvers to prepare him for fighting in Europe. He sailed across the Atlantic in November 1944, camped in Southampton, Great Britain, celebrated Christmas with complete strangers who were quickly becoming his best friends. He and his new friends heard about the Battle of the Bulge—Hitler's latest offensive into Belgium. They all wanted to be over there, to use what they had learned, to lick the Jerries. And on January 10, the 304th made the six day voyage across the English Channel and onto French soil.

They marched through the Ardennes Forest, where the Nazis had attacked. The battle was far from over and Albert's superiors feared another push from von Rundstedt, the ruthless general of the *Wehrmacht*—the German army. The countryside was littered with evidence of the recent fighting. A dusting of snow covered most of the wreckage—the splintered trunks of bombed trees stuck out like burnt match sticks, burned out jeeps, tanks and buildings reduced to rubble. The acrid smell of burnt metal stung Albert's nostrils and lungs. This was his new home.

They settled near the German border, in a deserted town called Dickweiler near the Sauer River. It was January and bitterly cold. Albert's platoon assumed a defensive position. They had walked twelve miles that morning to dig ditches and fox holes near the Sauer River. Albert surveyed the landscape. The snow covered the rolling hills. Blackened tree shards interrupted the solid white. Albert stamped his feet to try to get some feeling back into his toes.

His eyes traveled across the Sauer River to the Siegfried Line—the dreaded German defense that they were sent here to smash through and bring about victory. The grey concrete pylons, the Dragon Teeth, jutted out of the snow, waiting to swallow them. Somewhere, on that side of the river, holed up in their bunkers and machine gun nests, was the German army. Albert shivered, not from the cold, but in fearful anticipation of the next few days and weeks. The two sides had been exchanging artillery fire for days. It was continuous background noise, something that Albert couldn't quite get used to, but was able to block out after a while.

His thoughts turned, as they often did on these monotonous days of digging, to Rosemary. He went to the Paddock club on his last leave before shipping out. It was October of '44 and the war in Europe was hot. The Allies had successfully landed in France, but were still having quite a fight. He had his orders; he would be shipping out soon. Now he understood the boys on leave, longing for normalcy, a return to the familiar. He walked into the Paddock Club in his dress uniform, brass buttons shining, his coat hugging his frame. His company insignia, an oak tree on a blue and white shield, was sewn high on his shoulder. He knew what every patch, every stripe meant now. He felt the younger boys follow him with their eyes, wanting to be him, just as he wanted to be the army guys two years earlier.

Then he saw her, Rosemary, sitting at the end of the bar with her sister Norma. Her hand rested on the neck of a beer bottle. The sadness in her eyes had deepened, turning her eyes from steel blue to grey. Albert rushed over to her.

She looked up as he approached, a flash of happiness unclouded her eyes, but the veil dropped as quickly as it had lifted. Albert wasted no time.

"Rosie, I need to talk to you," Albert started. Her face had taken an angularity that wasn't there before he had left. Had his absence caused it? He didn't know, but he wanted to make it right.

"Go ahead," she said, twirling her hand towards him. Her head was down, eyes riveted to her bottle of beer.

"Can we step outside?" Albert asked, all of his military bravado dissipated with two words from her.

"Sure," she said and slid off the barstool. She walked ahead of him, back straight, arms stiff. Albert could feel her anger flowing from her like an icy comet's tail. She pushed the door open with the heel of her hand, not bothering to hold it open for him. His shoulder banged the closing door and he stumbled.

Rosemary turned to him, something like hatred showing on her face.

"Rosie, I'm here one last time," Albert said. "I've seen a lot in my training and will be going overseas soon, in a few weeks. But I needed to see you one last time. I know you said you couldn't wait for me, but I want you to reconsider." Albert was hoping that his time away from her would make her soften to him.

"Please, Rosie," he said as she remained silent. "I can't live without knowing that you will be here for me when I come home. I want us to laugh together, to love each other, to build a family…" his voice trailed off. Rosemary covered her face with her hands. She turned from him, shoulders shaking. He put his hands on her shoulders and turned her around. Her hands dropped and tears fell down her face.

"I've thought about you so many times. Wondering where you are, what you are doing. I hate not knowing where you are, I hate seeing my friends get war telegrams saying their beau was wounded or killed. I hate it, I hate it, I hate it!!" she beat on his chest, fresh tears welling in her eyes. Albert took his hands in hers.

"Please say you'll marry me, Rosie, I can give you a life together. I'll fight harder knowing you are waiting for me."

She looked up at him, all the anger gone and deep sadness replacing it. "But what if you don't come back? I can't be a war widow, Al."

"I will come back," he said, pulling her towards him. She fell into his arms with no resistance, clutching him around his waist, her arms trembling. He smoothed her hair. Everything will be all right, he thought, everything will be all right.

"Day dreaming again, Sarg?" Eddie Castillo teased. Al scoffed, pulled out of his reverie; he didn't feel like a Staff Sergeant in Charlie Company, 304th Infantry. The war was not what Albert had expected. Bone-chilling cold, mind-numbing boredom, and trenches—endless trenches and defensive positions to dig. He rolled his shoulders back, feeling the groan from his tight muscles, wishing Rosemary was there to knead his tired muscles.

Eddie's helmet slipped down over his narrow head, covering his eyes. He was thin and wiry with black hair. He was one of the original members of the 304th from New Haven, Connecticut, home of Yale University, but Eddie was not one of the fortunate to attend the college. He came from a poor Italian immigrant family, one of eleven children and joined the army upon turning eighteen. He and Albert became friends fast, seeing who could out-shine the other by telling stories. Albert made a snow ball and lofted it at Eddie. Eddie ducked, laughing. Albert picked up his shovel and began digging once again, focusing only on the trench growing in front of him.

When the sun had dipped below the horizon, turning the gray sky to shades of purple, pink and orange, Albert called for everyone to stop digging. They hoisted their shovels onto their shoulders and trudged back to camp. Albert admired the Catholic Church they passed on their daily walks. Eddie made the sign of the cross as they walked by, held up his gold crucifix and kissed it. He thought of Rosemary, praying for his safety in St. Anthony's. He didn't know if God was on their side or the German's, but he hoped that He was on theirs. Behind the wrought iron fence were tombstones of various shapes and sizes. Cemeteries used to calm Albert, the quiet that fell over everything soothed him. But now, the sight of the cemetery just made him realize how close to death he and everyone in his company and his battalion were.

They ended their trek at the mess hall. As they sat at the long tables, the drone of the Piper Club shook the ground, rattling the tin plates and cups on the tables. Albert was relieved to hear the Piper Club planes overhead, he knew that while they were in the air, the Germans would not fire their artillery for fear of disclosing their locations and bringing on the Piper Club's fire power.

Eddie threw his fork onto his plate. "Damned food. Damned Krauts are messin' up my eatin!" he said, mouth down turned. "Know what I want? A nice braciol' with some fresh mozzarell'. Awww... that's the stuff!" Eddie had a habit of cutting off the last syllable of his favorite Italian foods.

"Yeah, I miss my ma's halušky," he said, imagining the buttery egg noodles dissolving in his mouth.

"What the hell is halušky?" Eddie asked.

"It's butter and potatoes and noodles with cabbage. Mmmmm," Albert groaned.

"Kinda like gnocchi, minus the cabbage?" Eddie asked. Albert shrugged. He had never heard of gnocchi. There were a few Italians in Streator, but Albert never talked to them.

"D'ya hear about Marshall?" a guy from another company at their table said, leaning in. "Took some shrapnel in the hand."

"He okay?" Thomas Behrendt asked.

The guy nodded, "Yeah, he's fine, but makes ya realize how close we are, huh?"

"Alright, that's enough. I want to enjoy my damned army food. Quit jawin'," Albert said sharply. The boys quieted at the tone of their sergeant. He steadied himself, shook up at the first casualty of their unit.

The entire regiment was taut. The artillery was placed, the cannons and antitank guns aimed. In the morning, the 304th's sister regiment, the 417th, was attempting an initial crossing of the Sauer River at Echternach. They would be crossing into Germany.

Albert went to the tents to drift into a restless sleep. A little before midnight, they would engage the Germans—real fighting. This would be their first engagement and most men were eager to get in there, to not be "green" anymore, and to gain fighting experience. Albert wanted to do his part, he wanted to fight, was not afraid to fight. But he knew now that he had been naïve in his thinking when he was still in Streator. Being a hero, stealing behind the enemy lines—these were not easy tasks, not undertakings for some hick from the country. The bullets were hard and real, they could rip through a man's flesh and bleed the life from him.

Albert drifted to sleep, imagining his life with Rosemary. He knew now what her fears were, how they had influenced her decision. He thought of the panic in her blue-gray eyes when he showed up in his uniform, the alarm. In his mind, he put his arms around her slender shoulders, kissed her rosy lips again.

It felt like Albert had just closed his eyes when he was awoken—it was time. He grabbed his rifle and shook Eddie awake. Eddie opened his eyes drowsily and Albert motioned. Time to go. Eddie sprang out of bed and followed Albert. They joined the rest of their battalion and marched towards Echternach. The artillery began its mournful booming, shells lofted with a thwunk and exploded on the other side of the river. They were to provide cover for the 417th as they crossed the Sauer. Albert's company dug into a defensive position behind a stone wall that had been reduced to rubble. They were to take out the pillboxes and entrenchments that fired on the boats. Albert raised his rifle to his shoulder, pushed aside some small rocks with the barrel. He had a clear view of the pillboxes on the other side, but also adequate cover.

The boats pushed off the south shore, into the rushing stream, trying to get over and take the high ground on the German side. Machine gun fire peppered the river. Albert was given the order to fire. He squeezed his trigger, round after round popping out of his gun. He aimed for the nearest pillboxes where he saw flashes of white light exploding like little firecrackers. He kept shooting until no more firecrackers came from the bunker. He then moved onto the next pillbox, methodically, calmly in the chaos. The boats had reached the other side and were taking heavy fire. An American cannon launched a mortar shell and the pillbox spraying the boats went up in a great ball of fire, a loud boom filling the sky, blocking out the rifle and machine gun fire.

The gun next to Albert went silent. He looked over to see one of his men, Floyd Gussman, shot right through the forehead. Blood gushed from the perfectly circular wound, gray matter oozing out. His mouth was gaped open in horror and his eyes were glazed and empty. He was dead. Albert gagged. He'd never seen a dead person before. He closed Floyd's eyes, trying to keep the bile down. He gritted his teeth, turning his revulsion to anger. He placed his rifle into his small hole, roaring as he emptied the rest of his magazine.

"Ammo!" he called out. His men were watching him, looking to him for direction. "Keep firing!" he yelled. They quickly turned back, firing at the pillboxes.

The fighting continued as the sun rose, reached its apex and descended before Albert's company was relieved. They went back to camp for a quick meal and rest and then it was back to their defensive positions. They needed to build a bridge across the river. The days had been warm, melting the snow into the river. It raged past, swirling and churning, white caps forming and breaking as it surged by. Several attempts had been made to bridge the river, all made while taking heavy shell fire. The river was as unwilling as the Germans to be defeated. It capsized boats, sending several men to their icy deaths.

Finally, on the third day of fighting, the river was breached, floats and duckboards laid and the bridge began to take shape. Eddie crawled over to Albert, leaving his position. For the moment, the enemy was retreating, back to better defended pillboxes and entrenchments. Albert's company was on watch, guarding the bridge and the embankment.

Eddie whistled, offering Albert a cigarette. "Hell of a three days, huh?" Eddie said, his cigarette dangling dangerously off his lip. Eddie had a way of making the cigarette stick to his lip without falling. Albert could never do it.

"What are you doing here, Eddie? Get back to your post!" Albert hissed. He was the staff sergeant, in charge of keeping his platoon in position. If he couldn't control his men, he was not a good leader. Eddie knew this, but deliberately disobeyed rules when he felt like it.

"Eh, the Jerries are on the run, and I'm bored," he said, leaning against the rubble pile, his hands resting behind his head. Albert grabbed his arm and pulled him up, shoving him toward his position.

"Come on! You know we all need to stay in position. You're going to get somebody killed, acting like that," Albert was cross. This may have been his first battle, his first look at the enemy, but he had been listening in training and he knew that disobeying an order put the whole company at risk, in danger. He had to trust that his superiors knew what was right and would give orders that would put them in the least amount of danger—if they all followed directions. Eddie begrudgingly went back to his position.

Albert watched the supply trucks lumber across the bridge, providing much needed ammo and other supplies to the boys over there. He was relieved; his first encounter with the enemy was a success! He had seen the wounded, writhing in pain, being carried back to the medic's hospital. He shuddered, thinking of Floyd, the emptiness in his eyes. They had lost men, but it was worth the gain, worth the bridge, advancing into Germany, forcing the Nazis closer to surrender. Then he could go home. He could marry Rosemary.

Rosemary

Jack returned from filling the heater in the basement with the coal that they had collected that summer. Was it three years ago that she and Junie had done the same chore? The fall had passed in slow motion. The summer heat cooled, the trees turned their brilliant colors, but Rosemary saw none of it. She was riddled with worry about Albert and Junie. It blocked out all else. *This damned war!* She thought. It kept dragging on and on. Then came the news in December of Hitler's offensive, the Battle of the Bulge.

Rosemary, Norma, Wilma, Jack and their mother were glued to the radio every night to hear what had happened that day. The announcer read a letter from a local soldier—his unit trapped for seventy-two hours by the Germans. He and several men managed to escape, wounded by shrapnel. Dressed only in light jackets, they trudged through icy water that flowed over their boots. "My Christmas dinner was pieces of rye bread and an apple. It was a Christmas I'll never forget," he wrote. Rosemary read between the lines of his letter—read the misery of walking in wintery conditions, with wet legs, no relief or warmth. Where were Albert and Junie? There was no word on casualties or death to either one, so Rosemary breathed a sigh of relief—for now.

Albert hadn't written since he left for overseas. When she

saw him at the Paddock Club before he shipped out, anger bubbled over her. How could he leave her? She knew, she knew why, but it didn't make it any easier. Then he promised her all that she wanted in life—a home, love, a family, security. How could she say no? But at the same time, how could she say yes, knowing that he was leaving her, going overseas? In the end, she said nothing and let him think whatever he wanted. She'd deal with it later, if he came home.

She sat curled up under a knitted blanket on the sofa, reading *Wuthering Heights*. Her heart went out to Catherine. She loved Heathcliff with all her heart, but could never marry him. Instead, she married Edgar because he was stable and could provide her security. Oh, how Rosemary felt she could relate to Catherine. That was what she wanted too, the stability that Edgar provided.

Jack came and sat next to Rosemary on the couch, pulling at her blanket, exposing her bare feet.

"Hey!" she exclaimed and pulled the blanket back over her feet, tucking it beneath her. Jack missed Junie the most. He clung to Rosemary and Virginia, needing their attention. Christmas had been somber for the whole family. They had put up a tree, but the trimming of the tree lacked the usual festivity without Junie's practical jokes.

Virginia walked into the living room carrying a bottle of whiskey and two glasses. She put them down on the coffee table and filled each with a few fingers of liquor.

"Here," she said, pushing the glass towards Rosemary. The winter was so brutal—emotionally and physically. Although it was only January, their store of coal was quickly diminishing, even though she and Jack collected it each morning. There seemed to be fewer and fewer coal trains and more trains full of soldiers. They drank in the evenings to warm themselves, but also to numb their feelings, to lose the fear if only for a moment. Rosemary picked up the glass. The brown liquid swished over the sides of the glass, leaving a translucent residue. She tipped the glass to her lips. The whiskey was strong; it burned her tongue as it slid down her throat, burned her esophagus and solidly sank to the pit of her stomach. She preferred the taste of beer, but liked the effect of whisky. It warmed her.

"Give me some," Jack said, reaching for her glass. Rosemary pulled it away, deflecting his hand. He was only fifteen, too young to be drinking! Jack should be worrying about school and the upcoming baseball season, not drowning his worries in alcohol.

"Oh just give him some," Virginia said crossly. She wore a pinched expression, as if breathing pained her. Rosemary relented, not wanting to argue, and handed the glass to Jack. He drained it in one gulp, grimacing. Virginia and Rosemary both laughed at him.

"What?" he asked. "You two make faces!" Rosemary knew she wrinkled her nose when drinking the hard liquor. Virginia could drink like a sailor though. Her sarcasm became sharper after a few drinks.

"You drink like a girl, Jackie," she said. She refilled both glasses and flopped back into the overstuffed chair. She looked worn; the stress of raising two children and working full time was showing. She was still having problems collecting child support from her ex-husband. Their divorce had been granted. She was a free woman, a free woman with two dependent children. Thankfully, the judge deemed Ernie not worthy to have custody of the kids. If Rosemary had agreed to marry Albert and had had a baby, that could be her too. She shuddered, knowing she was not strong enough to raise children on her own. She wanted an equal partner, not a chump like Ernie had turned out to be. Deep down, she knew Albert would be that equal partner, wanting to be a part of their children's upbringing. But there had been no word from Albert, no letters of reassurance. *Albert, where on earth are you?* Her stomach churned. She chewed a Tums, popping it into her mouth like it was candy. She drained the whiskey from the glass and filled it another time.

"So they picked you to be a pin-up girl, huh, Rosie?" Virginia asked, a slight jealousy rising in her voice. At Owens, they chose a pin-up girl every month to put in the Nine 'O Line newsletter to send to the boys overseas. Rosemary had been chosen to be in this issue. The photo shoot was exciting. She had brushed her hair into soft waves, curling back from her face and securing it with a white silk daisy barrette. The light of the camera caught her eyes, making them look light blue instead of gray. Her cheeks were rosy and her lips perfectly colored crimson. She wore a white sweater with a square neck to accent her heart-shaped face. Wilma lent her a golden locket that she'd received as a wedding gift. It glittered as the flash hit it.

Rosemary was the beauty of the family. She didn't want to provoke jealousy from Virginia. She was sure that to Virginia, her life looked easy and care-free. But it wasn't. If Virginia only knew the internal struggle Rosemary went through every single day, she wouldn't be jealous. Rosemary prayed for peace of mind, to ease her worries, but the only thing that worked was the whiskey to calm her. It scrambled her thoughts and let her drift off into a blissful unawareness.

"I just wish this war would hurry up and be over," Virginia said, sighing. Her eyelids lowered in a whiskey haze. Rosemary felt the same way.

"Where do you think Junie is right now?" Jack asked, worry creeping into his voice. Rosemary didn't know where Junie was, somewhere in Italy, in the middle of this brutal and ugly war. He was probably in a muddy trench, shooting at the Germans, pushing into Austria and closer to Berlin and Hitler. Maybe he was dodging mortar shells and machine gun fire. Maybe he was hit and lying in a pool of blood, screaming for someone to help him. Rosemary shivered.

"I bet he's lying on the beach somewhere, chasing Italian girls, if I know Junie," Virginia said, in a rare moment of optimism.

Jack grinned, "Yeah, he's probably told the general that he's going on a secret mission to free the Italian countryside and he went to the Mediterranean Sea to get some sun and a pretty girl."

Rosemary laughed at them both, thinking that it was probably true; Junie was probably either causing trouble or chasing girls. Or both. She thought of him sunning himself on the warm beach, the shimmering aqua water crashing the shore. It comforted her to think of him doing that rather than the alternative.

The red bricks of the train depot shone warmly, belying the brisk January temperatures. Rosemary wrapped her coat around her, attempting to keep out the cold. She rushed into the building, which had been turned into the Free Canteen. The majority of the troops were being moved by the Santa Fe railroad, which came through Streator. Since the town only had one small restaurant, Mary Plimmer suggested opening a free canteen to serve the boys coffee and a quick meal as they came through. Mary's own son was serving overseas, and Mary hoped that some other mother had shown her son the same kindness.

Mary was making a fresh pot of coffee in anticipation of the next train coming in. "Morning, Rosie," she called as Rosemary stamped the snow off her shoes. Rosemary waved and went to work, setting up cups, putting out freshly made donuts from W&W Bakery. The first train usually came in around 6:30am. Rosemary glanced at the large clock on the wall. Five more minutes.

Rosemary felt a sharp poke in her side. She snapped her head around and saw Norma's smiling face. Norma came to volunteer at the canteen too, with her toddler, Marcia, in tow. Rosemary picked her up. The little girl looked sleepy, her eyes drooping. Rosemary didn't blame her, she was tired too. Tired of the war, tired of the shortages, tired of living in fear. She was tired of the lack of sugar and sweets, gasoline, rubber, coffee, and nylons. But mostly, she was tired of worrying that today would be the day that the Western Union telegram would come with the information that Junie had been killed in action. She didn't even know how she would know if Albert had been killed; she had no contact with his family and she wasn't his wife.

"Auntie Rosie, can I have a donut?" Marcia asked, her angelic face framed with blonde curls. Rosemary smiled, handing her one with extra powdered sugar. She set her down so she could eat it.

"Any word from Al?" Norma asked. Rosemary had confided everything to Norma about Albert. She had laughed when Rosemary told her that he had gotten fresh with Rosemary and she threw his car keys into the cornfield. "He's got his hands full with you, Rosie," she had chuckled. Rosemary still didn't think it was very funny.

"Nothing since he shipped off," she said.

The train whistle blew in the distance, a long shrill call, warning them to get ready. The women filed out to greet the approaching train. It came screeching to a halt, the metal brakes grinding and squealing as the wheels slid along the metal rails. A blast of wind followed the train, blowing cold air up Rosemary's skirt. She shivered, pushing her skirt down.

The men exited the train. They were fresh-faced and eager, their uniforms pressed and clean, brass buttons shining. *They have no idea what they are going into,* she thought as she handed each man a cup of warm coffee. They stretched their legs and their backs, stiff from the miles of tracks they'd covered, the miles they still had to go.

"You're a sight for sore eyes," a young man said as he took the coffee from Rosemary's hand. His cheeks flushed from the cold. His breath came out in white spurts. Rosemary smiled at him. She heard this many times each day as the trains rolled through Streator. The guys were starved for female attention. They all became a blur of faces, blondes, brunettes, freckles, noses, eyes. The train emptied, coffee was drunk, donuts and cookies eaten. Then they boarded the train and were whisked out of town, to their next destination.

Once the train pulled out of the station, the women cleaned, washed the empty mugs and prepared for the next train. On average, they served a thousand soldiers a day.

The next train pulled in a few hours after the first one left. Rosemary stood ready to hand out her coffee. A young man approached her, his head bowed, hat covering his face.

"Coffee?" Rosemary said to him, putting on her best smile. He looked up. His eyes were the same intense brown as Albert's and he had the same cleft in his chin. Rosemary's breath caught. For a moment, she thought Albert had come back to her.

"Thank ya, ma'am," he said in a southern drawl. Rosemary's heart sank. He wasn't Albert.

"Where are you off to?" Rosemary asked, trying to cover her disappointment. Maybe Albert had been comforted by someone working in a canteen too.

"We're going to Great Lakes for training. And then, who knows? Europe, the Pacific. It's an adventure," he chuckled.

"Where are you from?" Rosemary asked, annoyed at his naivety.

"Houston, Texas, ma'am," he grinned, chest puffed out.

"I've never been there," Rosemary said, smiling in spite of herself.

"Well, if you're ever fixin' to go there, you'll have to look me up," he said. "My daddy owns a huge ranch outside of Houston. We've got steer and cattle. Do you ride horses?" She nodded, knowing she would never be in Houston Texas. But it was nice to pretend.

He held out his hand and said, "Name's Jesse."

Rosemary took his hand. It was calloused and rough. He squeezed her hand, the bones crunching. Rosemary yelped in pain.

"Sorry," he smiled, "I don't know my own strength." He released her hand, looking remorseful. Rosemary waved it off.

"So if you come down south, we could ride down by the creek. My ranch is beautiful," his teeth were crooked, his canine tooth higher than his other teeth. That sounded nice to Rosemary, to ride horses all day under the open sky, with no war news to worry about. She wanted to go to Houston that moment, to forget about the canteen, the cold.

"Is it warm there?" she asked.

He nodded. "Yes, ma'am. I didn't know it was so darned

cold up here. It's colder'n a well-digger's rear end! Pardon my French."

Rosemary laughed at his sayings. She missed talking with a young man; they were all gone to war. She wanted him to stay and talk to her.

He walked back towards the train, climbed the steps, turned and tipped his hat at Rosemary. "Remember, if you're ever in Houston…" he let his sentence trail off, the rest implied. Rosemary's insides warmed. She said a quick prayer to keep him out of the line of fire. *Please, God, keep him safe. Let him go back to his ranch.* She hoped that if Albert had made a stop in a similar town, another lady was praying for him as well.

After the last train pulled out of the station at 10:30 that night, Rosemary walked home. Flurries of snow hung in the wintry air, suspended, defying gravity. Rosemary stuffed her hands into the pockets of her coat. The snow provided a natural sound barrier, muffling the car noises, and creating an eerie stillness. Yellow bulbs illuminated the brick road, tiny swaths of golden light. She walked down the center of the street, noticing how many homes had the white service banners with the red borders, signifying a family member in the service. Each blue star sewn onto the banner represented one member. House after house had banners with one, two, three stars. And then there were the houses that had a gold star sewn on their banner. The gold stars represented a service member who had been killed. Rosemary hated seeing those stars, knowing another life had been sacrificed, wasted. Her stomach lurched and she popped a Tums into her mouth, grinding it, her mouth filling with the chalky powder.

"Please God, let Junie and Albert return home safely," she said, looking skyward for a sign that God heard her prayer. All she saw were the falling snowflakes, sticking to her eyelashes.

Albert

They had been assessing the enemy position for weeks. Albert's company sat on the Luxemburg side of the Sauer River, gauging the strength of the German position, how many bunkers and pillboxes were active. Days became routine—get up before dawn, patrol route, eat, wait. The waiting was agony. Albert had watched the 417th secure the opposite side of the Sauer, yearning to be on that side of the river, to do anything but sit and wait. He was tired of reconnaissance work, tired of plotting the enemy position. It was time to fight, to cross over into Hitler's territory and drive the Jerries back to Berlin. Then he could go home to Rosemary.

"What d'ya say, Al?" Eddie said, coming into his bunker. Albert nodded at Eddie and watched him pace back and forth, wearing a path in the floorboards.

"What's going on, Eddie?" Albert asked, taking a drag off his cigarette. Eddie tossed a letter onto the table. It was written in a feminine script, a letter from his mother.

"Anthony's been drafted," he said, lighting a cigarette with a shaking hand. "He can't handle this. He's too soft, he ain't cut out for war." Albert knew from Eddie's stories that his brother Anthony was a genius on the piano.

"Maybe he'll play in the band," Albert suggested to ease

Eddie's nerves. Eddie just shook his head, picking up a deck of cards and shuffling, his hands still shaking.

"Say, did I ever tell you about Mikey Poo-tie?" Albert asked, anxious to break the silence, to fill the heavy air. Eddie smiled weakly and nodded. Both men fell silent, the sound of the cards fluttering under Eddie's hands filling the space between them.

"Mail call, Al!" A head poked into the tent and threw an envelope at Albert. He turned it over to inspect it. It was his Line 'o Nine, the Owens-Illinois newsletter. He ripped it open, eager for news from home, something to remind him that there was normalcy to return to. There was an article about the bottles that Owens made for the troops. He flipped the page and his heart stopped. Owens chose a pin-up girl for each issue, a small reminder of home. Staring up at him was Rosemary's angelic face. Her small mouth was curled into a smile, but the smile stopped short of her eyes. Albert felt the sadness, the anxiety. His heart ached to hold her, to make all her worries go away.

"What's got you so tongue-tied?" Eddie asked, yanking the newsletter from Albert's hands. He saw Rosemary's photo and whistled. "She's quite a looker. Wonder what she looks like without that sweater." Eddie grinned, raising his eyebrows up and down.

Albert scowled and snatched the paper back. "She's my fiancée," Albert said.

"Fiancée? Al, you dirty devil! You never even mentioned her!" Eddie slapped Albert on the back. "If I had a girl like that, I'd be telling everyone about her!"

Albert smiled. Rosemary was someone he wanted to keep to himself, separate from this war. She was pure and good and Albert needed to hold onto that. He stroked Rosemary's cheek, pretending he was touching her downy skin.

When they crossed the Atlantic on the U.S.S. Brazil, the band had struck up "Moonlight Serenade." The clarinets pulsated the notes across the briny air. Albert thought of the Paddock Club and Rosemary—her rosewater scent, her blonde hair, the way her skirt swished around her narrow hips and calves. Her skin was soft. He couldn't believe that he had left her.

On February 22 came the orders: Charlie Company would cross the Sauer at dawn. They prepared in the dark, loading supplies, ammo, and their weapons. They walked towards Echternach, Albert leading his company. It was eerily quiet, the animals hibernating in the chilly morning air. The sky streaked cobalt blue, not quite light yet. Albert clutched his rifle to his chest. They entered the city and marched down the main road toward the foot bridge. Everywhere was evidence of the fighting only weeks earlier. Broken glass clung to window panes, entire walls were missing, exposing the skeletons of buildings, piles of rubble crowded the streets. Telephone poles were twisted and splintered, wires frayed. Albert looked into a burnt-out truck. The wheels were bent outward as if a two-ton elephant had sat on it. The windows were shattered, the metal charred from a direct hit, probably an 88mm shell. Inside, the seats were burnt, bits of blackened flesh splattered against them. Albert's stomach heaved.

The company walked single file down the hill and onto the foot bridge. The Sauer raged under them. The days had been warm, melting the snow and swelling the river. Albert stepped onto the bridge, a narrow row of two by four planks floating on raft boards, with only a thin rope as a guard rail. The bridge swayed under the weight of the men. Albert teetered close to the edge. The river jumped at him, daring him to fall in, wanting to sweep him up, drown him. Albert steadied himself; he knew that if he fell in, he would be dead. His father had never thought it important that Albert learn to swim. Now, he wished that he had. Swallowing his fears, he marched across and then waved his men over.

After they crossed, he paused. He was on German soil, in Hitler's Reich. This was the enemy's homeland. A shiver ran up his back, a sense of foreboding. Now, the real fighting would begin for the 304th. They would become seasoned veterans, not inexperienced dough boys running drills. Albert glanced up the river bank to the burnt-out pillboxes. The Germans would hold on tighter. This was a defensive war for them now. Albert swallowed hard, and rushed up the embankment to get to their task and get away from his thoughts.

The landscape was mountainous. At least, it looked mountainous to Albert who had only known the flat land of Illinois. He struggled to get air into his lungs, the altitude making everything difficult for him. Albert trudged through the slop—a mix of melting snow and mud. His boots sunk ankle deep with every step. He looked back and saw his men struggling. Eddie slipped onto his hands and pushed his helmet back with a muddy paw. Albert gritted his teeth and barreled through the muck, trying to be the leader they needed him to be. As they climbed, the trees thickened and Albert breathed in the pine scent. It cooled his lungs and invigorated him.

They crossed an open field. Albert looked at a country lodge in the distance, shelled and broken. It must have been beautiful before the war, he thought. The mountains and pine trees surrounding the cottage were dusted in a brilliant white carpet of snow. Albert thought he would like to live there, away from everything. If he and Rosie had a house like this, full of little children running around, that would be heaven. She would have a fire glowing in the hearth and he would come home from a long day tending to the crops, or maybe herding some sheep or cows. He'd sink into a chair in front of the fire and Rosemary would rub his shoulders, her small hands kneading his knotted, stiff muscles. He'd grab her slender wrist and pull her onto his lap. She'd laugh and tell him that she had to finish making dinner, but Albert would not let her up. He would wrap his arms around her waist, feeling the solidness of her body against his, her sweet scent filling his nostrils as he kissed her. She would respond by entwining her arms around his neck and kissing him with an open mouth.

A shell exploded to Albert's right, bringing him back to the present.

After marching all day, they arrived at Fernschweiler. C Company took up residence in a bombed-out building's cellar. It was cold, but dry. They lit candles as the lieutenant laid out the plans for the morning's attack.

"Gather around, boys," he said and everyone moved in. The map showed the topography of the country side between Fernschweiler and Holstrum, every hill and stream. The lieutenant pointed. "The artillery attacks at 2300 hours. We'll cross the Prum north of Holstrum and take the high ground." He pointed to a slight rise north of Holstrum. "Green Company will take Holstrum and then we'll move in to hold the town while they push south. We'll remain in Holstrum until the heavy bridge is installed across the Prum. It is now 1845. Synchronize your watches."

He paused, his face softening. "Gentlemen, I don't have to remind you that this is our first attack. It must be successful. I know you're capable. Good luck."

He turned on his heel and headed up the dark stairs to deliver his message to the other companies. Albert was exhausted. They had been marching for two days straight and were told that in four hours, their first real battle would begin. His heart raced as he thought of the fighting tomorrow—coming face to face with the Jerries. He fell into a restless sleep, his brain reeling. He wanted to make sure he led his men proudly, but more importantly to Albert, was that he led them safely.

Rosemary

Rosemary missed butter. She longed for a roll, warm from the oven, dripping with golden, melted butter sliding down her throat. She couldn't remember when she last had a good buttered roll, her mind fried from the endless inspections of the bottles, more bottles, always bottles. They rolled by like soldiers going to the front, ready to fight. Rosemary's heart heaved.

There was still no word from Albert, no reassurance of his love and safety. Hitler's offensive was being repelled in the Ardennes Forest, somewhere in Belgium, but Rosemary knew American boys were losing their lives with every inch they gained. Was that where Albert was? She didn't know and had no way of knowing. Did his parents know about her? Would they contact her if something happened to him? Rosemary doubted it. Her heart felt as if it were in a vice. She placed her hands on the side of the belt to steady herself. The weight was becoming too much to bear, not knowing if today would be the day that she found out he was not coming back to her.

She entered the locker room after her shift. Betty sat on a bench, half undressed.

"What's the word, Betty?" Rosemary flopped next to her.

"Bud... he... his family heard from the War Department," she said, her voice shaking, but eerily calm. Rosemary's heart leapt into her throat.

"Is he... okay?" *Dead* was what Rosemary really wanted to say, but that seemed inappropriate.

Betty nodded, brushing back a shocking white curl from her forehead. It gleamed against the shining black hair, a crown of worry. Dark circles ringed her eyes.

"He was in the South Pacific, no specifics of course," she gulped. "His mother came over and told me he had sustained burns when a boiler burst on their ship. Really bad burns—covering most of his body."

"Oh God!" Rosemary was sympathetic but also jealous that Betty at least had news. Horrible news, but it was something. "What are you even doing here?" she asked, unable to understand how Betty could be at work.

"What else was I going to do?" Betty shrugged. "It's not like sitting at home crying was going to do me any good."

Rosemary bit her lip, thinking. "Let's forget about all of this for a while," she said and grabbed Betty's hands. "Let's go roller skating." She knew it sounded childish, but she wanted to do something for her friend. She had seen Betty worrying, suffering for three years, worrying about Bud, getting his censored letters that said everything and nothing at all.

Betty forced a smile and nodded.

Rosemary threw her arm over her friend's shoulders. She didn't want to think about anything anymore, no Albert, Junie, the war. She just wanted to be free.

Betty drove downtown to the roller rink, which was above the furniture store. Rosemary ran up the stairs, unable to contain herself, just wanting to forget it all. She laced up her skates and pushed onto the wooden floor. Her wheels rolled over the wooden slats, clicking rhythmically. Her hair blew off her face as she raced around the oval, the skirt of her green gingham jumper flapping behind her. Her face flushed under the exertion, blood pulsing. She skated up behind Betty and grabbed her waist, pushing her along.

"Rosie! Quit!" she cried, "You'll make me fall!"

Rosemary let go of Betty's waist and pushed herself to skate faster and faster, until the background blurred into a streak of color, all her worries flying from her head.

"Bet I can beat you. Wanna race?" Rosemary heard over her right shoulder. She turned to see her challenger. He had a long, narrow face, with a straight nose and brilliant blond, almost white, hair. It was slicked backward, one curl twisting over his forehead.

She momentarily lost her balance, tilting backward to see him. Her arms waved once, twice and then she regained her balance. This strange man laughed. Rosemary thought, *I'll show him who's clumsy!* She nodded at him and took off.

She felt him behind her, like a silent wind against her back. She pumped her legs, determined to show him that she was not a weak female. He overtook her, his long legs gliding effortlessly as she huffed. He spun around, skating backward, smiling as he drifted away from her. She ground her teeth and used the last bit of energy to launch herself forward. His smile fell as she surged past him.

Rosemary was elated; she had wiped the smug smile off his face. She turned around to see the stranger, to revel in her victory. His legs pumped to catch her. She giggled, watching his face turn red, his nostrils flaring. His arms swung as if they were eels gliding underwater, with no bones to cut his movement short, jerk him forward.

She got so caught up watching him that she forgot to look where she was going. Her arms and legs entwined with another person's and she fell, her momentum hurling her forward, colliding with the wooden floor. Her palm smacked the ground, pain shooting up her arm. She sprawled out, half on top of a little girl, her hand throbbing.

"Are you alright?" she heard. Her vision blurred, her head spinning. She looked up at the man she had been racing with, his blue eyes full of concern. He held out his hand to help. Underneath her, the little girl wailed. Rosemary sprang into action, pulling herself off the floor and lifting the little girl onto her skates.

The girl's mother ran onto the rink. "You should watch where you are going and slow down!" she said, her face screwed up into a scowl. She marched off the floor, dragging the girl behind her who protested, "But Mamma, I'm not hurt, I want to skate!" Rosemary looked at the blond stranger, and they burst into laughter.

"Well, you beat me. Can I buy the victor a drink?" he asked. Rosemary flushed, savoring her victory, however small.

"Yes, you may," she said, smiling. He led her from the skating floor, placing his hand on the small of her back. *Like Albert did*, she thought. Albert... his serious eyes, chiseled jaw. A pang of guilt shot through her and she went rigid. She slipped away from him, darting to a booth. His eyes were veiled and Rosemary couldn't tell if she had offended him or not. This stranger went to the counter, ordered drinks, then came back where she sat. He placed a bottle of coke on the table, slipping into the seat opposite her. She put her hand around the bottle and winced in pain.

"Here," he said. "Let me see your hand." He reached for her, his palm long and narrow. She placed her hand in his. He bent forward to examine her. The butterflies fluttered against her stomach for the first time since Albert had left.

"It's going to be a pretty bad bruise, but I think you'll live," he said, lifting his head. "I'm Harry, by the way."

"Rosemary."

"So what do you do, Rosemary, other than skate fast?" He draped his arm over the empty chair next to him. His eyes tilted downward, giving him a sleepy appearance.

"I work at Owens–Illinois Glass Factory," she said. His eyes penetrated her. She felt naked and bare, like she could hide nothing from this man.

"And are you a doctor?" she asked, wanting to take his focus off her.

"No, a manager for Gebhardt's, selling auto parts," he said.

"I bet business isn't that great with the war going on."

"You'd be surprised. What, with no new cars being produced, the old ones breaking down. Business is pretty good." His eyes never left her face. Rosemary wasn't sure if she felt flattered or disturbed.

"I guess everyone still needs to drive, even though soon there won't be rubber left for tires or any gas rations," Rosemary said, and instantly regretted it. She didn't know how this man felt about the war. He might think she was unpatriotic. She changed the subject again. "I've never seen you before, are you from around here?"

"No, I live in Taylorville, down by Springfield, but I travel up this way for work," he said, his blue eyes shrouded. Rosemary couldn't read him; it was as if she were looking into a murky lake. She nodded and broke his gaze, looking out over the rink. Her heart pounded, blood coursing through her. After a long winter of numb feelings and being blanketed in heavy sadness, this buzzing in her body reminded her that she was alive.

"So Miss Rosemary of Owen-Illinois Glass Factory, would it be okay if I were to take you out dancing some night?" He leaned forward. Rosemary hesitated. She knew she should say no, but it had been so long since she'd been dancing. Albert's face flashed before her, his brown eyes beseeching her to wait for him.

"I'll be a perfect gentleman," he smiled, his eyes twinkling, anticipating her argument.

"I, I kind of have a beau," she said. But did she really? Albert was half a world away, putting himself in death's path. Even though he promised he would come back to her, it was a promise he wasn't in a position to make.

"I'm not asking you to marry me, just go dancing. Is that a

crime?" he laughed, leaning back in his chair. Rosemary relaxed. What harm could there be in going dancing? He was here, sitting across from her. If she went out with him, she wouldn't have to worry about him not coming back. He wasn't in the war. A thought came into her head.

"Why aren't you in the war?" she asked. Immediately, she regretted her words. Her blood pulsed, crashing against her eardrums.

He didn't hesitate. "I have a hernia that keeps me out of it."

Rosemary flushed, embarrassed. "I… I'm sorry, asking such a personal question."

"Not at all, it's quite a normal question, given the times," he said. Rosemary was not satisfied. Every able-bodied man wanted to be fighting in the war. Why was this guy different?

"Can't a hernia be fixed?" she asked.

"Not if I don't want it to be." He leaned forward and dropped his voice. "I'm not going under the knife just so I can get shot by some Jap or Jerrie."

"So you won't join up for the war?" she asked, shocked, but intrigued at the same time.

"Not even if they would let me! Don't get me wrong, I appreciate all the boys who have gone over and made the sacrifice, but at this point, I can't go and I won't. Besides, the war is over. Hilter is licked and we've got the Japs on the ropes. They don't need me and that's just the way I like it."

Rosemary sat back, trying to decipher her feelings. He wouldn't go and join the army; he *couldn't* go and join the army. She was disconcerted that he was not fighting when Junie and Albert were, but at the same time, there was a perverse comfort that came from his confession. She shook her head, not wanting to think about it anymore. She leapt up from her chair, knocking it backwards.

"Let's go skate again," she said.

"It would be my pleasure." The words sounded rehearsed, but still Rosemary flushed. He probably said these things to every girl he met, but for the moment, she allowed herself to believe she was the only girl in the world that he cared about.

Harry took her hand as they skated onto the oval ring. Rosemary allowed herself to be pulled along. For the first time in almost three years, her worries melted away. Thoughts of Albert and Junie trickled from her consciousness. She and Harry moved as one unit, pushing left, then right, swaying like leaves in a soft spring breeze. Rosemary trembled as she felt her body reawakening. Her heart soared; she felt light, the burden of her fears lifted. She glanced at Harry, smiling. He was easy, had none of the complications of Albert, none of the feelings of duty. He would not ditch her for the war.

He skated with a supple spine, leaning slightly forward, relaxed and confident. Feeling her stare, he looked at her. His eyes were deep blue, with swirling green and yellow strands melding together. Rosemary couldn't help but smile back at him, his smile was easy and infectious. Warmth radiated from his hand, through hers and up to her head, spinning. This was what she was looking for, the security and comfort, the absence of abandonment.

"There's my friend, Betty," Rosemary pointed at Betty gliding along in front of them.

"Let's go and get her," he grinned. He skated off to catch Betty, and the butterflies flew with him. She hurried after him, wanted to feel the whirling inside of her again. She reached Betty a moment after Harry. He said something to Betty and she glanced over her shoulder, grinning. He was already charming her, getting her to smile in one second, which Rosemary had not been able to do for days.

Rosemary skated up and took Betty's hand. It was clammy and cool. Her face was slick with sweat. Harry skated ahead of them, spinning around and skating on one foot to impress them. They giggled, as if they were school girls again.

"He's quite a charmer, Rosie," Betty said, caution creeping across to Rosemary. It was something that Rosemary had been thinking herself, but she rationalized that she should be able to just have fun for one afternoon. She chose to ignore the uneasiness that bubbled behind the butterflies. The butterflies were more exciting.

"He's a gas, Betty! Let's just enjoy skating with a good-looking fellow for once!" Rosemary laughed. She just wanted to be free and for Betty to forget all of the seriousness in their lives. She pulled Betty along after Harry. Betty shook her head and followed along.

"Can you two skate on one leg?' he asked. They shook their heads. Harry reached for Betty's hands and told her to lift her leg. Rosemary felt a spike of jealousy stick in her ribs. She had hoped Harry would reach for her first. Betty's face was frozen in fear as she clung to Harry's hands, wobbling on her right leg, her left leg bent behind her. Harry held onto her, pulling her as he skated backward. Betty let a whoop of glee as she relaxed and allowed Harry to pull her, allowed herself to let go and enjoy herself. Have we all forgotten how to have fun? Rosemary thought. It is all worrying and fretting?

Then Harry let go of Betty's hands and came over to Rosemary.

"Are you ready?" he asked, his blue eyes twinkling.

Rosemary pursed her lips and shrugged, trying to look coy. She held out her hands and pushed towards him on her right leg. She collided with him. He placed his hands around her slim waist to catch her from falling. She shuffled on her skates to regain her balance.

"Whoa, I wasn't ready!" Harry protested. Rosemary froze, mortified, thinking she has somehow offended him. She opened her mouth to explain herself.

"I was only joking," he whispered in her ear, his breath blowing her hair. The flesh raised on her arm.

He released his hands from her waist and took her hands. He skated backward, pulling her along. She felt like a fallen leaf floating in a current, powerless against where she was going, and she just let herself go and float. Harry was looking at her, devouring her with his eyes. Rosemary looked away, both wanting the attention and not wanting to lead him on. She was spinning with thoughts of duty and her wants—they were butting against each other, violently thrashing about in her head. She just wanted her head to be quiet, for it all to lie down and just let her be.

Harry slowed, releasing her hands. She skated past him, balancing on one foot, steadying herself with outstretched arms. She glided along, lost in her confusion. Guilt crept in, the old familiar guilt. Was it wrong to skate with a man when the one who had her heart was fighting? What was the harm in just wanting to have a little bit of fun? Like so many unpleasant thoughts, she pushed them down.

"I could skate forever!" she said, spreading her arms out wide. Harry laughed, a deep belly laugh. His teeth shone like wolf's teeth.

"I bet you could," he said, his eyes flashing, "I bet you could do just about whatever you wanted."

"I can," Rosemary said, not sure if that was a compliment or a complaint. She jutted her chin up.

"You got spunk," he said, skating up behind her. He leaned into her hair. "I like spunk," he whispered, his breath sending shivers up his spine. Somewhere deep down a warning bell was ringing, but Rosemary was flying with the fluttering butterflies. She wasn't hurting anyone, she was just living her life.

———————

Betty skated over later and said she needed to go home, it was getting late. Rosemary nodded, exhausted from the excitement of meeting Harry and fighting her guilty conscience.

"I'll be seeing you soon," Harry said. Rosemary's heart soared, even as her head wrenched with guilt.

Albert

It was an hour before midnight. The cellar was pitch black. Albert lay on his back, his eyes open, straining against the darkness, trying to form a mental picture of Rosemary before he got up. It was no use, the war pushed all thoughts of her out of his head; he had to focus on their mission. It was time. They would be forming up soon. Albert dragged himself off the straw mattress. He elbowed Eddie, who slept opposite him. They woke the rest of the men and climbed the stairs, Albert's heart in his throat.

The night was overcast, no stars shining. The melted snow had refrozen into a slippery carpet. Albert's hands were already numb and they hadn't left base camp yet. He led his men in silence north of Fernschweiler, east of Holstrum.

They came to a stack of metal canisters. He hefted one to his shoulder. "Everyone grab one," he said, repeating the orders given to him.

The men walked to the Prum River. The inky black water swirled past, gurgling as the current surged. Albert took a deep breath—they would be crossing this river on foot, carrying heavy ammo. There was no foot bridge. He paused, fear seizing him. What if he fell and drowned? But this was not the time to think about that. He hoped the river was not deep and trusted that his men would catch him if he needed them to. Following the staff sergeant from the 2nd battalion, Albert plunged his feet into the icy water. The cold shot up his legs, into his arms, numbing him. For a moment, he was frozen with fear and with cold. The metal canister burned his hands as he balanced it on his shoulders. He felt the current pushing him sideways. How deep was this river?

His men watched. Eddie's mouth gaped open. For the first time, Albert saw fear in Eddies' eyes, in all of their eyes. Albert strode ahead, his limbs stiff, feeling like he was made of ice himself. The water rose to his chest, freezing his muscles. His breath was short and shallow. The night was so dark. He felt he could slip into unconsciousness and float down the stream in the darkness. But he was reminded yet again of his duty—to lead his men. "Come on!" he barked, "Let's go!"

They forded the river and climbed the steep banks. The heavy undergrowth grabbed at Albert's legs, and he slipped and fell. A boulder sliced his knee open. The blood gushed down his leg, but he kept churning, crawling up the hill. Once everyone was at the top, they shed the heavy canisters, picked up emergency ammo and rations, and waited for dawn.

An eerie gray light fell over the battle field. Albert watched from atop the craggy hill as the first battalion crept to the edge of the open field. They pitched themselves down, rifles aimed and ready to fire. A sea of dark green crossed the gray. Two single shots rang, and two men fell. Albert tried to swallow, but his mouth was dry; he stifled a cough. His hands shook seeing the two men writhing in pain, but there was no time to focus on those men. The order was given, and Charlie Company jumped up. Albert waved his men forward, walking through the dead grass. Suddenly, the field came alive with machine-gun and rifle fire. Bullets slashed through the grass. The tell-tale sound of a mortar pierced the air. Albert dove into the grass, feeling it crunch under his weight. He hit the frozen ground hard as the shell exploded behind him. Men fell, ripped through by bullets.

Albert looked for his men. He saw Eddie's ill-fitting helmet bobbing through the grass as he crawled for the barn in the center of the field. Albert crawled toward him, his elbows scraping. He felt his knee open up and bleed again, but he focused on the barn, getting to safety. A staccato machine-gun fire filled the air. Albert heard men screaming as they were hit. He kept his head down and crawled faster, faster. The barn was a few feet away.

He heard the drone of an airplane engine. *Please let it be one of ours*, he prayed. Albert looked up and saw the underbelly of a P-47 Thunderbolt, dropping bombs on the German position. Albert heard the loud booms of the heavy artillery behind him. He watched two machine-gun nests go up in an orange ball of fire.

He reached Eddie at the barn. The stone walls were scorched from bombings and only the charred rafters remained of the roof, but it was enough protection for them.

"You alright?" Albert asked. Eddie nodded, his eyes wide with fear.

"We've got to provide cover for these boys coming," Albert said, watching more men fall and hearing the P-47 make another pass. Eddie exhaled slowly, deeply. Albert nodded. They both stuck their rifles from behind the barn and shot into the pill boxes in the woods where the white flashes popped.

"You boys holding up?" a soldier with dirt smudged across his face asked. He dropped new rounds of ammunition for Albert and Eddie.

"Yeah, we're good. Thanks for the ammo," Albert barked, trying to sound tough. His voice was drowned out by the planes and the *rat-tat-tat* of German machine guns. Albert's stomach heaved; he was glad he'd not eaten breakfast or it would have come back up. The soldier gave a salute and headed back out across the open field to distribute more ammunition where it was needed.

More soldiers reached them at the barn. Albert pointed out the pillboxes as they raised their rifles.

After several hours, the German firing slowed and then

stopped. Albert gathered the men to cross the field, where they would defend the high ground until Green battalion captured Holstrum. Albert shouted for his men to make a break for it and provided covering fire for them. There were few shots fired from the Germans. They had abandoned their positions, dropped back to reinforce Holstrum.

Work began on setting up a station for the wounded. The medics ran onto the field and collected the injured men—men with arms mangled, stomachs blown open, legs ripped off, heads cut. The moaning from the tents was constant, but the medics worked to save as many as they could. Albert grabbed some bandages off a cart, tied up his bloody knee and joined his men.

Albert and his men were positioned at the defensive front. The field was clear of Germans. They could get a few hours rest before they started all over the next day. He closed his eyes and could almost feel Rosemary brushing her hand across his forehead as he slipped into an uneasy sleep.

Holstrum was a village built where the Ens Stream emptied into the Prum River. On the west side of the river were a few scattered houses and crumbling buildings. The main town sat on the east side of the Prum, on the gentle slope beyond. There had been two bridges in Holstrum across the Prum, but the Germans had blown both up. Scouts from the 76th Infantry had snuck into Holstrum and taken a building on the west side of the river known as the Castle. From the attic windows, three stories in the air, they had a front row seat for the battle about to happen. They could see the German's positions seventy-five to a hundred feet away on the opposite side of the river and fed this intel back to the officers on the ground.

A thick fog covered everything as the morning dawned. Albert heard the machine-gun fire from across the river. The mist was so dense that Albert could not see the sparks firing but knew they came from inside Holstrum. Able and Baker Companies moved towards the river and crossed over the rickety foot bridge. Albert and his men followed, but then headed to the north of Holstrum. Their mission was to capture and hold the high, wooded area. Albert strained to see through the gray fog. The town was destroyed, shelled into rubble, only shadowy skeletons of buildings stood. Albert maneuvered around a dead, bloated horse in the center of the street. It smelled foul, thawing and refreezing for days. Albert gagged, but pushed past it. His men followed him, their heads lowered, blocking out the devastation.

Albert heard the shells shrieking overhead, landing in the town, turning the rubble into rubble. Able and Baker Companies had been successful in taking their part of Holstrum. Now, he must lead his men to do the same.

They marched to the eastern-most part of the town where the Germans were dug in. Albert was worried about the action they would see. He knew the Germans were burrowed in tight. Suddenly, a soldier leapt out from behind a pine tree, screaming in German. Albert had just enough time to pull his rifle to his shoulder and squeeze off a shot before the German doused Charlie Company with lead. The German fell immediately, shot in the throat. Albert looked at the man he had killed. He had stubble on his cheeks and chin. He looked like any one of them. Albert realized that if he had been a second slower, he would be lying in the mud instead of this man.

Albert told his men to spread out, take defensive positions. The Germans came at them with a full company, but Albert and his men were able to drive them back. The fighting continued throughout the day, the Germans attacking, Charlie Company driving them back. Finally there were no more counter-attacks.

Eddie had just lit a cigarette when the lieutenant came with their next orders. Able and Charlie were to capture the high ground south of Holstrum.

"Shit!" Eddie spat. "More fucking high ground!" Albert shot

Eddie a look. He wasn't happy about it either, but they had their orders.

"Alright, boys, we've gotta get the Jerries off the high ground," Albert rallied his tired men. "Let's go kick the shit out of them!" They picked up their rifles and met Able Company to move south of town.

As they crept up to the southern high ground, the Germans launched a massive counter-attack. The machine-gun fire buzzed all around them. Albert dove behind a fallen tree, lifting his rifle and shooting anything that moved toward him. The sun was falling, throwing an orange light on the battlefield, masking the fire from the machine-guns. He heard the mortars—the screaming meemies—dropping on them. The sound was ear-piercing and horrific, but the devastation was worse. Behind him, he heard the booming of his heavy artillery, driving back the Germans, creating deep craters in the earth before him.

After hours of attacks and counter-attacks, they finally drove the Germans off the ridge. In the twilight of evening, as the last light of day was fading away, Albert looked over the ridge. The woods were destroyed, trees split and burning, giant holes in the ground—and the bodies. German bodies twisted, blood gushing from wounds, arms and legs blown to bits. This sight no longer affected Albert. He was used to seeing blood and guts and carnage. He had become a soldier.

Rosemary

Rosemary stood amidst a sea of worn clothing in the gymnasium of St. Anthony's school. The church collected clothing for the Children's Clothing Crusade, an annual event held to support the Save the Children Federation. The clothing would be distributed to needy kids in the United States and Europe. The gym was alive with a flurry of clothing being tossed across tables, sorted into piles of shirts, pants, dresses, coats. A rainbow of colors flashed across the open space.

"Well, hello there."

Rosemary looked up and saw Harry. In the bright light of the gymnasium, he glowed, his hair a golden wave, his skin shining.

"Hi," Rosemary said. "What are you doing here?"

"Just because I can't fight, doesn't mean I don't want to do my part," he said. He picked up a shirt and tucked the arms under, smoothing it under his long fingers. Everything about him was slow and deliberate, calm and relaxed. She flushed, embarrassed that she had insinuated that he didn't care about the war efforts.

"And of course," he continued, "I wanted to see the famous Rosemary Ruhrmann again." He grinned at Rosemary. His teeth were long and wolfish.

"Famous? You've got the wrong girl."

"Everyone knows the beautiful Rosemary Ruhrmann. She's Owens' pin-up girl."

Rosemary was thrown off balance—he had done his homework. She was flattered that he had sought out information on her. But she wondered what else he knew as his eyes rolled over her. There was nowhere to hide from his penetrating gaze.

A flash of guilt struck her as Albert's face crossed her mind. Here she was, flushing under another man's attention while Albert was overseas fighting for their country's freedom. She turned away from Harry and pretended to sort clothing.

"Okay, I'll confess the real reason why I am here," Harry said. Rosemary glanced at him. He looked at a coat, holding it out and then tossed it to the side.

"I want to get a definite date out of you," he looked over at her, daring her to say yes. She wanted to say no because of Albert, but she also wanted to bask in Harry's attentions. *What could it hurt just to go dancing with him?*

"Whenever you would like," she said, feeling a little faint and disloyal.

He stepped back, his face stretching into a wide grin. "Good, good. I'll pick you up tomorrow at six," he said, turned on his heel and walked out of the gymnasium, before Rosemary could protest.

Remorse washed over her when she thought again of Albert. *But it's only a date,* she rationalized. *And anyway, he left me.* If he wouldn't have gone off and joined the stupid army, she wouldn't have to make a decision like this. As she did with many things lately, she pushed the thoughts from her head and went back to sorting the clothing.

True to his word, Harry was at her house at six o'clock sharp. He looked dashing in a navy suit. It deepened the blue of his eyes. He looked Rosemary up and down, drinking her in. She blushed and shifted, nervous under his glance. She felt like a defenseless deer trapped by a hungry wolf. As quickly as the feeling came over her, Harry smiled and it vanished. He held out his arm. She laced her arm through his and he led her to his car.

He drove to Indian Acres, a local dance hall. Rosemary's heart leapt. She was looking forward to jitterbugging, to losing herself in the music. They walked into the open hall, the band on the stage at the far side of the dance floor.

"Come on! Let's dance," Harry said, taking her hand and pulling her onto the dance floor. She wanted to protest; no one else was dancing and she didn't want everyone to stare at her and Harry, but he was oblivious, a wide grin stretching across his face. He started swinging his long arms back and forth. His legs moved in and out like a wooden puppet. Rosemary smiled. He was a horrible dancer! She wondered how he could look so graceful on skates and manage to be so awkward on his own two feet. But seeing him dance with complete abandon, she threw away her reservations and danced with him, her arms swinging in time to the music. He took her hand and tried to spin her but knocked her off balance.

She stepped backward, catching herself. His face fell in horror.

"Maybe we should get a drink and watch for a little while," Rosemary said.

"I think that is a grand suggestion," Harry said. They took a seat at a table on the side of the dance floor. Harry brought over two beers. Rosemary took a long drink, letting the cool liquid glide down her throat.

"Whoa, slow down!" Harry said.

She was embarrassed to be caught drinking like a man. She just wanted to drink away these conflicting feelings—the guilt of being with Harry, but wanting to be with him all the same. She looked down, peeling at the label on her beer bottle. Harry reached out and put his hand on hers.

"I was only joking. You can drink however you like," he said, but something in his voice seemed insincere.

Rosemary looked off onto the dance floor. A couple danced closely. The woman's head rested on the man's shoulder, her eyes closed, a contented smile playing on her face. That was how she and Albert had danced. Her heart thudded as she thought of how his arms felt around her.

"What are you thinking about, Rosemary?" Harry asked, his eyes fixed on her face. She shook her head, her eyes filling with tears.

"I... it's just... oh, I don't know why I'm crying," she laughed at the tears welled in her eyes, not willing to confess the truth. "It's been so stressful. My brother is overseas, and I worry about him."

Harry patted her hand. "Poor Rosemary. You need a break. You need to stop worrying. Listen, he made his choice and worrying is not going to bring him back, right?"

Rosemary nodded, dabbing at her eyes.

"I wanted to bring you dancing to put a smile on your face," he said. Rosemary smiled at him, grateful for his efforts. He was right, worrying was getting her nowhere, but she couldn't stand the unknown. Well, maybe just for tonight, she'd leave that worrying at the door.

"So, how do you not worry?" she asked, curious as to how he lived so freely.

He shrugged. "I only live for today. The future comes whether you worry about it or not."

Rosemary laughed; his way of thinking was freeing, almost irresponsible. It was just what Rosemary wanted.

"See, I got you to laugh," Harry said, grinning with pride.

"So how do I live just for today?"

"For starters, you have to dance—often and wildly!" Harry said and pulled her out of her seat. Rosemary suddenly needed to move, to rid her body of the nervous energy that shook her. They went back onto the dance floor. Rosemary let herself go, stamping all of the guilt onto the dance floor.

When the band played the Star Spangled Banner, Rosemary was surprised. The evening had passed so quickly.

Harry drove through the town.

"Oh, I had so much fun tonight!" Rosemary said, sinking into the car seat.

Harry chuckled. "Me too. Isn't it fun to not worry?"

"Yes, I'm just afraid my worries will be back tomorrow," Rosemary said.

"So don't think about them. Do something you've never done before."

"Like what?" Rosemary looked at Harry skeptically.

"Haven't you ever done anything impulsive?" he asked. Rosemary thought about it. Had she done anything impulsively? Her family thought she was impulsive, but Rosemary felt as if she always acted out of responsibility, at least in matters that counted. She thought of riding Yankee Clover and the freedom she felt. She shrugged.

"Well, you should try it some time. You might surprise yourself," he said. He killed the engine in front of her house, got out, and walked around to her side of the car.

Rosemary inhaled deeply. This part of the evening she had been dreading. Would Harry expect a kiss? He opened her door. She decided that she would take Harry's advice and not think about it.

They walked in silence to the door. Rosemary watched her breath form white puffs in the crisp winter air. The sky was ink black, the stars twinkling and reflecting the white snow. She remembered walking up the sidewalk with Albert. Her heart fell. She stole a glance at Harry. He walked straight, oblivious to Rosemary's thoughts, her doubts. She shouldn't have gone out on this date, but she'd had fun. What was wrong with that?

They reached the front door, the dim light casting a yellow shadow on the steps.

Harry grabbed her hands. "I had a wonderful night, Miss Rosemary."

"I did too," she said, reluctant to admit it. Her heart hammered against her chest.

He kissed her hands, right then left. "I hope we can do this again," he said. Rosemary nodded, her tongue stuck to the back of her throat. Her heart pounded in anticipation.

"Good night and adieu," he said, bowing. He released her hands, turned and walked back to his car. Rosemary stood, paralyzed. A lump of disappointment sat in her chest, her head swirling—feelings of joy, frustration, and disloyalty. She closed her eyes. She didn't need to figure it all out this evening; she turned and walked into the house, closing the door on all of her feelings for the night.

Albert

Albert looked across the river—*another friggin' river*. The Nims River ran through a wooded lowland. He took a final drag off his cigarette before tossing it aside. He was exhausted. Since the campaign began, he'd had little more than a few hours of sleep here and there. And that sleep was never good because he was anxious about the fighting the next day, keeping his men safe, getting back to Rosemary. *This war business is for the birds.* He glanced behind him to see Eddie trudging along, his helmet sliding back and forth with each step he took. Eddie's brother had been sent to the South Pacific. They had heard about MacArthur landing in the Philippines and the heavy fighting. After seeing the horrors here, Albert knew what Eddie's brother was going through, and the fear Eddie felt for him. He felt like he even understood Rosemary's fear for Junie after seeing another person go through it.

The 2nd Battalion and Charlie Company were marching through the German countryside, clearing pillboxes as they went. The main German army had pulled back, but there were still pockets of resistance. The men moved in the cover of night, the darkness their shield against the machine guns and artillery fire. Albert and his men climbed another hill, fighting through the underbrush and mud. Albert's lungs were getting used to the altitude and exertion. Maybe it was the adrenaline coursing through his blood.

Right before dawn, Albert climbed atop a ridge. From a mass of low bushes and brush came rapid fire—a hidden pillbox! Albert dove down into the brush and set his rifle, pulling off shot after shot. His heart was racing—he had not even seen the pillbox! It was well camouflaged, but Albert should have known it would be up there. Stupid! That could have cost the lives of some of his men, or himself! With his anger swelling, he stood and screamed, firing into the hole.

Albert felt a hand on his shoulder. He spun around, frightened, thinking that a German had somehow snuck behind him. Eddie was standing there with his hands raised in surrender.

"Al, there's no return fire. I think we should throw a grenade in there and flush them out," Eddie said in a low voice, to make it seem like it was Albert's idea. Eddie didn't want to overstep his rank and tell Albert what to do, but Albert was relieved that he stepped in. He shook his head, clearing the fury, thinking of what a good leader would do next.

"Cooper!" he barked. "Grab a frag grenade and toss it in there to flush them out!"

Cooper reached into his pack and was about to pull the pin of his grenade when they heard, "*Kamerad? Schiessen Sie nicht!*" *Don't shoot!* Two German soldiers, weary and frightened, came out of the pillbox with their hands raised.

"Anyone speak German?" Albert called back to his men, while keeping his rifle aimed on the German soldiers. Thomas Behrendt came up to Albert.

"Yeah, I do," he said, gruffness covering his embarrassment at speaking the enemy's language. He was a first generation German and still spoke the language, like Albert spoke Slovak. Albert nodded at him and he questioned the Germans.

"They say there's only two of them, that they were left behind to throw up fire. The main force fell back to Helenenburg," Thomas reported to Albert. Helenenburg—according to intelligence, the Germans were gathering their forces there, digging into the city to make a stand against the Americans. A shiver passed up Albert's spine.

Albert nodded, "Fine, we'll take them as our prisoners."

"Helenenburg?" Eddie snorted, "They may as well just call this whole place Hell!" Albert shot him a look, even though he was thinking the same thing. Eddie shrugged and lit a cigarette.

They marched over the hill and towards the base camp that was set in a small village of Meckel. Albert and his men turned the prisoners over and were given permission to rest. Albert remembered a bombed out farm house just west of the village. He and his men walked, hoping to get some much needed rest before the next order to march was given.

The small two-story house set off to the side of a glen, an open field in a depression between the hills. Albert hopped a battered stone wall, anxious to just lie down under a shelter and get some rest. The roof of the house had been bombed and collapsed, but the chimney still stood erect. Maybe they could build a nice fire, Albert hoped.

Albert pushed the wooden front door open with his rifle and surveyed the room. The wooden floor was clean and dry. There was a stack of wood next to the fireplace. Albert and his men filed in, flopping into worn chairs, lying on the floor. Eddie went over to a closet to see if there were blankets while Albert busied himself getting the fire ready. He hefted the logs into the hearth and looked for kindling to start the fire.

"Holy shit!" Eddie exclaimed. In the closet was the farmer, his wife and daughter. They were cowering in the corner, the farmer's arms reaching around his wife and daughter. Their eyes were wide with fear. Eddie motioned for them to come out of the closet. Thomas stepped in to speak with them. As soon as the farmer realized that they were Americans and not Nazis, he relaxed.

Thomas said, "The Nazis destroyed this place while they were retreating. They slaughtered and carried off all of his pigs and then used the house as target practice, shooting 88mm rounds. That's how the roof collapsed. Nearly burnt the entire house down."

The farmer's wife came out and busied herself, cutting turnips and onions to make soup. The soldiers eagerly handed over their rations for her to turn into a delicious stew. Soon, the house was filled with the aroma of wood burning and hearty food cooking, a wonderful combination! The farmer brought out blankets and told them to stay as long as they liked.

"*Haus kaput! Hitler kaput! Alles kaput!*" he exclaimed. *Everything is finished!* Albert liked that phrase—*Alles kaput*. It seemed so fitting when he thought of the devastation of the countryside, the mangled and ruined bodies, the battered buildings.

When their bellies were full, the men settled in for a good night's sleep. Albert lay on the floor, a thick wool blanket wrapped around him. The embers of the fire warmed the room. It was the first time in weeks that Albert was not cold. He flexed his fingers, trying to work out the stiffness. He felt like he was a hundred years old. Every joint ached, his muscles sore. He settled into the warmth, the wool blankets smelling slightly of animals, the wet, earthy smell—like a wet dog. It was comforting to Albert.

He slipped into a deep sleep and dreamed. He was back in Streator, looking for Rosemary, but he couldn't find her. He ran down Main Street, but the buildings were bombed out, rubble crowding the street which had huge craters, red bricks thrown in all directions. The sky was a menacing, glowing orange. He ran to Owens, but that was bombed too, the roof gone, walls broken and collapsed. Where was Rosemary? What had happened to Streator? He saw people shuffling in two rows down the middle of the street, like prisoners. He saw Rosemary's blonde hair, her curls hanging limply as she plodded along. He ran up to her, touched her shoulder, which was thin, all bones. She turned around and her face was a bare skull—her nose gone, teeth bared in a garish smile, her eye sockets empty and dead. Albert shrank back from this monster. This was not Rosemary!

What had happened to her? She moved towards him, and her body became all bones, the flesh peeled off. Then all of her bones disintegrated into a pile at Albert's feet. He screamed.

Eddie was shaking him. "Al, you were having a bad dream," he said. Albert looked around. His men were watching him. He looked at his wrist watch—0630.

He barked at his men, "Get ready to move out."

Only Eddie saw his hands shaking as he picked up his rifle. They thanked the farmer and his family for their hospitality and started on their four mile march to Helenenburg. The sky was streaking with the first color of day. It was brisk and chilly, Albert's breath coming out in white puffs. The cold seeped into his bones and he was once again stiff, an old man shuffling along. He looked up and saw a lone black crow gliding across the grey sky. The raven of death. Its ebony wings stretched out like fingers grasping for him. He shivered, foreboding creeping over him like the cold, sinking into his bones. He shook his head to focus on the march ahead of him, the wooded area where he needed to lead his men, to get his next orders. But the ominous feeling followed him like an invisible cloak.

Rosemary

Rosemary lay in her bed, watching the snow fall. The whole world outside her window was white—the sky was white, heavy with low clouds, spitting out little flakes, which covered the houses, cars, streets, turning them all white. Individual crystals stuck against the window pane, frosting the inside. They were mosaic, some six and eight sided, each one unique.

"Rosie, are you going to lie in bed all day?" her mother called. Rosemary sighed, wondering what her mother wanted her to do now. There was always something to do, cleaning or cooking or something. It had been snowing for two days, and she was tired of being cooped up in the house. She kicked the blanket off her feet and slipped a heavy wool sweater over her head. The sweater was rough against her skin, but it was warm.

She padded through the living room and into the kitchen. Jack stoked the coal furnace, getting some warmth into the house. Sandy sat bundled up in her high-chair, her cheeks rosy from the chill. Rosemary ruffled her blonde curls. They felt like silk between her fingers.

"Can you do the dishes?" her mother asked, as she bounced a crying baby Carol on her hip. "I need to change this baby."

Rosemary turned on the water to fill the sink. She held her hands under the warm water, feeling it flow over her. She stared at the snow falling out the window. Was it snowing in Europe? In Italy, Germany? No word yet. No letters, no news. Only the endless winter that dragged on and on. And then she remembered her date with Harry. The guilt stabbed her side like a rusty dagger. Even though she hadn't heard from Albert, was it appropriate to go on a date with another man? Could she be in love with Albert and have had a great time with Harry?

She felt instantly old, a spinster. All of her sisters were married by the time they were Rosemary's age. Was it wrong that Rosemary wanted some security and comfort like they had? She groped in her pocket for her Tums.

"Ma," Rosemary said, "How did you know that Father was the one you wanted to spend your life with?"

Her mother wrapped Carol in a clean cloth diaper. Rosemary bit her lip, longing for some advice, wanting to spill her feelings about Albert and Harry to her mother. But her mother was hard to read. Rosemary had never seen her express her emotions. She remained behind her stoic German façade.

"Well, I just knew," her mother said, not looking up. Rosemary felt herself deflate. She knew that her mother wasn't one to talk much, but she had hoped that maybe she would open up and let Rosemary in. "There we go, baby," her mother said and lifted Carol high into the air. The baby giggled.

"But how did you know, Ma? What made you so sure?" Rosemary tried again. There was some compulsion within her that demanded answers—from someone, anyone who could tell her what the right thing was. Her brain was too full to discern the right thing.

"Well, he took care of me. And he was a good man and father, before he got sick. Wasn't he?" Her mother turned her full gaze on Rosemary. Rosemary blanched, afraid that her mother would see her turmoil, that her mother would think she was a bad person.

"What are you fishing for, Rosie?"

Rosemary wanted to answer, *I want you to tell me the future. Does Albert come back safely and I'm wasting my time with Harry, or is Harry the one for me because Albert isn't coming home?*

"I… I don't know, Ma," Rosemary said, slamming the silverware into the soapy water. "I, I'm confused, I'm scared, I can't stand worrying anymore."

"We're all worried, Rosie. All we can do is pray and know that God is protecting William," her mother put her hands on her shoulders. "We have to be strong for him. We have to believe that he will be coming home."

Rosemary turned to her mother. "But what if he doesn't?"

Her stomach clenched thinking of Albert not returning, not seeing his deep brown eyes, his kind smile. Not talking to him again, laughing with him, discovering herself with him. And then there was Harry. He was stable, like Edgar—Catherine's Edgar. And like Catherine, Rosemary felt that her heart could rest if she could give herself to him.

"It's in God's hands now," her mother said. Rosemary sighed and looked up into the white clouds for a sign from God if she should wait for Albert or move forward with Harry. If only He would give her a sign, then she could be calm and her heart could slow to a normal pace.

———

A few days later, the telephone rang. It was Harry. Rosemary felt her heart rise and fall in the same breath.

"I'd like to take you out on another date, if you're not busy with your pin-up duties," he said. Rosemary felt herself blush, annoyed and flattered at the same time.

"I don't have any duties as a pin-up girl," she said. "They just took my picture."

"Good! Then I'll pick you up on Friday."

"And what are we going to do?" Rosemary asked.

He chuckled. "You'll just have to wait and see." He hung up.

Rosemary stared at the receiver, more aggravated than happy.

———————

He picked her up at seven sharp. Despite feeling annoyed, Rosemary was excited to be going out again. She wore Virginia's dress again, guilt creeping up her throat as she remembered putting it on for her first date with Albert. She smoothed the skirt over her legs, brushing the guilty thoughts off her. Albert hadn't tried to contact her, no letter, nothing. She felt betrayed by him, that he'd left her and she hadn't any idea if he were coming home to her. This date was out of spite—spite that he hadn't written to her, that he had left her. When Harry knocked on the door, she flew into the living room, surprising her mother.

"Bye, Ma. I won't be home too late," she said, turning the wool collar of her coat up. She slipped out the door before her mother could ask who she was going with.

Harry stood, smiling, ever smiling.

"Here, take my arm, it's slippery out here," he said, holding out his arm. She slipped her arm though his, feeling the warmth radiate off him. The sidewalk was covered in ice, but they managed to get to the car without falling.

"So are you going to tell me now where we are going?" Rosemary asked as he drove away from her house.

"We're going to see a boxing match!" he said, grinning like a school boy. Rosemary wrinkled her nose. What was so fun about watching two guys beat on each other's faces?

"Can't we just go to the Paddock Club? There is a good swing band playing there," she said, hoping to change his mind.

"You can go to the Paddock Club any time. The Golden Gloves championships are only once a year. And you're lucky enough to be going with a fella who knows all about boxing," he said. Rosemary fidgeted with the button on her coat, reminding herself to just enjoy the evening.

He pulled up at the armory, and they hurried toward the

building to get out of the wind that had kicked up. He led her to the third row, his hand cupping her elbow. She sat in the wooden chair and looked around. The cavernous space was warm from all the bodies, the windows fogged over. The ring was in the center of the room, a white canvas square with brown ropes encircling it. The next fight began. Harry threw her a smile and leaned forward in his seat.

"This is gonna be good," he said, his knees bouncing. The referee touched the two boxers' gloves together and a bell sounded. The boxers took their fighting stance, hands covering their faces, legs wide. The boxer in the white shorts, Rosemary didn't catch any names, skipped to the left and threw a hook. The boxer in the green shorts bobbed out of the way. They circled each other like two dogs. Finally, the one in the green shorts stepped in and jabbed the other boxer right in the nose. His head jerked back and Rosemary heard the cartilage crack.

"Oh right in the shine box!" Harry yelled and threw his arms in the air.

Rosemary's hands flew up to cover her mouth. The white shorts's nose swelled and turned bright red, but there was no blood. Rosemary's stomach heaved. Green shorts moved in, a little too close. White delivered an upper cut to his chin. Rosemary winced, squeezing her eyes shut. She didn't want to see any more.

"Rosemary, it's fine. They are trained to do this," Harry said, prying her hands from her face. Rosemary looked down, feeling embarrassed that she was behaving like a little girl.

"I've never been to a fight is all. I wasn't sure what to expect," she said, hoping she sounded more confident than she felt. Harry laughed and patted her leg. She swallowed down the bile that crept up her throat.

"You can cover your eyes all you want if it makes you more comfortable."

Rosemary smiled, feeling foolish. The fight was a draw, and soon, the next fight was about to begin. The next boxers entered the ring. A boxer in a blue robe skipped back and forth, warming up his legs. He turned to Rosemary. His black hair was slicked back off his face. His brown eyes were focused on his opponent, a clef in his chin deepening. Her breath choked off. Was this Albert's ghost?

She grasped at the program in Harry's hand.

"What's the name of the boxer in blue?" she said, frantic.

"Why? You got a crush on him?" Harry asked, a sharp jealousy flashed across his icy blue eyes.

"Oh, no, no. He looks like someone I work with," she said, which wasn't actually a lie. Harry opened his program to look for the boxer's name, but the suspicion stayed on his face.

"His name's Steve Jedoga."

"Did you say Jedoga?" she asked, her voice little more than a whisper.

"Yeah. Is he the guy you worked with?" Harry said, not even trying to mask his jealousy. Rosemary shook her head. No, it wasn't Albert. It was someone else, his brother. He had to be, he looked just like him. The fight began and Harry turned his attention to the ring. Rosemary struggled to breath. She felt as if she had been caught red handed, weapon in hand, murdering someone. And maybe she was. If Albert found out about her being here with Harry, would he do something foolish? Would he care? She sat like a statue, numb. The feelings of betrayal ran out from her and the guilt rushed to replace it. Had Albert told his brother about her? Her heart squeezed inside her chest, as if Albert's hands were squashing it. She had to get out of there.

She jumped up and bumped past a surprised Harry, stumbling over legs to get to the aisle. She ran away from the ring as a roar went up from the crowd. Steve had knocked out his opponent. Was he after her next? She paused in the entry to see if Steve was charging down the aisle after her. Her heart pounded and she struggled to catch her breath and decide what she was going to do next.

"Rosemary," Harry said, panting. "Are you alright?" Rosemary squeezed her eyes shut and nodded. She didn't want Harry to see the pain she was feeling, to know her confusion.

"This was a bad idea," he said, rubbing the back of his neck. "I'm sorry. I thought you would have a good time."

Rosemary shook her head, unable to answer Harry, wanting to reassure him that it wasn't his fault, but not able to articulate anything.

"You're right, we should have just gone to the Paddock Club," he said. She continued shaking her head, the vibration moving down her arms, her hands trembling. She wanted to cry, but no tears came. Why was she feeling so guilty? Albert left her, not the other way around. She hadn't promised him anything. Oh, if only the pain in her heart would dull.

She looked at Harry, his blond curl waving over his forehead, blue eyes concentrated on her. Maybe Harry was her answer. If she fully accepted Harry and gave him all of her affection, then she wouldn't be conflicted about Albert.

"I just wanted us to have a good time," he said, taking her hands. They felt warm, solid, slender. She didn't pull her hands away. If she could just forget Albert...

"You are so beautiful, I just wanted to put a smile on your lovely face," he said, squeezing her hands. "I didn't realize how sensitive you are."

"Yes, I have a very sensitive stomach," Rosemary finally answered, fumbling in her coat pocket for her Tums roll. She twisted one out of the foil wrapper and popped it into her mouth. Her already dry mouth was coated in a chalky paste. Yes, she was just sensitive, she thought to herself. It had nothing to do with her guilty conscious. If she tried really hard, maybe she could love Harry like she loved Albert.

"Hell, Rosemary, I just wanted to take my finest girl out on the town," he said.

"I know, Harry," she said, "I'm sorry I ruined the evening."

"No, it's not ruined at all! It's a little chilly, but do you want to walk by the river?" His eyes raised in anticipation. Rosemary nodded and was rewarded with his dazzling smile. He took her arm and they started towards the dike.

"Rosemary, I've never met anyone like you before," he said.

"How's that?"

"You don't seem to need anyone. You're very independent."

Rosemary felt her insides crumble. She did need people; she wanted someone to love, to start a family with, to make a home with. He made her feel like she was a cold fish.

"I need people," she said quietly.

"We all need people, but you seem to be able to take care of yourself. And I bet that if you found the right guy, you would take good care of him."

Rosemary smiled, "You've got that right. I definitely will take care of my husband and our house."

"I like that about you," he said, dropping his hand from her elbow and entwining his fingers in hers. Her fingers were icy, but his palm was warm. Rosemary fell silent and they walked along the dike, the river flowing beneath the snow-covered branches in a quiet trickle. He was different from Albert—not so serious, lighter. When Albert stared at her, she felt as if she unattainable, like a goddess. But she wasn't, and that expectation could topple her over under the weight of it. Harry didn't have that expectation. *He* was more nebulous, harder to read. If she let him, would he melt away all of her worries and help her to relax?

Lost in her reverie, she wasn't watching the path. Her shoe hit a frozen root and she pitched forward. Harry grabbed for her arm and lost his balance, falling in the snow next to her. His arms and legs sprawled across hers. She turned to find his face inches from her, his breath warm on her cheeks. She heard the blood rushing inside of her, heart pounding. Harry moved his hand to her cheek, caressing it with his long fingers. She decided she would let him.

He leaned in, his lips pressing against hers, cold from the winter air. Before Rosemary could react, he pulled away.

"I just wanted to make sure you were real and not some winter fairytale," he said, pulling himself to his feet. He held out his hand for Rosemary. She grasped his hand and stood, wondering if he had kissed her. The remnants of his cool kiss hung in the air, suspended like a snowflake, and quickly dissipated into the night.

She wanted to tell him that it was okay that he kissed her, that he could do it again. She pushed Albert out of her mind to try to fill it with Harry. But her mouth would not say the words.

"What a mess we've made!" he said in a loud voice. A cardinal fluttered from the tree above them, a flash of red. Rosemary looked down at her coat and dress, which were soaked. She shivered as the cold inched up her bare legs. Harry noticed her shivering.

"Let's get you home," he said, wrapping his arm around her shoulders and walking her back to his car. He turned the heat on high and started towards her house.

"I'll be in town for another month, Rosemary. I'd like to see you as much as I can before I go back to Taylorville," Harry said.

"When will you be back after that?" Rosemary said, an abandoned panic settling over her. Was he leaving her too?

"Oh, I come up here about once a month, but that's not enough for me. You see, I want to spend all of my time with you."

Rosemary felt the heat rise in her cheeks, relieved that he was not abandoning her.

"I want to make a home with you. One day."

That was what Rosemary wanted too. So maybe Albert couldn't give her what she wanted most in life, but Harry was offering it to her. Not as quickly as Albert, but he wasn't going to war either. They could get to know each other and work slowly on their relationship.

She was about to answer Harry when she noticed Norma and Wilma's cars in front of her house. Her heart froze, fear gripping her. Something had happened, she knew it. Harry cut the motor in front of her house.

"I've got to go," Rosemary said, her eyes not leaving the cars.

"Is everything alright?" Harry asked.

"I don't know."

"Do you want me to come in with you?"

"No, no." Rosemary couldn't explain who he was to her family. She was focused only on finding out why Wilma and Norma were at her house. She leapt out of the car and ran up the porch steps.

She burst into the house and found her mother weeping, her arms flailing. Norma and Wilma were on either side of her, trying to calm her down, tears coursing down their faces. Jack was off to the side, trying not to cry. Even Virginia, who was usually stoic, was crying. Rosemary looked from face to face and she knew. Junie.

Virginia came up to her and put her hands on Rosemary's shoulders, guiding her to the overstuffed chair.

"Rosie, we got news about Junie," Virginia started. The room spun, Rosemary felt her face drain of blood. "Don't you dare faint!" Virginia shook her. "We got a letter from the War Department. Junie was injured in Italy. They didn't say how, but they did say that they had to amputate his right leg."

Junie? Rosemary swooned again. Virginia released her and let her sink back into the chair. Her breath was choked off; she put her hand to her heart to feel if it were still beating. It beat against her hand, vibrating her rib cage, her entire body. Junie was hurt, lost his leg.

"At least he's alive," Wilma, the oldest and most practical, said.

Her mother cried, "What if he gets an infection and dies?"

She couldn't imagine him with his leg missing. How would he drive like a maniac and scare Rosemary half to death? How would he go fishing? What had happened? She wanted to know every detail, every movement, everything that had happened. Tears fell from Rosemary's face, onto her sweater. She hadn't even known she was crying. She licked the side of her mouth and tasted the salty tears. Her eyes burned.

"At least he's alive," Jack said, echoing Wilma as if he never heard her.

Rosemary suddenly thought of Albert. Had his mother received a letter like this? Or worse, a telegram saying that Albert had been killed in action? Rosemary ran into the bathroom and vomited. She looked in the bathroom mirror. Her eyes were sunken, dark circles underneath. Her cheeks were hollow, weight lost from worrying. Albert—she was suddenly frantic to find out if he was okay. She ran into the living room and threw on her coat.

"Where are you going?" Virginia wanted to know.

She ignored them and ran out of the house, through the slushy streets, melted snow splashing onto her bare legs. The night was black, wind licking at her face. She leapt across the railroad tracks, never breaking her stride. Her lungs burned. She forced herself to keep running, down Main Street, turning onto Otter Creek.

Snow clung to the roof, the porch railing. A light was on in the front room of Albert's small, one story house. She smelled the faint odor of manure from the pig sty out back. Rosemary's chest heaved up and down. Her legs felt like a newborn calf's, wobbly and unstable.

Illuminated in the window she saw a white banner with a red border. There were two five-pointed stars. The lower one glistened behind the frosted pane. Was it a gold star shimmering? Gold star meant death. Oh god! Was it Albert's star? Rosemary stood, frozen. Her arms and legs tingled, her breath cut off from fear. The frost was thick, and the night was dark, but Rosemary swore it was gold.

Albert

The sun was climbing over the trees as Albert and his men approached the wooded area north of Helenenburg. Their mission, of course, was to capture the high ground south of the city. Eddie swore under his breath. Only Albert heard. The town lay ahead of them in a valley of the Eifel Mountains. Albert's feet hurt from walking. The blisters on his heels had been rubbed raw. Not even the cold numbed the pain. He held his rifle in both hands stiffly. They crept through the underbrush and pine trees. Albert was focused on getting his men to the Bitburg-Trier Highway, the main highway between the two cities, to cut supplies coming down to reinforce the German troops at Trier. Fox Company was dug in on the highway. Their dug-outs were battered and rough.

"Boy, are we glad to see you!" the staff sergeant said as Albert and his men fell into the dug-outs. "Those Krauts are dug in good! We've been fighting 'em off all morning."

"What's their position?" Albert asked. He knew they were at a disadvantage, the Germans had a good position. But how good?

The staff sergeant pointed up the road, toward the town. "They've pulled back into the town. Probably holed up in every goddamned rubble pile there is!"

"Great. We'll take it from here," Albert saluted and the staff sergeant began leading his men out of the dug-outs.

Albert swallowed hard. The highway was wide open, there was no cover. But he had his orders to march up this road, into the town and take the high ground in the south. The Germans may be out of sight, but their guns were pointed directly on this road. That's where he would aim his guns.

Albert motioned his men forward, giving hand signals to stay as close to the tree line as possible. Albert himself hunched over, his knees touching his chest as he crept along. When they got close enough to make out the details of the town's buildings, the mortar fire started. They had nowhere to go, no foxholes to lie in, no rubble piles to hide behind. The only thing to do was run. Albert followed the lead of fellow officer, Lieutenant Rohrbaugh, who was waving his men on and running for cover. The sky was alive with exploding mortars, raining fragments and shrapnel down like a black blizzard. The screaming pierced Albert's ears as he ducked and ran. He dared not stop for fear that he would be hit. At least if he was moving, he would have a better chance of surviving. He hoped his men were following him, but his instincts for survival took over. He only thought about saving himself for the moment.

Lieutenant Rohrbaugh led them to an abandoned cemetery at the edge of the town. The troops took cover behind the tomb-stones. It was not a great defense, but they needed to catch their breath and decide what the best action to take was. To Albert's left, there was a freshly dug mass grave. The smell of turned soil prickled Albert's nose. An 88mm shell exploded to Albert's left with a sickening blast. Albert leaned his back against the tombstone to catch his breath, looking back at the short distance he had covered. The ground was littered with bodies, rifles and ammunition strewn everywhere. Men writhed in agony from fragments and shrapnel wounds. Albert recognized two of his men, the anguish on their faces. He started to get up, but Lieu-tenant Rohrbaugh put his arm across his chest, stopping him.

"There's nothing you can do for them now, Sergeant. You'll

only let the rest of your men down if you do something foolish," he said. He was right. Albert still had other men who were counting on him. He searched the crouching forms behind the tombstones, looking for Eddie, but could not find him. The shells kept screeching through the air.

Albert looked up and saw a crow a top a blackened tree stump. The raven looked right at Albert, its beady eyes said, "You're going to die." Its head swiveled as a shell whizzed by, blowing its ebony feathers up. It shook itself, settling the feathers back into place. It cawed at Albert, daring him to go back and get his men, not to be a coward. Albert's heart skipped a beat, his head spinning.

"Goddamned bird!" Lieutenant Rohrbaugh grumbled. He aimed his rifle and shot the bird. It fell from its perch and hit the solid ground. The bird didn't move. Albert exhaled, the tension in his shoulders releasing and slumping them forward. He was released from the raven's spell. He could move again and peeked around the tombstone. The shelling seemed to be letting up. Rohrbaugh motioned towards an abbey two hundred yards away. They could hole up in there.

Albert motioned to his men, who were ready to move, to get out of this death trap. He sprung up from his coiled position and charged across the open grass, his eyes trained on the abbey wall. Just let me get to the abbey wall, he prayed. The shells and machine gun fire hurled all around him, but he kept going. He felt, rather than saw, men falling. The groans mixed into the gruesome cacophony. Albert heard his blood pounding inside his helmet as he ran.

He reached the edge of the abbey and tumbled inside, pushed by someone from behind. He rolled onto his knee, the cut one, and felt the wound open anew. He couldn't think about the pain; he waved his men in, counting them as they entered, one, two, three. Where was Eddie?

He positioned his men. *You! At the window! You, cover the doorway!* And then he took position himself, firing from the window. The medics arrived at the abbey, carrying a stretcher with a wounded soldier. He was gritting his teeth, trying not to scream. Albert looked and saw that his leg had been ripped through by shrapnel. Ugly bits of metal stuck out of the pink flesh. In the center, his shattered bone jutted. Albert couldn't think about that now, he had to guide his men safely into the abbey.

Staff Sergeant Hardesty ducked out of the building and ran to a wounded soldier, throwing his arm over his shoulder and dragging him back inside. Albert stuck his rifle through the broken window pane to provide cover for him. He made several runs while Albert and his men provided the cover. The fire slowed and then stopped completely. Albert glanced at his watch. It had been less than two hours since they stood in the woods and planned the mission for the day. Being holed up in an abbey definitely was not the objective, but it would have to do until the artillery could flush some of the Jerries out and they could complete their mission.

Albert surveyed Helenenburg. Shells of buildings stood like skeleton sentries, crumbling chimneys teetered on broken legs. The cobble stone streets were pocked with mortar shell holes. Metal twisted in strange shapes and was strewn in the street. More burnt out trucks and vehicles. And rubble—rubble everywhere. The once pristine white snow was blasted into a black pulp. The bodies of the dead lay where they fell, in pools of quickly freezing blood. This was destruction on a grand scale.

———————

As more troops poured into the abbey and surrounding buildings, stories of courage flew around, boosting the men's moral. Albert took the down time to search for Eddie. There were so many men, wounded, in various states of consciousness. Heads were wrapped, arms in slings, legs in splints. These were the lucky ones, the soldiers who weren't critically wounded and screaming behind the white curtain.

"Al," a weak voice called. Albert spun around to see Eddie lying on the floor, his stomach wrapped. His eyes jumped back and forth wildly as if he could not hold them still. Albert dropped to his knee and took Eddie's hand.

"Are you alright?" Albert asked. The white bandage was red with Eddie's blood. He was too weak to lift his head. He nodded and tried to smile, his lips curling into a snarl. Albert patted him on the shoulder and sought a medic to see what had happened.

"He took some shrapnel in the stomach. His spleen is shot, ruptured through. Looks like spaghetti in there. We got him on morphine. He's not going to make it much longer," the medic said.

Eddie's eyes rolled back. His head lolled limply. Eddie was dying. Eddie—the one guy who had calmed Albert and kept him under control, the guy he could jaw with and forget about the war for a down moment. He clenched his jaw to block out his frustrations. He sat by his side, taking his hand again.

"Al," Eddie's voice was hoarse, barely above a whisper. Al leaned in to hear him. "I didn't have time to write a letter…"

"Don't talk like that!" Albert said, knowing he was giving false hope, trying to comfort himself more than Eddie.

"Listen," Eddie started, but then began coughing. Albert held up a white handkerchief. Specks of blood stained the cloth. "You gotta write a letter to my ma."

"Of course. I'll tell her that you died a hero," Albert said, knowing it was what Eddie wanted to hear.

Eddie nodded and fell deeper into his pillow, closing his eyes. Albert looked at the blue veins cross his translucent eyelids. He felt so utterly insignificant. Eddie had been alive this morning, keeping Albert in check, pushing him when he couldn't push himself. And now, he was dying. Albert watched the final death gurgle escape Eddie's lips, which were ringed with blood. His shoulders heaved with dry tears. *Take him home, God,* Albert looked to the sky. Then he stood, pulling his shoulders back, and said, "Medic, he's gone."

Albert crossed the abbey and joined his men.

"Everyone here?" he asked.

"Everyone who's not dead or injured," Thomas said, his head drooping. Albert snarled.

"Look, it was a rough day. I know it, you know, the Germans know it. But we still haven't succeeded in our mission. We need to keep it together for all the boys who are left out there in that cemetery and on the road!" He quickly counted his men, cutting off any retorts. Of the men who started, half were not sitting there now. Fury boiled inside him at the useless wasting of lives that the Germans were causing. He wanted to go and kill them all! He wanted to drive all the way to Berlin and blow up the Reichstag, the government building, with Hitler in it! His skin burned, fueled by his rage. He ground his teeth, like a wolf closing in on its prey.

"Charlie Company!" the captain summoned. "You will be starting the attack tomorrow morning. Your mission will be to take the high ground east of Windmuhle." This was a small rise on the east side of Helenenburg, an area strongly defended by the Germans. *Good*, Albert thought, *I want to blow those Jerries off that hill.* He sat by himself, segregating himself from his men, the anger coursing through his body.

———

Albert lay awake all night, waiting for the first light, gnashing his teeth to get out there, to kill the people who killed Eddie. He spoke hard to his men as he relayed their orders. More fucking high ground, as Eddie would say. *We're going to take this high ground for you, Eddie.*

Major Reithel walked up to Albert and his men. Albert clicked his heels and saluted. His men all followed suit.

"At ease, boys," the major said, waving their hands down. "I'm going to go along for the ride with you fellas." Albert was shocked. A major participating in a mission? These sorts

141

of things just didn't happen. But Albert was eager to show his bravery and courage. The major waved them out, onto the cobble-stoned avenue to the rise. The men marched smartly, following Major Reithel, who was covered by several men in the abbey. Albert's heart was in his throat. The men hugged the edges of the broken down buildings, bypassing rubble piles and scrap metal. Major Reithel carried only a pistol, which he held in front of him. The Germans opened their artillery, bombarding the street. A stone wall fell in front of Albert, kicking up a brown cloud of dust and pebbles. Albert deftly stepped back from the falling stones and hurried around it, leading his men.

He saw the sparks of machine gun fire from atop the ridge and dove behind an overturned jeep, firing. The air was thick with artillery and gun smoke. It crept like a slow fog. He could see Major Reithel a hundred feet ahead of his men. He waved them forward, ever forward, toward the Jerrie's position, to take them out like they had taken Eddie out.

The ground rose, and Albert's legs churned in the wet ground, his boots slipping on the wet rocks and mud. He kept firing and firing, not knowing if he was killing any Germans or not. The ascent continued, mortar shells exploding over their heads, overshooting them and landing at the bottom of the rise. Out of the corner of his eye, Albert saw one of his men, Pfc. Aaron, running past him, a long, low bellow exploding from his mouth. His eyes looked wild, yet determined. Albert charged with him, his men following.

An 88mm shell zinged past his head, so close he felt the heat from the shell burn the tiny hairs inside his ear. His heart was pounding, but he pushed ahead. The shells were closer now. He could see the German shooting from their fox holes, their positions atop the ridge. He shot two in the head, *bang, bang*!

Major Reithel was atop the ridge with Albert close behind him, Pfc. Aaron was to his right, nearing the top, Albert's men following behind. Albert placed his foot at the top of the crest. The sky was lit with a blinding white light, a white phosphorous shell exploding near Pfc. Aaron, throwing him to the ground, searing his clothing and exposed skin. He writhed in pain, as did two other men who were near the shell.

Albert made a lunge toward him when the sky again lit up, this time with the orange light of an 88mm shell. The shell hit the ground and exploded, projecting dirt and shrapnel outward. Albert was enveloped in the muddy cloud and felt a heavy pain in his left side, throwing him backward onto the ground. His left arm and chest felt like it was on fire. White flashes of light sparkled behind his eyeballs. He looked down at his left side. His entire left shoulder had been ripped open, metal fragments and shrapnel protruding from the bloody mess. He smelled burning flesh and saw smoke steaming off the metal jutting out of his arm. He screamed, the world tilting and rolling him onto his back. He clutched his shoulder and scorched his palm on the smoldering metal shards. He looked at the exposed pink flesh, red blood running down his arm and chest. The metal was deeply embedded into his skin, cutting down to the bone. The tip of his clavicle bone lay open, burning in the acrid air.

Albert could not feel anything but extreme pain radiating from his left side. The pain came from everywhere, pulsating and wide. It blackened out all else. The world spun faster and faster, until the only thing Albert felt was the red-hot pain coursing through his body.

Rosemary, he thought, recalling her sad eyes and waving blonde hair before all went black.

Rosemary

Albert! Rosemary sat up with a start, jolted out of her sleep by a horrific image of Albert lying in a pool of his own blood. She looked around her bedroom in confusion. How had she gotten here? She remembered being in front of Albert's house, seeing the banner with what she thought was a golden star, a symbol of death. The pigs squealed and the curtains shifted in the front window. She dashed off, back towards her house, her vision blurred by tears.

Albert! How could you have left me?!? She cursed him, cursed God, and cursed the damned war! She didn't care if it was a sin! Obviously God hadn't listened to her prayer to bring Albert and Junie back safely, so why shouldn't she curse him?

She pulled at her hair, hoping the physical pain would take away the emotional pain, the pain deep in her heart that she could not outrun. She put her hand to her chest—it was being crushed, crushed from the inside out. The weight of her anger and sadness was a two ton load of bricks. She sat in the snow and cried. She beat at the snow with her ungloved hands, the snow flying up as she pounded and screamed.

Exhausted, she picked herself up and trudged home.

"Where did you go? What happened to you?" Questions were thrown at her when she entered the house. Her sisters and mother stopped when they saw her bloody hands, wet skirt

144

and shoes, and the frozen tears on her face.

Her mother put her arms around her and led her into the bathroom. She drew a hot bath, undressed Rosemary and eased her into the water. Rosemary could not react, could not think. She allowed her mother to move her like she was a huge ragdoll.

"I… I think Albert's dead," she whispered, a tear hanging off her bottom eyelash. Her mother's face was drawn and worn. She didn't ask Rosemary who Albert was.

Somehow, she had fallen into a deep sleep, until she was shocked out of it by the vision of Albert.

Albert!

Her room was silent. Rosemary could hear voices in the kitchen and smell coffee brewing. The sky was gray, the snow still sticking to the tree branches outside her window. It was another day. If only she could see if Albert was safe, if the star had been gold. She couldn't be sure now, in the light of the morning. In her dream, she saw the cobble stone street, the bombed buildings, the piles of rubble. She smelled the acrid odor of charred metal and busted buildings, the crumbling mortar. She saw Albert in a pool of his own blood, his life force fading. Was that real?

She put her head in her hands and began weeping once again. She thought she had no tears left to cry. Her eyelashes stuck together, glued by her tears. She didn't have the strength to pry them open. Why had Albert left her? She couldn't pretend that her life would be normal once the war was over. Nothing was going to be the same. Ever.

She dragged herself from her bed and looked at herself in the mirror. Her eyes were raw and red from crying. And vacant—so full of pain that they appeared empty. Like Rosemary's heart. Empty, barren. All alone.

———

Rosemary was a zombie. She lifted the bottles at work like an automaton. Her life became like the belt moving the bottles—the

145

sun rose, moving her out of bed and along to work, she inspected the bottles, the sun set and she shuffled back to her house. But the sun hadn't shone in weeks either—it was hidden under a blanket of grey clouds, as if it were in mourning as well, mirroring Rosemary's mood.

She went to church on Sunday with her family. Kneeling, she glowered at Jesus on the cross. *You were supposed to keep Albert and Junie safe. Now, Junie is coming back without a leg and Albert is probably dead!* She stifled a sob, clenching her hands together.

She lost her grip on time. How many days had passed, she didn't know. It took all of her energy to drag herself to work and check the bottles. Everything else was too much effort. Her life was a black misery.

She was about to crawl back into bed after a day at the factory when a knock sounded at the front door. She heard her mother talking to someone in a low voice. There was a soft knock on her bedroom door.

"Rosie?" her mother said, opening the door a crack. "There's someone here to see you."

Rosemary rubbed her eyes, smoothing her hair. "Who is it?" she asked, bewildered.

"He said his name is Harry Connor," her mother said. *Harry.* She had forgotten about him. He had been calling and calling her, but Rosemary couldn't explain what she was going through. She didn't have the energy for this, not now. But she pulled her robe around herself and pushed past her mother.

Harry stood in the center of the living room, gripping the collar of his heavy wool jacket.

"Well, hello there. Long time, no see," he said. His eyes twinkled and his mouth twisted into a smile. She had been avoiding this conversation, the reality of her life. And yet, here he stood, fidgeting with his coat. She felt she owed him an explanation and the truth.

"Can I take your coat?" she asked him. He handed her his coat, his fingers touching hers. She felt a sharp spark when he touched her, almost a pain reminding her that she was alive. She jerked the coat out of his hand, breaking the connection to him, not wanting to be reminded that she was still here.

"Let's go into the kitchen," Rosemary said, walking towards the back room and away from the questioning stares from her mother, Ginny, and Jack. Harry followed behind.

He sank into one of the kitchen chairs. She positioned herself across the room, out of his reach.

"I need to talk to you, Harry," she said.

"I heard about your brother. I kept calling to see if you were okay, but you wouldn't answer my calls. So I had to come by and see for myself," he said. "Are you okay?"

Rosemary felt the tears welling in her eyes, her throat constricting. Was she okay? The pain radiated over her. She had to come clean with someone, and so why not Harry? It was as if he were a priest, and she was confessing her sin. She collapsed against the sink, holding on so she didn't collapse under the waves of hurt that crashed against her.

"I don't know. I don't know if I'm okay. Or if I'll ever be okay," she said, sighing.

Harry sprang out of his chair, taking her hands in his hands.

"I'm so sorry, Rosemary," he said. "What can I do to make it better for you?"

What could he do? Rosemary didn't know if he could do anything. She just wanted to escape her pain.

"I need to tell you something. It's not about my brother. It's about someone else," she paused. She didn't care if Harry left her once he found out about Albert. She wanted to tell someone, release the pain. "His name is Albert. I... he... well, he wanted to marry me before he went to Europe. I never gave him an answer. And now, I think he's dead."

She pulled her hands out of Harry's and covered her face. Shame wrapped around her like a red cloak, marking her as a sinner.

"If you never talk to me again, I'll understand," she said from behind her hands, too afraid to look at Harry. He gently pulled her hands away from her face. She looked up at him and saw compassion in his blue eyes.

"I'm not leaving you, Rosemary. This is war. We've all sacrificed and done things we wouldn't normally have done," he said. "I've missed you. All I've thought about is seeing you again. I had to stop by one more time before I left town. I'm glad you told me. Were you in love with this man?"

Rosemary shrugged her shoulders. She didn't know anymore. The summer when she met Albert seemed like it had been another lifetime. She couldn't be sure if it had been real or imagined. The hurt was too great for her to think about anything except the pain radiating from her heart.

"Rosemary, I don't want to leave you. I want to take away your pain, regardless of where it came from. But what do you want? That's all I want to know," he said, pulling her hands to his chest.

"I just want to get away from it all," she said.

He pulled her to him, breathing into her hair, "I can take you away from it all."

Rosemary melted into his arms. Take her away… no more pain, no more worrying. Warmth radiated off Harry's body, cocooning Rosemary in a comfortable bubble. Maybe he could take away her pain.

"I can take you away from here," he said again, pulling back from her.

She blinked her eyes to try to clear her head. Her head was pounding, breath choked off.

"Harry, I…" Rosemary trailed off, her thoughts knotted.

"Rosemary, I want to spend the rest of my life with you." He was serious, the smile going out of his blue eyes. Rosemary widened her eyes, her mouth agape.

"What… what do you mean, Harry?" Rosemary whispered. Harry grabbed her hand in his, his deep blue eyes searching her face.

"I mean that we can make a good life together. I want you to be my wife, Rosemary. Will you marry me?" he asked her. She wanted—no, *needed*—a constant in her life. Here was Harry, offering her stability, her Edgar. Her hands shook as she looked at Harry and knew he would never leave her, he would never abandon her. He wouldn't be like every other man in her life—her father, Junie, Albert.

Albert. For a split second, Rosemary felt a flash of—what? Guilt, regret. Her heart was broken, crumbling inside of her chest. The life she had imagined building with Albert had been blown to bits, like the mortar shell had blown him to bits. She couldn't live with this pain, this misery. She wanted her life to be complete, to be secure. She wanted to know that she would never be abandoned again. She swallowed hard and said, "But I don't know how I feel. My insides are all torn up."

"Do you think you could love me, once your hurt is gone?" he asked her. This is what she'd wanted, what her sisters had, what she dreamt of.

"I don't know. Maybe. Maybe I could," she said.

"Then marry me. I'll take you away from this pain," he said. That is all Rosemary wanted at this moment in time. She wanted a good, stable life. She needed to know that her life was not a waste, in ruins, waiting for someone that may never come.

"Okay, Harry. I'll marry you!"

He threw his arms around her, lifting her into the air before placing her on the ground and tilting her backwards, kissing her hard on her mouth. Her lip started bleeding, reminding her that she was alive, not lying on the cold ground with the life seeping out of her.

———

Harry wanted to tell her family together—immediately. "*Why wait?*" he said. She wanted to move forward with her life, even though she was still unsure of what that exactly would mean for her. Harry was offering her security, and that was all that mattered for now. Rosemary tried to smile as they burst into the living room.

Virginia rocked the baby, Sandy played on the floor with Jack, and her mother lay on the sofa. They all looked up.

"Mother, Ginny, Jack—Harry and I are getting married," she said, with an enthusiasm that she wasn't sure she really felt. Her body was numb, her emotions blank. She waited for them to rush around her and congratulate her, surround her in happiness and love. She wanted them to validate her decision, to let her know that this was all right. She was met with gaping mouths.

"When did all of this happen?" her mother asked. Rosemary blushed, knowing she should have confided in her mother about Harry.

"I know you've been concerned about your son, so Rosemary probably didn't give you details," Harry said.

"Yes, that's right," Rosemary said, believing Harry's story.

"It is a little faster than we would like, but it is wartime and this calls for quick decisions," Harry continued, "I'll take good care of her." The finality of his tone dared questioning.

Rosemary looked to her mother for approval. Her mother's eyes were veiled as she said, "Well, it sounds like everything has been decided already. Congratulations, Rosemary." She remained on the couch. There was a tightness in her eyes. Rosemary wished her mother would be happy for her, get up off the sofa and put her arms around Rosemary and really wish her well. She wished that her mother was more emotional, not so robotic with her feelings.

"Thank you, Ma," she smiled, pretending it had been a positive blessing. Jack and Virginia remained silent. A harsh tension vibrated the room. Rosemary twisted her hands and looked to Harry to step in.

"We'll get married in Taylorville," he picked up her cue, breaking the awkward silence, "And live with my grandparents until we can find a house together."

Live with his grandparents? But she didn't even know them. She hadn't thought of the logistics of her life with Harry. When he said he would take care of her, Rosemary envisioned a cute little bungalow of their own, large oak trees providing shelter from the summer heat and winter winds. Reality smacked her in the face. What did she know of Harry, really? Had she made a mistake? She began to swoon. Harry caught her elbow, smiling at her.

"Easy, Rosemary, I know you're excited," he laughed. She smiled weakly back at him, willing herself to believe that everything would work itself out once they were married.

"Taylorville? What about Rosie's job? What's she going to do down there?" Virginia asked, her eyes narrowed in open suspicion. She sized Harry up, not trusting Rosemary's judgment. Always treated like the little sister she was.

"Well, of course she won't work! No wife of mine will work. She will need to be at home to take care of the children," Harry replied.

Children? Rosemary's plastered smile sagged a little. Harry hadn't said anything about children so soon. She was only eighteen, still a child herself. But she shook it off. They would talk about that later.

"And where will the wedding be held? What church do you belong to?" her mother asked.

"Oh, I don't belong to a church," Harry scoffed. Rosemary looked at him, her eyes wide with shock. She had assumed that they would be getting married in a church, like normal people do. Her heart twisted. Not get married in a church? Would God recognize their marriage if they weren't married in a church?

"No church?" her mother said, unable to keep the disgust out of her voice. "Where will you get married at?"

"We will have a civil ceremony at the courthouse. Nothing elaborate, just a simple ceremony so we can start our lives as man and wife. Lots of couples are doing that now, with the war and all," Harry said, as if he and Rosemary had already discussed all of these details. "I just want to be married as soon as we can."

Rosemary understood that. She wanted to be married quickly too. The hole in her heart could begin healing once she was married, she told herself. She would lose herself in her new life, building a new family, and bask in the security that Harry was offering, even if that looked a little different than Rosemary imagined. And so she let Harry convince her family that a courthouse wedding was what they both wanted.

The next two weeks were spent packing her things to move to Taylorville. Harry came and loaded up his car on an unseasonably warm February afternoon. The sun radiated its warmth, melting the snow. Rosemary inhaled, taking in the scent of wet soil, new growth. This was a good beginning to her new life. She took it is an omen of good things to come. Her heart was light for the first time since Junie had gone, since Albert had left her. She felt the black weight lifted off her. It was not her burden anymore.

But Albert—Albert had left a scar that would take time to heal. But she knew, in time, she would heal. She looked over at Harry, his wavy blond hair and deep blue eyes. He was different than Albert. Rosemary had so many questions for him, was so eager to know about his life. He was a mystery in many ways. But he was here, and they would work on the rest together. Rosemary was not alone anymore.

Rosemary fidgeted with the collar of her taupe suit. The day was finally here. She stood before a mirror in the restroom of the court house and adjusted her pillbox hat. The room was empty, every sound echoing off the marble floor and austere walls. Her stomach lurched, bile creeping up her throat. The nerves were normal, every bride felt an anxious anticipation before her wedding, she told herself. Her hands trembled as she fluffed her hair. She took a deep breath to relax herself.

She inspected the image in the mirror. She smoothed her hands down the front of her suit. The jacket had a notched collar and padded shoulders which accentuated Rosemary's narrow waist. The face in the mirror stared back hollowly, the light of life vacant from the steel blue eyes. She sighed, wishing her mother was there to calm her down, to help pin her corsage onto her lapel. Her mother, always the pragmatic, would know what to say, to calm her.

But her mother was not there. She knew her mother didn't come because she did not think Harry was a good match for Rosemary, didn't approve of the hasty courthouse wedding. A church wedding she would have attended, but not this. Her absence was her open disapproval of Rosemary's choices.

Rosemary took the corsage and held it to her lapel, pushing the pin through the fabric. It pricked her thumb and Rosemary jerked back, dropping the corsage. The pale carnation lost a few petals as it hit the marble floor. That was how Rosemary felt—like a dying flower, losing a piece of herself. This should be a happy day, but it was not like Rosemary planned it, not how she wanted her wedding to be. They should be in the vestibule at St. Anthony's Church. Harry had been adamant about not getting married in the church.

"But I don't understand what you've got against church," Rosemary said, trying to make him understand that their marriage was not recognized if they weren't married in the church. That they would be living in sin in God's eyes.

"That's a bunch of superstitious nonsense. Evolution has already proven the Bible wrong. Only stupid people who can't think for themselves go to church," he said, using the same daring tone as if he wanted an argument. Rosemary snapped her mouth shut. She knew church wasn't superstitious or wrong, but there was no way to convince Harry of that. So she caved and agreed to the courthouse ceremony, she didn't want to fight before they were even married.

She picked the corsage off the floor and pinned it on, moving her pulsing thumb out of the way. The carnation drooped, yearning to be anywhere but pinned down, held against its will. Rosemary tried to smile at her reflection. *Everything will be okay*, she told herself. *This is just pre-wedding jitters. This is normal, everyone feels like this.*

Albert's face flashed across her consciousness. His brown eyes were sad, crying. Rosemary shook her head. No, no, she wouldn't think about him today. This was her new beginning and she wanted this, she needed this to feel whole again. She turned on her heel and walked out of the restroom

Harry was sitting on a wooden bench outside the courtroom, waiting for her. He looked so handsome in his navy suit. He smiled when he saw her. They could make this life work together, despite their differences. Rosemary tried to smile back, but it felt like a grimace.

"Nervous?" he asked, standing up. He towered over her like a scarecrow. Was she the pesky crow that kept flying around? Sometimes she felt as if she were a bother to Harry, that her opinions were an annoyance. She felt like he wanted her to be seen, but not heard. Maybe that was what a good wife did. She swallowed hard and nodded. Yes, she was nervous.

"Well, soon it will all be over and you will be Mrs. Connor," Harry said. Rosemary swallowed a huge, dry lump in her throat. Harry took her hand, which was slick with perspiration.

They were called into the courtroom. Rosemary glanced about, looking for her mother to reassure her. Then she remembered once again that her mother was not there. She shook her head and followed Harry to the judge's bench.

The judge, in his black, draped robe, stood and said, "We are gathered here today to celebrate one of life's greatest moments, to give recognition to the worth and beauty of love, and to add our best wishes to the words which shall unite Harry Connor and Rosemary Ruhrmann in marriage."

Rosemary felt her kneels buckling, the room spinning as if

caught up in a tornado. Harry caught her elbow and held her up. The judge paused, but Harry nodded for him to continue. This was the end of Rosemary's single life. She was becoming a bride, a wife. Harry repeated his vows confidently. Rosemary wanted to believe that all would be well, but fear gnawed at her consciousness. She felt wooden, propelled forward by a wind which she was powerless to stand up against.

Harry slid the slim golden band around her left ring finger and Rosemary repeated the action, slipping a golden band around his finger. They were man and wife, married, at least in the eyes of the state, until death do they part. It was done. Let no man break this bond.

Albert

The light flickered in and out, accompanied by radiating pain. Albert tried to open his eyes as a burst of orange lit the sky over his head. He heard the shell explode, but it was muted as if he had heavy woolen mittens covering his ears. Dirt sprayed over him, thrown up by the shell hitting the ground. Albert spit, trying to clear his mouth of the earth, remove the metallic taste. He heard men yelling, screaming in agony, barking orders. He could not move, felt paralyzed. He shifted his gaze to the left and a sharp pain started in his shoulder and jolted his heart. His breath was shallow, but he was alive. He had to be—there couldn't be this much pain if he were dead. This must be hell. It looked like hell, Albert thought as he moved only his eyes to assess his situation. To his right was Pfc. Aaron. He lay motionless, his shirt bloodied, his legs at odd angles. Albert couldn't tell if he was unconscious or dead.

The ground which was so firm this morning when they had climbed the ridge was now pocked with shell and mortar holes. The pine trees which stood tall and green were now blackened, branches on fire, others blown to bits, only splintered trunks standing, still others uprooted, twisted and gnarled. And blood… It mixed with the soil, creating a metallic scent that Albert breathed in with every shallow breath.

It covered the smoke and smell of wood and flesh burning.

There were still men coming up the hill, holding the hill. Albert saw them cut down as the machine guns rained bullets on the ridge. He tried to locate his rifle and sit up. As he lifted his shoulder off the ground, he felt like he was hit with another mortar, this one full of searing heat and pain. It came from inside him and washed over him, blanketing him in blackness. He slumped back against the ground and looked at his shoulder, the source of the discomfort. It was a bloody mess. The metal was twisted into his shoulder muscle, blood spurting out. Albert felt weak, saw flashing white stars behind his eyes and thought he would faint again. *No! No!* He told himself. *Stay awake, stay alive!* He didn't want to be overrun by the Germans and be bayoneted to death. At least if he was coherent, he could save himself.

He tried to pull himself along with his right arm, to take cover behind a smoldering tree trunk. With each movement came a flare of white pain, threatening to overwhelm him and knock him back into unconsciousness. He gritted his teeth, his lip snarling. He would make it to the trunk. Inch by inch, he dragged himself through the shell holes, over the low bramble, his shirt getting stuck on a thorny bush. He yanked at the shirt and it came off with a loud rip. Albert remained very still, not knowing how loud the rip was, if he had given his position away to the Germans. They must have heard it. They were probably aiming the 88mm mortar gun on him now. He scrambled on his knees and one arm, his left arm dragging as he crawled.

Finally he reached the tree trunk and collapsed against it, relief washing over him. He cradled his left arm, holding it against his chest. His shoulders heaved, despite the shooting pain. Would he get out of here alive? Eddie's head bobbing swam in front of him, beckoning him. He was too weak to fight anymore. His vision narrowed, and he was sucked into the black tunnel of unconsciousness.

"Hey buddy, we're getting you out of here," Albert felt an arm slip around his back. He looked up and saw the white arm band with a red cross. The medic! Albert tried to tell them he was alright, his mind alert.

"Don't try to talk, we've got you now," the man said as he swung Albert's legs onto the canvas stretcher stained with blood and dirt. Albert tried to sit up, to show them that he could walk, he was fine. The world spun and he fell back onto the litter. The other medic patted his good shoulder, "I know you're ok. But you'd better let us carry you back just in case."

Albert laid back and tried to relax. They carried him down the ridge, back towards the outskirts of Helenenburg, to the orphanage that had been transformed into a hospital. Mortar shells exploded in the air, although not as many as earlier in the day. The sun had rounded the sky and began its descent back into the underworld. There were bodies strewn everywhere. Albert closed his eyes—so much destruction. So much had been sacrificed.

"Did we hold the ridge?" he asked hoarsely.

The medic nodded. "You boys did real good!"

Albert nodded, satisfied that at least they had completed their mission and taken that ridge. Then he passed out.

The orphanage bustled with activity. The make-shift infirmary had a surgical room, a convalescing room, and a prep room. Albert was given a few stitches to cauterize the splintered artery and close up his wound.

"They'll need to take out that shrapnel when you get back to Britain," the doctor said as he sewed Albert's shoulder, injecting him with morphine. The drug coursed through his veins, blocking all pain. Albert floated above himself, feeling like he was not in his body. He watched the doctor push the needle into his shoulder and pull the string through, sewing his gaping wound, but he could not feel a thing. It was probably better that way.

"Wait, what did you say?" Albert asked. The morphine made it hard to concentrate, to connect the doctor's words.

"They'll take out the shrapnel when you get to Britain. You know, England?" he laughed.

"No, I can't go to England. I have to lead my men," Albert slurred. The doctor finished sewing Albert up.

"Nope, no more fighting for you, buddy. You're going to England for surgery. I can't take the shrapnel out here without you losing more blood. That shrapnel is stuck in an artery. It's all that's keeping you from bleeding out right now. I doubt you'll be doing any fighting for a while," the doctor packed up his kit and left. Albert drifted into sleep, wondering if this was all a dream.

———————

He awoke later—how much later, he didn't know. His bed swayed, bobbing up and down. Was he going crazy? He called a doctor over. "What's going on?" he asked.

"We're crossing the English Channel, taking you to a hospital in Southampton. Just get some sleep, there's nothing to see anyhow," the doctor gave him another shot. Morphine. It surged through his body and he drifted into sleep.

He had a dream, Rosemary was leaning over him. He breathed in her scent—rosewater and that unidentifiable womanly smell. Delicious. Her hair waved back from her forehead, caught at the sides with tortoise shell combs. Her small mouth was pursed as she dabbed a cool washcloth across Albert's head. He grabbed her wrist with his left hand—no pain in his shoulder. She smiled, her pearly teeth glowing. Albert rubbed his thumb over the inside of her wrist. It was smooth and soft, like satin. She cocked her head in a questioning gesture. Albert reached for her face. He stroked the gossamer down hair on her cheek.

He wound his hand into the back of her hair to hold onto her. Her slate blue eyes were clear, no underlying worry or sadness. She put her hand on his face. It tingled as she brushed her fingers across his cheek, over his lips. He kissed her fingers. She ran her hand over his lips. He closed his eyes and just felt her hands on his face.

"Easy now."

Albert was roused out of his beautiful dream. He opened his eyes and was in another hospital, endless hospitals now.

"Ah, he's finally awake. Hello, mate! Welcome to England," an orderly dressed in white grinned at Albert as he adjusted the bed. The springs creaked under Albert's weight. There was a dull ache up his left arm, which had been bandaged and placed in a white sling. He leaned back against his pillows and surveyed his new home. His bed leaned against the wall, in a long row of metal bed frames lined up against the wall. Across the room was an identical row of metal beds. The linoleum flooring was waxed and shiny. It smelled like antiseptic and industrial cleanser. Overhead, fluorescent lights flooded the cavernous room with artificial light. Albert didn't know what time it was, what day it was or even where he was. He passed out again.

When he awoke, the room was filled with sunlight from the windows on the side of the room. Albert flexed his shoulder and immediately regretted it. Pain shot down his arm, numbing his fingers and seizing his chest. He cried out, alerting the orderly that he was awake.

"Good morning, old chap," he said. "We're going to get your shoulder all fixed up today. We had to pump a few pints of blood into you so we didn't lose you!"

Albert looked down and saw the IV in his arm and paled. He hated needles. The room started spinning, but Albert fought the urge to pass out.

"Where am I?" he asked, still groggy from the morphine.

"You're in a hospital in England. Do you remember what happened to you?" the orderly asked.

Albert saw the blinding orange lights of the incoming mortar shell. He saw the blackened trees, the shell holes marring the ridge. He saw Pfc. Aaron go down as the phosphorous shell exploded. He felt the searing pain in his shoulder as the shrapnel was flung in every direction, embedding itself into Albert's shoulder, knocking him to the ground. And he remembered clawing his way to hide behind the blackened tree stump, using it as cover from the shells and machine gun bullets. Albert remembered it all. He nodded at the orderly.

"I'm going to give you some more morphine and then we'll be taking you into surgery." The drug hit his bloodstream with a *whoosh*—heat radiating over his body, numbing out all of the pain, the mangled bodies, the ravaged countryside of Germany. Albert nestled into his pillow, content to just let the world slip away for a moment.

———————

Albert didn't remember going into surgery, being moved onto the gurney and wheeled into the surgical room. He was given a topical anesthesia, which numbed his shoulder. The morphine was wearing off, but the anesthesia blocked the pain from his shoulder. He watched the surgeon cut open his injury with a shiny, sharp scalpel and then take a pair of stainless steel tongs and yank on the metal shards. Albert felt like he was being shocked, pricks of pain shooting up his arm. He tried not to cry out, to show weakness. The doctor cut around the metal with the scalpel, freeing the metal from the pink muscle. His assistant mopped up the blood with white gauze. After all of the large metal pieces were removed, the surgeon took the needle and sewed more stitches into Albert. He felt the needle go in and tug the skin as it pulled the two sides back together.

It wasn't a pain that he felt, just a weird sensation of knowing that a sharp needle was piercing him.

After the surgery, he was wheeled back to his bed to recover. He asked for paper and a pencil. He wanted to write Rosemary a letter, to let her know he was safe and that he was thinking about her. How long had it been since he was with her?

"My dearest darling," he began, "Another day is almost gone, darling, and still we are so far apart. Day after day I just hope the Jerries would hurry and give up so I could be near you again. But I guess I'll just have to keep on praying to the Good Lord and hoping he will soon bring this bloody massacre to a close so all of us fellows can get home to our loved ones and above all our sweethearts."

Albert paused, pen midair. He wanted to keep the horror of the war out of this letter, but the morphine was a truth serum. But it was the truth. Albert did wish that God would intervene and the Germans would give up, stop this senseless murdering of both sides. The end was inevitable, and Albert just wanted it to be finished. He wanted to return to Rosemary, who was pure and good. He needed that normalcy.

He looked out the window at the gray sky. The sun never seemed to shine anymore. It was as if the earth knew the devastation that was happening and couldn't even let the sun come out and brighten the world. In the stark sunlight, the blood would be redder, the soldiers' expressions could be read, the utter destruction clearly visible. As long as the sky is overcast, the details of this war remain blurry and softened. Albert shuddered to think of how awful everything would look once this war was finished and the sun came out again.

Rosemary

Rosemary bustled around the kitchen, checking that the potatoes weren't boiling over, that the chicken was not getting too dry. She tried to open the window to let the fresh spring air into the kitchen, but the sash was jammed. *Damn window!* She thought as she shoved against the window with all her might. Living in her grandparent-in-law's house drained Rosemary. Harry had told her it was temporary, that they would move as soon as he had the money saved, but it was not coming fast enough for Rosemary.

Grandma Weston, Harry's grandmother, was relentless, always grouching at Rosemary for one reason or another. *You're letting too many bugs in! You're letting the potatoes burn! You can't keep the house clean!* Rosemary gave one good thrust, and the window opened with a groan. She breathed in the lilac blossoms.

Her mother-in-law, Beulah, was a sweet woman. Rosemary felt sorry for her. She had gotten pregnant with Harry and then the father took off, *probably on a drunken bender,* Beulah had said. He showed up at the hospital when Harry was born and named the baby Harry Junior. Beulah was furious. But the name stuck. Harry's father hopped a freighter back to England and married another woman and had children whom Harry had never met.

Rosemary usually was not allowed in the kitchen by Grandma

Weston, who was afraid Rosemary would burn the house down. But today was a special occasion; her mother was coming this afternoon for her first visit. She had not been to see Rosemary and Harry since they had left Streator.

Junie was coming home. They had gotten a letter from him. He didn't mention any details about his injury. Rosemary jabbed at the potatoes in a metal bowl. She was so angry at Junie for joining the war. So angry he had left her, just like Albert. She shook her head, trying to forget Albert, smashing the potatoes.

Being married was not so different than not being married. She and Harry fell into a routine. He worked at the garage until late in the evening, leaving Rosemary home alone to dodge Grandma Weston's barbed insults. She tried to stay out of the house as much as possible, taking the dogs for walks in the evenings when the sun dipped below the horizon. Or she would hide out for as long as possible in the outhouse. The Weston's didn't even have an indoor bathroom! Rosemary wrinkled her nose, but then relaxed it, remembering that she had chosen Harry and had to accept his way of life. At least, until they got their own house.

On their wedding night, Harry had told her what he expected of her, what her duties as a wife were. She came into the bathroom in a new cream chemise embroidered with blossoms. It had a high neck and fell to her ankles. Harry lay on the bed in only his cotton striped underwear and white undershirt. His eyes lit up as she stepped into the room. He licked his lips and for a second, Rosemary felt as if he were the big, bad wolf and she were Little Red Riding Hood.

She froze in fear for a moment, unsure what she should do. Her blood thundered in her ears. Again she felt disappointed by her mother whose sex education had been letting her watch the birth of Virginia's first baby. Harry reached out for her, beckoned with his hand for her to come closer. She walked towards the simple brass bed as if treading through quicksand. The cotton bedspread wrinkled under Harry as he shifted his weight. She sat on the edge of the bed, pulling down her night-gown, feeling exposed despite being fully clothed.

"Don't be nervous. I'll show you everything you need to know," Harry murmured into her ear as he pulled the chemise up, revealing her thin, milky legs dangling over the side of the bed. She fought the urge to yank the dress back down, to cover herself. Harry began kissing her neck, her earlobes. His lips were moist and clammy, like a dead fish. She thought of Albert, and how strong and warm his lips had been. How her heart raced as he kissed her in his car. She thought of the night on Airport Road, of him tracing the Big Dipper with her hand. Had she made a mistake? She turned to kiss Harry on the mouth to drive the thought from her mind.

As he made love to her, Rosemary wept. Her child-like in-nocence was being taken away from her. Harry cooed into her ear, trying to make her relax and enjoy the act of love making, but Rosemary only cried harder. She cried for Albert being lost in the war, for Junie losing his leg, for her carefree days of collecting coal and riding horses, for her father getting tuberculosis and leaving them to fend for themselves.

She knew her life was changed forever now. And she knew that she had been naïve in thinking that just because Harry would not leave her, her life would be transformed into a life of security and comfort. She had been so naïve.

Rosemary put her hand on her flat belly. And the result of their love making was a pregnancy. There was a flutter in her abdomen, a rush of blood flowing and creating a new life. She missed her period and calculated that she must be about six weeks or so along. She had not expected it to happen so soon, but Harry had been determined to start a family as soon as possible.

"Why can't we wait a year or two?" Rosemary asked, trying to keep the whining tone that Harry hated out of her voice. He admonished her for what he called "being womanly." That included having cramps at her period, complaining about any-thing, and whining about situations that he could not change.

The charmer who had courted her had changed into an over-bearing, condescending overlord. She was trying so hard to make him happy, but it felt like there was always something else to change and improve so she didn't irritate him.

"Why should we wait?" he scoffed, making Rosemary want to shrink inside of herself, wishing she had never asked the question. She shut her mouth and hoped that she would not get pregnant so soon. But she had.

She could feel the baby forming, which she knew was not possible because the fetus was not even the size of a peanut. But still, when she lay on her back at night, after Harry had drifted to sleep, she placed her hands on her abdomen. There was a pulsating right below her belly button. She could see it pumping the life force to her new baby, lifting the thin pale skin of her lower abdomen. She could feel the arms growing out of the trunk, extending, fingers forming. It frightened her. In nine months, she would be responsible for another human being. She hadn't told Harry yet, she wanted to talk to her mother about it first, to see how she should break the news to him.

There was a knock at the door at noon exactly. Her mother was always prompt. The kitchen was bright with the late morning sunshine streaming through the windows. Rosemary wiped her hands on her apron and went to the door. Her mother's face was drawn and tired. Her shoulders were hunched, giving her a defeated appearance. Rosemary threw open the door and stopped short of hugging her.

She guided her mother into the kitchen, onto a wooden chair and went back to the stove to check the chicken once again.

"So how is everything in Streator?" Rosemary asked, trying to keep her voice light and airy. There were deep lines of worry in her mother's forehead and next to her mouth.

"The same. Virginia met a nice young man at the factory. His name is Ed Norman," her mother said in a monotone.

"What is he like?" Rosemary said, holding the metal bowl against her hip and whipping the potatoes. Her mother shrugged and looked around the kitchen. Rosemary had made sure she had cleaned well, that every surface shone. But she still felt disapproval wafting from her mother, filling the small kitchen.

"How is everything going with you?" her mother asked, looking her straight in the eyes, reading the thoughts that Rosemary tried to ignore.

She put on her best smile. "Everything is good. Harry has been working a lot, but I've been keeping busy here at the house."

Her mother studied her, tilting her head to the side. Rosemary fidgeted under her scrutinizing stare. She concentrated on the potatoes, making sure she was getting all of the lumps out. Her mother had always been able to tell when Rosemary was lying. Rosemary prayed that she was a good enough actress to fool her mother this time.

"So you are happy?" she asked, peering at Rosemary, following her every move with her eyes. Rosemary nodded, a weak smiling pulling at her lips.

"You are really happy?" her mother asked again. Rosemary knew her mother could still see through her. She covered her anxiety with anger, slamming down the potatoes.

"Yes, Mother. I'm happy. I'm happy! What else do you want me to say?" Rosemary held her arms out in surrender to her mother.

Her mother reached into her purse and pulled out a letter. It was in a Red Cross envelope.

"I wasn't sure if I should bring this for you to read or not," her mother fingered the letter. Rosemary could see that it was addressed to her at her mother's house. Albert! She ripped the letter from her mother's hand. The writing was faded, as if it had come a long way. She pulled the letter out of the envelope, unfolded the paper and inhaled the ink and sea salt.

"My dearest darling," the letter began. Rosemary felt the world spin, her head feeling light. Her chest was tight and her breathing choked off.

"When did you get this?" she whispered to her mother.

"It came after you left with Harry. I couldn't very well send it here. I didn't know how Harry would react," her mother said. She didn't mask her disdain.

Rosemary turned her back to her mother and read the letter.

March 12, 1945
Somewhere in England

My dearest darling,
Another day is almost gone darling and still we are so far apart.

Rosemary's heart was in her throat. All the months of worrying, wondering what had happened to him, moving on, and now, now she had her answer. He was not dead after all.

Darling, I can't wait until that day arrives when peace will reign all over again and I can hold you so close to me and know I can be seeing you every day. Oh darling, how my heart keeps beating out those same words all the time—I love you, I love you. I hope before long, darling, I can be whispering those exact words into your ear.

Also, darling, when we make it 7:00 in the morning at the George Hasckak place, we will make it either St. Anthony's or St. Stephen's, whichever one you please. That will surely be the happiest day of my life. For right now, darling, that is a tougher fight than the one of fighting the ole Jerries.

I'll close with Good night, Sweetheart.

Your future hubby,
"Al"

Rosemary held the letter, her hand steady. He held onto his promise. He was planning on marrying her when he came home, planning on meeting her at George Hasckak's place. Oh God! She hadn't kept her part of the deal! She had caved and married someone else. All because she wanted a guarantee. And so she agreed to marry a man who could never leave her for the army, never leave her wondering if he was lying on a battlefield, his life bleeding out of him.

Albert was alive. And she was married to someone else. She opened her mouth and a blood-curdling scream erupted from her. It was coming from her soul, invading her body, this scream of pain, of broken promises. She saw Albert's face, the high widow's peak framing his dark eyes, his strong nose and wide smile. She wailed, for not being stronger, for not trusting him, for not waiting.

She felt herself swoon. The kitchen became a black hole and she sunk into it, screaming as she fell.

Albert

Albert received updates from the front daily. He followed the movement of his unit as they drove the Germans back through Koblenz and into the Rhine valley. On April 12th came the news that President Roosevelt had died. Albert hung his head, saddened for the president who had done so much to first keep America out of the war and when war was inevitable, campaigned to put the best generals and training in place to protect the troops as best he could. To have done so much and not see the conclusion was heartbreaking. He heard about the liberation of Buchenwald, the Nazi concentration camp. He was sickened by the descriptions and photos of the Jews, the walking skeletons who the Nazis used as slave labor, with as many as 6,000 dying each day. Albert could not believe the brutality.

The Soviets were closing on Berlin, their bombs carpeted the city, demolished it. They said that Hitler was in an underground bunker, but no one knew for sure. Albert had hoped the Americans would reach Berlin first and claim the capitol of the Reich for themselves, but the Soviets were moving faster.

Other than his daily updates, Albert's days consisted of playing cards with some boys from Pennsylvania, writing to Rosemary, playing catch in the small grassy yard between two hospital buildings. Try as he might, he could not find a Catholic

Church—only the Church of England. He had tried to go to a service, but he missed the Latin and the ceremony of the Catholic Church. He would not go back into combat, but that didn't stop the nightmares. At night, he could still see the mangled bodies, faces contorted in pain.

He lay back on his bed, watching the white clouds float across the deep blue sky. Spring had finally come to Britain, a reprieve from the damp rain that hovered for months over the country. Albert had never been to a place that was so dreary and overcast. He was glad to see the sun and watch the clouds morph into different shapes as they danced across the sky.

"Mail call, Albert," the mail clerk dropped a letter onto his lap. He glanced at the handwriting—Rosemary! He swiftly sat up and ripped the letter open. His heart was singing to finally hear from her. Maybe she hadn't known where to send her letters, maybe they were getting sent to his unit, not knowing that he had been sent to Britain to recuperate. In any case, this was the first letter he had received from her since he'd gotten to Europe. He ripped it open.

"Dear Albert," it began. Her handwriting was cramped and slanting, reflecting her anxious disposition. "I don't know how to write this to you. I married someone else. I thought you were dead and I couldn't bear the thought of living alone without you. Please forgive me. I never meant to hurt you. Yours, Rosemary."

The letter was cold and impersonal. Had Rosemary written it? A weight crushed Albert's heart, pushing on his rib cage. His shoulder wound began throbbing, beating in place of his heart. He placed his right hand over his heart, to try to hold it together, keep it from exploding and coming out of his chest.

The letter couldn't be real. He told her he was coming back. Why? Why had she done this to him? He reread the letter, but it made no more sense to him than it did the first time he read it. He slumped back against his pillow. *Rosie*, he mouthed. How could you have such little faith in me? Albert willed his thoughts across the ocean to enter Rosemary's brain, demanding answers from her.

He had no more tears left to cry, he was bone dry. They had all flowed out of him during his combat, seeing Eddie die, thinking he was going to die himself. Those pains were nothing compared to the emotional pain. His heart was broken.

"The Nazi's surrendered!" a soldier, dressed in a hospital gown ran into the big room, his fists pumping over his head. A loud roar went up from the beds, celebration. Albert couldn't even muster the excitement that the Germans had surrendered; the end he had been wishing for now seemed trivial. He had lost his reason to live through this, to go home.

The next day was overcast, but not even the weather could dampen the spirits of the crowd gathering in the street to celebrate V-E day. Red, white and blue bunting had been draped from building windows, over door sashes, across streets, everywhere. Albert sucked on the end of his cigar, which he had been handed as he left the hospital and wandered into the streets. The whole city seemed to be buzzing with excitement, except Albert. He shuffled along, past a bugle corps playing Stars and Stripes, his head down, studying the cobble stones. He headed up towards the Council House to hear the proclamation of peace. Young women rushed past him, giggling with excitement, elated that the war was over and their lives would return to normal. Whatever "normal" was, Albert thought. Normal for him was to return to Streator, to work at Owens-Illinois Glass, to marry Rosemary. But his version of normal had been blasted away from him, blown into shrapnel bits that cleaved him in his heart as painfully as the metal shards had opened his shoulder. Albert felt his shoulders droop just a little more, the weight of his broken dreams shoving him down. He concentrated on putting one foot in front of the other, determined to make it to the Council House, to hear the King's proclamation, to live his life in the new version of "normalcy" that had been created for him—to live alone, without Rosemary. As he neared the building, the crowd closed in, making it impossible to pass. He stood off to the side, studying the gray slate stones, the Union Jack flapping in the slight breeze. The sun was trying to peek through the clouds, but they were just too thick to let the sunlight through.

A woman walked past him, brushing his chest and murmuring excuse me as she shuffled her children closer to the Council House. Her hand was on the top of a small girl's head. Her blonde ringlets bounced as she ran to keep up with her mother and older siblings. She was carrying a tiny Union Jack flag on a stick, dressed in a Union Jack dress and had a big red and white striped bow in her fine hair. Albert smiled despite himself. That child will never have to know what this war was really like. She'll read about it in history books, removed from the actual horror. It will become just another event in history, just another war to learn about for her. Albert wished he had the same luxury of not knowing what happened across the Channel.

Over the tinny speakers, King George VI's voice boomed into the street, "Today we give thanks to Almighty God for a great deliverance. Speaking from our Empire's oldest capitol city, war-battered but never for one moment daunted or dismayed – speaking from London, I ask you to join with me in that act of thanksgiving."

Thanksgiving that the war was over—no more men would go to their deaths on the soil of an enemy that many of them descended from. Hell, most of his friends were German. Half of Streator was German. He could not escape them. And he could not escape his memory of killing them.

The crowd was rapt, hanging on the king's every word.

They had hope again, hope that life would return to normal, that all would be well again. But Albert's world would never be normal, never be right again. The woman he had planned on making his life with had deserted him, had married another man. She may as well have died, for she was dead to him. All of his dreams, all of his plans were gone. He felt like a shell of a human, a part of himself lost, as real as if he'd lost an arm or a leg. Albert was grateful that he would recover physically from his injuries. But he doubted that he would ever recover fully from his emotional wounds. He turned away from the jubilant crowd and walked in solitude back to the hospital, unsure how to rebuild his own life.

1949

Rosemary

Rosemary dropped into the wooden chair and took a long drag off her cigarette. Georgie, her son, was sleeping in his pram. She had left him in there, afraid to move him to his crib and wake him. She rubbed at her eyes, which felt perpetually dry. There was a stain on her dress; she didn't know when she had gotten it or where. The past four years, which should have been the happiest of her life, passed in a frightening blur.

What had happened to her? Rosemary remembered the letter, Albert's letter, telling her that he was still alive and waiting for her. Her heart shattered into a thousand pieces, scattered across to Europe. She lost interest in everything, no longer trying to please Grandma Weston or avoid her barbarous tongue.

If only she'd waited, she chided herself. If only she had gotten the letter earlier. If only she hadn't been so weak and afraid of being alone. If only, if only, if only. The words banged around her head several times a day.

She had tried to put the regret out of her mind, tried to push it down and get on with her life with Harry. And that horrible letter—guilt crept over her every time she thought of that cold letter she dashed off. She had wanted to explain, to make Albert understand. But her mother hawked over her shoulder.

"Better to just be blunt and to the point," she said. "No point in prolonging the agony. Then he can move on too." So Rosemary obeyed her mother and copied her mother's dictated words.

She regretted the frosty tone, but she had been afraid that Albert would write back, talk her out of her marriage and back to him. And she was afraid that she would go. Instead, she put her energy into the growing baby, hoping that when it was born, her misery would lift. Her life could return to normal.

Her bourgeoning baby stretched her stomach. She felt a little arm or leg as it stretched against her stomach, trying to get out. It was fleeting moments of happiness to which Rosemary clung. On November 7, 1945, Kathleen Connor was born. In her angelic face was the promise of the happy life that she had craved. Her white-blonde hair curled around her delicate face. She looked so much like Rosemary had when she was a baby. In her was the salvation she longed for.

"When can we have her baptized?" Rosemary asked Harry when Kathleen was already four months old. Her soul was in danger. What if, God forbid, she died? She would be stuck in limbo forever!

"No child of mine is going through that brain-washing voo-doo! The Catholic Church is a cult. They only want your money so they can live high on the hog. They turn out imbeciles who can't think for themselves and will just hand over their money," Harry said, flicking his wrist at Rosemary.

"But, Harry, we…." Her voice faltered. "We have to get her baptized."

He jabbed his thumb at his chest. "No daughter of mine will ever be forced into those old-fashioned witchcraft ceremonies. Catholics are no different than other crazy cults. They brainwash you into thinking you are bad, you're a sinner, so you keep coming to church. I thought you were smarter than that, Rosemary."

He shook his head, and Rosemary felt herself shrink. She felt like a child being reprimanded. He dug into his dinner in front of him, signaling the end of the conversation.

But it plagued Rosemary. How was she going to start a new

life if he was rejecting God? She looked to the billowing clouds for answers. But God was silent. He had damned her because she had turned away from him. No amount of penance could clear her soul and bring her back into God's good graces. Even if Rosemary was damned, she was determined that her daughter's wouldn't be.

One Sunday, when Harry was off tinkering with his latest project at the garage, Rosemary made her first move towards saving her daughter from spending eternity in limbo—or worse, hell. Even though she feared Harry's wrath, she bought a baptismal dress from Woolworth's and hid it in her undergarment drawer, where she knew Harry would never look. She dressed Kathleen in the lacy dress, making her look like a cherub. *Her* little angel, *her* responsibility to lead into a religious life, to teach her not to make the same mistakes that Rosemary had made. The bonnet looked like a halo as her blonde curls spiraled from under it. This baby was sent from God, and Rosemary had to save her.

She pushed her in her pram to the Catholic Church. There was only one in town, despite the proliferation of other denominations. She suspected that the entire town was anti-Catholic, but she held her head high and pushed Kathleen on. The elm and maple trees were just budding, the tulips and daffodils pushing up from the dark, wet dirt, proving that God could do anything and He would save her baby. Rosemary's heart soared. Kathleen would be saved.

After the baptism, she hid the dress once again in the bottom of her drawer. Harry never needed to know that she had secured a place in heaven for their daughter.

Despite those moments of triumph and serenity, Rosemary's new life was obscured by a dark cloud. She never felt like she was able to get caught up. She was perpetually tired, which everyone told her was normal as a young mother, but Rosemary felt it went deeper than that. Ever since she found out Albert was still alive, she felt like an adulteress, even though intellectually she knew she hadn't consummated their love. She had no energy to fight, weariness seeping into her bones. A dark abyss surrounded her, threatening to pull her under.

Harry was no help in relieving her worries and anxieties. In fact, Rosemary felt as if he were adding to her miseries by keeping her away from the church. He also was not very helpful with the baby. He shied away from her when she cried or dirtied her diaper. She knew it was her duty to care for the baby, but it was exhausting for Rosemary. She wished Harry would help her, take Kathleen when she fussed, just give her a moment of peace. But he never would help her, he was always at the garage, working or messing with his cars.

"Harry, can't you just stay home this once with your daughter?" Her voice had taken a hard edge, brimming with frustration. She feared that he was sabotaging her efforts to build a happy life.

"Rosemary, you know I need to work all I can to save for this house that you want," he replied, his voice taking the smooth edge that Rosemary recognized now as just lip service. He used that tone whenever he wanted to placate Rosemary, and even though she knew it was a lie, it did calm her a little.

"But when, Harry? When are we actually going to get it?" She knew she was whining, which would cause Harry to flip from charmer to belligerent, but she didn't care. She was tired of the outhouse, of filling the tub in the kitchen to take a bath. She wanted privacy, she wanted a house of her own, not to feel like a burden on Grandma Weston, which she was quick to remind Rosemary. But never in front of Harry, oh no!

"Well, it's taking more time than I expected. You just need to be patient. You act like I can just blink and the money will appear!" he smiled, the swami charming the snake out of striking position.

Rosemary just wanted Harry to hold his side of the bargain, to keep his promises. She clamped down, holding in all of the insults and barbs she wanted to shout back at him, knowing they would get her nowhere. His voice held the same finality it did when he told her family that they would not be married in the church—no discussion warranted or wanted.

The little voice screamed that she was a sinner and this was what she deserved, so she might as well just deal with it. She watched Harry shake his head.

"I guess I should just go back to the garage and earn more money for your house," he said. Rosemary wanted to protest, this is not what she wanted at all! She wanted a break from the baby, just for a few minutes.

But he was already gone. She heard the gravel kick up as he peeled out of the driveway. Rosemary felt Grandma Weston's presence and disapproving head shaking without turning to see her.

When Kathleen was three months old, Harry started getting frustrated with Rosemary and her lack of interest in him. The charmer came back to get what he wanted from Rosemary.

"Leave the baby, Rosemary," he coaxed, "Come to bed."

She buried her head into the baby's neck, breathing her comfortable smell. The dual personalities frightened Rosemary. She never knew what she was going to get when he opened his mouth, soothing compliments or scathing digs.

Then Harry came home late one night, banging around the house in frustration. Rosemary was already in bed, pretending to be asleep. Even though she knew it was a sin, she had been thinking of Albert again, reliving their dance at the Paddock Club, humming "Moonlight Serenade," imagining his hands holding her, protecting her. He had been constant in his temperament. Rosemary had traded physical abandonment for emotional. Now she realized that emotional abandonment was worse. She squeezed her eyes shut as she felt Harry climb into the bed, the brass creaking as he shifted towards her. She could smell oil and alcohol exuding from him. He put his arm around her. She lay perfectly still, hoping he would give up. He pressed his body against her back.

"Harry, I'm sleeping!" she mumbled, shoving his hand away.

"Rosemary, I just want to love you," he breathed into her ear.

"Harry, I need to check on the baby," Rosemary said, turning her head and pushing against him. But Harry would not let Rosemary go.

"The baby's fine, Rosemary," he said, turning her onto her back and easing legs open with his knees, slipping into her.

Rosemary closed her eyes, accepting that she needed to do her wifely duty, that she needed to let Harry love her. She drifted into her own mind and pretended she was in a field, a green open field. Her hand ran atop the knee high grasses, purple flowers blooming. The sun warmed her back, her hair. She turned her head to get the sun on her face. The sparrows and larks twittered, calling to each other, to find a mate. It was like twenty flutes playing an unsynchronized symphony. The ground was damp, her feet sinking slightly into the earth and cooling her soles. She stayed in this field until Harry had finished.

She sprang from bed and ran into the baby's room, scooping Kathleen up and shushing in her ear, rhythmically bouncing her up and down. The baby started, but after a few moments, she settled, calmed by her mother. But nothing could calm Rosemary's nerves. She placed the baby back into her crib and headed for the kitchen. She poured herself a glass of straight whiskey, understanding now why Virginia drank. She tossed the brown liquid back, feeling the warmth sink down her throat and into her stomach, comforting her, numbing her feelings.

Rosemary constantly doubted herself with Harry, questioning what she used to know was right and wrong. Harry turned her thoughts inside out, calling her weak and brainwashed whenever she tried to bring up the church. She felt as if a part of her had been amputated, removed without her consent. But then Rosemary remembered. She had consented, had agreed to marry Harry. She had sacrificed her soul for the momentary relief of a man who wouldn't abandon her.

Seven and a half months later, Georgie was born. Thank God, Rosemary had insisted on going to the hospital and not having the baby on the Weston kitchen table, as all other babies had been born. He was a small baby, needed an incubator the first week of his life to keep him alive. Rosemary felt guilty when she looked at him.

"This has to be your side of the family," Harry attacked her. "No boys on my side are weaklings. We are all strong and fit."

"Hmph... let's hope he doesn't turn out like his grandfather," Rosemary shot back, trying to cover her hurt with sarcasm. Instead of letting Harry see how his comments cut her, she developed an icy veneer.

"At least he was a man. And look at what my mom had to deal with! She never complained. Not like you. You were always moping around while you were pregnant. No wonder my son is not strong. He's weak like you," he said.

"I... well, you're no help," she said, her voice barely rising above a whisper. If Harry had heard her, he made no indication.

Did she not love Georgie enough while he was growing in her belly? Was she passing her misery onto her child? Rosemary cried, believing that it may be true.

And now Georgie was two, still sickly and weak, an extremely light sleeper. But when he did sleep, he too looked like an angel. She wished he could be that quiet when he was awake, but his screams pierced ears. She felt a tug at her dress and looked down. A beautiful blonde girl looked up at her with big blue eyes. Her blonde hair was knotted and tangled.

"Momma," she said, "Georgie is crying."

Rosemary stared into Kathleen's sweet face, her concerned eyes. No child should have to worry at three years of age. Rosemary felt disconnected from it all, as if she were watching someone else's life and not her own.

Then, the words from Kathleen connected in her brain. Her baby was crying. She jerked up from the table, ran into the living room and the crib that held Georgie, knocking her shin against his carriage. Tears sprang into her eyes, from the physical pain, from the emotions she could not deal with. She picked him up, patting his back, trying to soothe him, but he kept screaming, his face red from exertion. It rattled her nerves to hear the ear-piercing cries. She was taut, like a rubber band pulled too tightly. She felt that soon, she was going to break.

She bounced Georgie up and down, anything to get him to stop crying. *God, please help me*, she prayed. And like so many of Rosemary's other prayers, it went unanswered.

She walked from room to room of her new house, the house that Harry had promised her and finally bought after Georgie was born, but no longer had the same appeal. Rosemary no longer had the drive to make this house her home. Kathleen tagged behind Rosemary, following her like a shadow.

Georgie finally stopped crying. Rosemary's ears rang in the silence, sharp tones that punctuated the quiet and filled her head with noise. They say that silence is deafening, and she never understood why they said that. Her brain never quieted, never gave her a moment's rest. She wished she could be internally deaf, so she didn't have to hear her own thoughts. She laid Georgie in his crib with a bottle, his cheeks pulsing, sucking the cold liquid. At least he was a good eater, even if he never seemed to gain weight.

She walked back into the kitchen, sat at the table and lit another cigarette, just one to calm her nerves. Harry didn't like her smoking in the house. He said it was unbecoming. Her hand shook as she lifted the slender white cigarette to her mouth, inhaling unsteadily. She wanted the ringing to stop, to leave her in peace. A tear fell from her blinking eyelid, a lone tear. She wiped it away in frustration, a lump creeping up her throat. She could not deal with this, could not handle the crying baby, the needy toddler, her feelings of guilt and shame. They were burying her under a sea of anxiety and frustration. *God*, she pleaded, *please give me the strength to deal with all of this*. But as soon as she completed her prayer for help, she remembered that she had abandoned the church, was being kept away by Harry, and that her soul and her children's souls were damned. She felt like she was drowning.

And Harry—Harry was no help. He worked such long hours, coming home well after the sun set and leaving before it rose again. When he wasn't working, he was tinkering with his car or working on his hair-brained invention of a one-seat plane. He always begged off helping with Georgie, claiming that it was Rosemary's responsibility to take care of the babies. His responsibility was to work and support his family. She wasn't so sure she believed him anymore. Too many things didn't add up. His total disregard of religion, his disinterest in the children. Was he in the KKK? This was southern Illinois, where there were as many bigots and racists as in the south, it felt like. Maybe his late nights of working were a cover for Klan rallies. Yes, that was much more reasonable.

And even though he wouldn't help her, she was not allowed to go to church for any relief either. He must be a Klan member. That was the only explanation that made sense to Rosemary. Yes, and he was trying to pull her family into his web of evilness.

Rosemary wiped her brow with the back of her hand, trying to wipe the negative thoughts away. This was her family. She needed to make the best of this. She made her bed, it was time to lie in it. This was all nonsense, her logical side told her. What time was it? The sun had already dipped below the horizon, its rays not penetrating the thick clouds which drizzled rain down, coating everything in slick moisture. Would this winter ever end? It was May, and she had not seen the sun in weeks. Rosemary watched the fog descend like a dirty blanket. It matched her mood.

Rosemary prepared dinner, waking Georgie and sitting him into his high chair, settled Kathleen and the three of them ate in silence, Rosemary's mind a million miles away. She wondered what Albert was doing. Was he sitting at his mother's table, eating halušky and stuffed cabbage? Was he working at

Owens? Rosemary had lost her right to know about Albert and what he was doing. But the loneliness made her feel desperate.

After dinner, she put the children to bed, reading *Little Red Riding Hood* to Kathleen. Her daughter loved and hated the story. She got so scared when the wolf ate Little Red Riding Hood, but then she cheered when the hunter came and cut open the wolf, and Little Red Riding Hood escaped unharmed. Rosemary smiled as Kathleen's expressive face scrunched up in fear and then opened with relief at the end. Rosemary longed to be that innocent again, to have her life to do over.

When the children were sleeping, Rosemary finally had some time to herself. She opened a beer and settled into the couch, lost in her thoughts. Her hand shook as she lifted the beer to her mouth. The amber liquid cooled and soothed her nervous body as it glided through her system. She wanted to be numb, to not feel, to just be. Where had the carefree seventeen year old gone? Rosemary got out old photos and clippings. She held the Owens pin-up photo. Her eyes connected with the girl, her blue eyes serene, the crimson lips curved into a smile, chin tucked softly into her neck. Rosemary could not remember being this girl, could not remember being excited for a date, driving out to Airport Road with Albert. Could not, or would not? She asked herself, draining the beer can. She walked to the kitchen to get a fresh beer and saw Harry's headlights pull into the drive way.

Harry—Rosemary narrowed her eyes. He had tricked her. He made her think that everything was going to be great if they got married, that he would take care of her. Well, he wasn't living up to his end of the bargain. She watched him get out of the car, without a care in the world, a lift in his step. He was whistling to himself as he opened the door and let himself in.

"Good evening," he said, his face sliding into his charmer's smile. Rosemary snorted and cracked open the beer. Of course it was a good evening for him, he hadn't had a baby screaming in his ear for hours, alone in his head with guilty thoughts. Rosemary's hand quivered with her building rage, shooting daggers at him over the top of her beer can.

"Well, I guess I'll get dinner for myself," he said, pausing. "That is, if you've made any." Rosemary sometimes forgot to make dinner. Not once did he ask if something was the matter that she couldn't make dinner. No, he just assumed that she was the bad wife neglecting her duties. The anger climbed into Rosemary's throat like a weed she couldn't stop.

"Yes, your children are fine, thanks for asking. I had a terrible day," Rosemary said in an even, angry tone. Harry sighed and sat down hard at the table, dropping a plate of cold stew. He didn't even acknowledge her. Rosemary's skin prickled in irritation.

"Georgie wouldn't stop crying all day," Rosemary continued, wishing he would for once show that he cared about her.

"Maybe you should have my mother come over and give you a break if you are so overwhelmed," he said between bites of stew. He never once looked up at Rosemary. Rosemary was livid. She didn't want his mother; she wanted him to help with the children! She emptied the beer and whipped the can at Harry's head, wanting to hurt him. It hit the wall behind Harry, echoing in the silent room.

"You missed," Harry said, still not looking up from his food. Rosemary screamed inwardly, wanting to gouge his eyes out, scratch him until he hurt as much as she hurt. She wanted him to do something, anything to show that he heard her, that he cared about what happened in this family. But his head stayed down into his plate and Rosemary gave up.

She walked out of the kitchen, her body weighed down in misery. This was not what she had planned when she had said yes to Harry. This was not the wife she wanted to be. Had she acted too impulsively? She knew she had, and always did. Taking momentary peace instead of thinking things through. She just hadn't wanted to be alone. But after four years of being married to someone who would not stand up for her to his grandmother or let her go to church, she longed to be alone, to not be trapped in this prison called a marriage.

Albert

Albert walked along the catwalk, high above Owens' factory floor. He looked down on the line, made up mainly of men once again, returned from war. Albert had gotten his job back once he returned from England. Owen-Illinois had reinstated many veterans upon their return. They made every effort to make it seem like they had only left for a few days. Had it already been four years since V-E day? Albert thought back to that day in May when he was recuperating in the hospital, when everyone was filled with joy and optimism, and he was miserable. Even listening to his beloved Chicago Cubs make it to the World Series did nothing to raise Albert's spirits.

He listened on the radio as announcers explained a disturbance during Game 4 against the Detroit Tigers.

"A local business owner brought his goat to Wrigley Field with a sign pinned to it that said, 'We got Detroit's goat.' The goat was paraded around the field," the announcer explained. Albert thought it was a distraction to the game. They were there to play baseball, after all! The announcer continued, "The ushers threw them out of the stadium. The man uttered a curse before leaving the stadium, 'The Cubs, they ain't gonna win no more.'" And they did not win the World Series that year.

Albert felt cursed too, cursed to live a life where he knew

Rosemary was married to someone else, someone else was living the life he wanted for himself. He moved like a robot, waking, going to work, making the bottle molds, returning home, eating, sleeping. The joy had gone out of his life. It was all he could do to just live.

His mother worried about him. "Albert, *zlatko*, you must get over this, this heart ache," she pleaded with Albert. She held his face in her large hands, peering into his eyes, her face furrowed. He shook off her hands. She didn't understand, would never understand what it felt like to have found the perfect woman, only to have her marry another. Rosemary was his innocence lost in Germany. His only grip on his sanity had been coming home and regaining that innocence in her.

Albert gripped the rail of the catwalk to keep himself from screaming. He dug his fingernails into the metal, feeling them bend under the pressure. He wanted his life back and until he had gotten that letter, he felt he could find his way home. He turned away from the void, blocking out Rosemary and the crushing misery.

"Say, Albert!" his buddy, Raymond Dudak, slapped him on the back. Albert exhaled with relief. He nodded a hello.

"We're still on to play euchre at the Paddock Club tonight, right?" Raymond asked as they walked along the catwalk towards the mold shop.

Albert nodded, he had forgotten that they were playing euchre that night. It was Albert's favorite card game because it required strategy and skill. Albert and Raymond were the best team in the city—they could beat anyone even if they were dealt the worst hand. Euchre is played in pairs, one pair against another pair. Your partner sits opposite you at the table. Five cards are dealt to each player—only the ace, king, queen, jack, ten and nine are used. Albert could lose himself in the game, block out all thoughts and feelings while he played. He needed that today to stop his mind from twisting.

It was his dream—the same dream kept haunting him. He was

hurrying for something, but he didn't know what. He needed to get *there*, where ever there was. He ran along a cobblestone street lined with destroyed buildings, rubble piles, a coating of brown dust over everything. An eerie silence reverberated in the street, his footfalls echoing off the exposed brick walls of the busted buildings. The sky was the same brown as the dust, horizon and ground meeting at an indistinguishable point in the distance. A building came into view; Albert squinted and made out the twin steeples, the cross atop. It was a church. He opened the heavy oak doors, the thick metal hinges creaking. His chest heaved, his breath cut off. It hurt to inhale, to get the oxygen to his muscles that he needed. He leaned over, his hands on his knees.

The organ blared shrill opening notes. Mass must be starting, Albert thought and hurried into the nave. The church was cavernous. The ceiling must have touched the sky, the pillars supported the gilded ceiling were spun like spirals, to support the additional weight. Two people knelt at the altar, heads bowed. The church was empty. Odd, for a wedding, Albert thought. His footsteps echoed in the emptiness, overpowering the organ blasts. Albert's heart began pounding, adrenaline surging through his body. The hairs on the back of his neck rose in alarm. There was something off about this scene. The groom turned around. Albert recognized the thin face, large dark eyes. Eddie! Albert broke into a run; he wanted to throw his arms around his friend, to feel if he was real. The bride turned around as Albert ran to the altar. It was Rosemary, her veil framing her face. She carried a bouquet of blood red roses. The smile continued all the way to her eyes, shining blue, no hint of sadness pulling at the corners. Albert stopped short, his breath cut off. His legs wavered, threatening to give out. She held her hand out and Eddie took her slim hand in his palm, squeezing it. It was as if they were squeezing Albert's heart out, wrenching it from his chest. Albert wished that she would, it would hurt less.

As Albert was deciding if he was happy to see Eddie, or sad that he was marrying Rosemary, a horrific boom sounded, a mortar exploding through the dome above the altar. It landed between Eddie and Rosemary, throwing them backward, separating them with a shower of crushed marble and dust. And blood—red blood mixing with the white marble and dust. Rosemary lay lifeless, her smile still on her face.

He awoke in a cold sweat. He knew he should let her go, but even his subconscious was not willing to. Albert shivered as he recalled the dream, the life that he knew he needed to forget, but he just didn't know how.

Albert walked into the Paddock Club and into the smoky haze that hung over the club. He craved a cigarette every time he walked into the place, as he walked towards the back of the club where the euchre tables were set up. In the corner of the club, just before the back room, Albert saw Virginia with her face close to a young fellow. Virginia, Rosemary's sister. He stared at her, willing her to look up and see him. She did, meeting his eye. Her eyes were the same deep-set, sad eyes that Rosemary had. He couldn't look at her anymore, it was too painful. He rushed into the backroom, ducking his head as he passed Virginia's table.

Raymond waved Albert over to their assigned table. Losers rotated to the next table when a game was finished. Albert and Raymond hardly ever needed to rotate. Raymond poured a schooner glass full of beer for Albert. Albert sat down and gulped the beer, wanting the alcohol to loosen him up, make him relax. He was keyed up from seeing Virginia, the resemblance to Rosemary. Raymond dealt the cards and Albert fell into the game. He was like a shark, circling his prey, making it feel safe and then swooping in and tasting blood. He slammed the card onto the table, Jack of Hearts, the highest card in this hand.

Raymond hooted, "You know how to make it exciting, Al!" Albert grinned, but it came out as a snarl, a killer's smile. Raymond filled Albert's glass again and Albert drank it down in one gulp.

"Whoa, Al! Slow down! We've still got to play the game," he joked. Albert grabbed the pitcher himself and filled it again. He was developing a plan. As the cards were dealt, Albert's mind clicked into place. He was going to talk to Virginia, get a message to Rosemary. Tell her that he was fine, better than fine. He was great without her.

Raymond and Albert beat their opponents. "Next time, come ready to play!" Albert barked as the guys got up to switch tables. Albert's hand slipped off the table and he almost fell from his chair. The alcohol bolstered his courage, all other thoughts vanished. He was biding his time until he talked to Virginia, once the alcohol loosened him up. Until then, he took out his repressed aggression on anyone who came near him. Raymond just shook his head, wanting to play cards, not get into a fight.

"I'll be right back," Albert slurred, his words stuck in his mouth as if he were sucking on cotton.

"Where're you going? We've got another game to play! AL!" he heard Raymond yell, but he headed towards the front of the bar, feeling the alcohol course through his blood. He rounded the corner and saw Virginia facing him. Her face registered surprise before falling into a deep scowl.

"Hey Ginny," he said, swaying backward. He grabbed a chair to stop himself from falling.

"Why don't you sit down before you fall down, Al," she said. Her voice was not like Rosemary's. Not light and melodic—it was harsh and scratchy. Albert nodded and tumbled into the chair. He wanted to look strong and like a man who was carrying on with his life. Instead, he felt like he was going to break down in front of Rosemary's sister. A lump formed in his throat, choking him.

"How are you, Al?" Virginia asked, her harsh voice softening. Albert shrugged. How could he explain how he was?

"How's Rosemary?" he asked, his voice squeaking. He wanted to know, but yet was afraid of the answer.

Virginia shrugged, "She's taking care of two children with an absent husband."

"What do you mean, absent? I'll kill him!" Albert balled up his fists. Even though she married him instead of her, he would not see her disrespected. Virginia placed her hands over his.

"Slow down," she said, "You're not killing anybody. It is what it is."

"Why couldn't she wait for me, Ginny?" he whispered, all of his emotions unleashed in his husky voice.

Virginia sighed, tilting her head to the heavens. "You know Rosemary, Albert. She never thinks things through. Never has, never will."

Albert laid his head on his arms atop the table. That was what Albert loved about her. She was a wild spirit and he had wanted to cultivate that.

"Albert," Virginia placed her hand on his elbow, shaking him. "She was afraid, she thought you weren't coming back and married him because she couldn't be alone. She could never be alone. First our father, then Junie, then you. She just didn't want anyone else to leave her."

Albert wasn't listening to her; he was lost in thought of Rosemary, her smooth, milky throat, her serious eyes, her spunkiness. He thought of "Moonlight Serenade," dancing close to her, smelling her rosewater scent, her soft hair curling around her face.

"She broke my heart. She broke my heart," he mumbled, trying to not let the tears fall. He stumbled from his chair, knocking drinks out of someone's hands.

"Hey!" the person protested. Tears blurred Albert's vision. He smacked into the front door, shoving it open with his knee. He fumbled to get the car door open. His head spun from all of the beer he drank, but he was determined to get away from there, to not let anyone see him crying.

He drove out of town, down Main Street, zig-zagging. The

center of the road kept jumping from right to left, making Albert dizzy. He closed one eye to drive straighter. His head hit the top of the car as he raced over the railroad tracks, the car propelled into the air. The car pointed out of town on autopilot. He turned left onto Airport Road, stopping at the rise where he'd taken Rosemary. The lights of Streator still twinkled in the distance, but they looked dull and dreary. It was May, too early for the crickets to be serenading each other. Albert heard "Moonlight Serenade" in his head. The melody filled the car, the clarinets wavering high above it.

In the silence of the evening, once his tears for Rosemary stopped, visions of the war came back, as they always did. He shuddered and tried to think of something, anything but the war. He saw Floyd, the blood gushing from the bullet wound in his forehead. Bile rose up his throat, gagging him. He saw the bloated, decaying horses left by the fleeing Germans. He saw the bodies littering the hillside after the battle of Hostrum, bodies lying broken, the life seeping out of them in a pool of thick red blood, staining the ground in a way that can never be cleaned. And Eddie. He saw Eddie lying on that gurney, his stomach busted open.

He opened the car door and vomited. The life he had dreamed of—being a hero in the war, coming home and marrying Rosemary—none of it happened. It was all for nothing—all for nothing! And Rosemary—Rosemary hadn't believed he would come back. He had broken her heart as he walked away from her that last day. He saw it in her eyes, but he wanted to believe that she would wait, that she could wait. And now, he had to accept that she was not strong enough for that.

Rosemary

Rosemary pushed the stroller faster, her legs burning. Kathleen struggled to keep up with her mother, but she knew better than to say anything when Rosemary was in one of her moods. The miniature schnauzers also struggled for breath, their little legs churning to keep up.

Rosemary was lost in her own thoughts, replaying the fight she and Harry had had that morning. It was Sunday, and she was counting on him to help her with Georgie, to give her a break from his incessant crying.

"Harry, please," she begged him, following him from room to room as he collected his gear to go to the stock car track. He loved racing and would spend every minute he could with his cars, but Rosemary needed a break.

Harry set his jaw, determined not to fight. The silence was worse than yelling. At least if he would yell, she would know that he cared.

"I can't take this, Harry. You need to take the children this afternoon. I feel like I'm losing my mind!" Rosemary knew she sounded desperate, but she couldn't help it. It was as if she were on a train and her life was flying past her and she couldn't move, she was stuck in a lightless prison, paralyzed.

"I told you, call my mother and ask her to come and help take care of the children," he said, finally stopping, placing his hands on Rosemary's shoulders. She looked into his eyes for a sign that he cared for his family. But Harry's eyes were blank. Rosemary never could read him, never get past the veil he pulled own. She clung to his arms, feeling the ground tilt underneath her. She was drowning, being pulled under by her responsibilities.

"No, I want you to help me, not your mom. Just take them with you, just for today," she said, hoping he would agree and she could slip off to church, to confession. She needed a few hours to confess everything that she had done in the past four years.

Harry turned on his charm, the charm that Rosemary fell for, the charm that held the empty promises that Rosemary believed. "Rosemary," he said, "I'll be home at three this afternoon. I promise. And then I'll help with the children, I really will."

Rosemary could only take shallow, short breaths. The ground decelerated to a slow rotation. Tiny white stars sparkled behind Rosemary's eyes, covering Harry's face. She released his arms; she had heard this story before.

He usually snuck out of the house before Rosemary had risen so he could avoid confrontation. Today, Rosemary had beaten him. Actually, she sat at the kitchen table and smoked cigarette after cigarette to try to calm her nerves. Georgie had finally gone to sleep in the early morning hours. Rosemary had ambushed Harry, scaring him as he slunk into the kitchen. And now, he was pouring on the charm, and Rosemary was too tired to argue with him.

"Take the kids to Grandma Weston's and I'll come and pick you all up after my races. We'll have a nice family afternoon together," Harry soothed. Her face was slack, she couldn't even make herself smile, it was too much effort. Her bones ached. And she knew he was lying, she knew it, but she wanted to believe it was true at the same time.

So after Harry had left, waving from his car window as he peeled out of the driveway, Rosemary packed up the kids and the dogs to go to church. If she couldn't go alone, she'd take the children. A little religion wouldn't hurt them. She wasn't going to take charity from his grandmother! She hated the way Grandma Weston looked at her over the top of her glasses. Her look confirmed that Rosemary was a failure as a mother. So instead of sitting in judgment of a person, she would sit in judgment of God. She needed a sign from God, anything to tell her what she should do. Maybe this would be the day that God answered her prayer, gave her the sign she needed, changed Harry and made him care about his family.

She tied the dogs to the rail in the front of the church, lifted Georgie's pram and entered the building. Confession was not for a few hours, so she would just need to pray on her own. She tugged at Kathleen's hand, pulling her towards the Virgin Mary's statue at the side of the sacristy.

"Momma, why are we here?" Kathleen cried.

"Shhh, this is God's house and you need to have respect and be quiet," Rosemary said in a harsh whisper. She shook her head, saddened that she needed to explain this to her child. Kathleen should already know this from going to church every Sunday.

She knelt in front of the statue and fumbled in her purse for change to drop into the votive offering box. She lit a candle, the glow blinding her for a second. But that was okay because this was God's holy light. The Virgin's hands were outstretched, reaching for Rosemary. She wanted to climb into those arms, let them soothe her worries.

She clutched her hands together. Kathleen knelt next to her, mimicking her mother's actions.

"Oh Holy Mother," Rosemary prayed, "please let me be more like you. Give me your patience. Please make Harry want to be a part of this family. Please help me! I feel like I'm losing my mind."

The words were tumbling in Rosemary's head, bumping into each other, struggling to be realized. She didn't know if she were speaking aloud or not. She didn't care.

"I don't know what to do. I'm so tired. He never helps me,

197

even for a minute so I can just breathe. I'm suffocating. And he's keeping me from God. I know that isn't an excuse, but I don't know what to do. Please help me, please help me, please help me, please help me."

She felt the tears on her cheeks. She sniffled and waited for a response. Kathleen looked expectantly at her. She smiled, knowing that soon she would have some answers. Mary, the Holy Mother, would not leave her when she was in greatest need. All they needed to do was wait.

Georgie started whimpering in his pram. *Please don't cry now!* Rosemary thought. *I'm so close to getting the help we all need.* She looked back up at the statue. Mary's face was serene, a small smile on her lips. Mary was the perfect mother and would help Rosemary to be as well. Kathleen held her breath. Georgie's cries echoed off the cavernous ceilings and marble floors. Rosemary heard her heart beating, pounding, pounding, pounding.

The wails interrupted her fervent prayer. Rosemary looked back, cooing at Georgie to try to quiet him. Just another minute. She knew that was all she needed. Just another minute, and Mary would help them. She shook the pram, pushing and pulling it, hoping the movement would lull him back to sleep.

"Momma, what do we do now?" Kathleen asked. Rosemary shushed her. How could she hear the Virgin's message with all their chatter? She began to panic. She swung back to the statue, searching the face for an answer. But only the enigmatic smile looked back. Rosemary wondered if the Virgin's look was serene or if she was taunting them. Oh God! She must be beyond help if even Mary couldn't give her an answer! This was all Harry's fault. If he let them go to church, if he cared about their family, if he helped with the children… then she wouldn't feel as if she were coming undone.

"Excuse me, ma'am."

Rosemary turned and saw a priest standing, hands folded. His eyes smiled.

"We are getting ready for confession. I'm afraid you'll need to take care of your baby before you can be heard," he said. Rosemary's eyes swung from the statue to the priest. But she needed an answer. The priest remained standing, hands folded. Rosemary sighed, pushing herself up from the kneeler.

"Come back without the baby, child," the priest's expression softened. "You look like something is weighing heavily on your soul."

Rosemary wanted to collapse at his feet and explain everything to him, about Albert, about Harry, about God punishing her. The priest shifted. No, she couldn't tell a priest. He would only tell her that she had gotten herself into this mess, she needed to make the best of it and get back to the church. Rosemary felt ashamed of her actions, of falling for a man and not waiting for him, of being weak, of allowing Harry to treat her as he did, of not fighting and going to church. No, she couldn't tell any of this to the priest.

"Sorry, Father. We'll be on our way," she said, trying to smile. She pushed the pram past him and hurried out of the church. The only place for her to go was Grandma Weston's.

As she walked, Rosemary's eyes blurred with tears. She was reminded once again of her mistake, her rash decision to marry. Why was she impulsive? Why hadn't she waited?

"Mommy, slow down!" Kathleen panted, her little legs pumping quickly to keep up with Rosemary's pace. She stopped in her tracks. A flash of guilt came over her. She was too wrapped up in her own thoughts to notice Kathleen struggling to keep up with her. Perhaps she wasn't any better than Harry. Maybe this was why God never answered her prayers. She deserved what she was getting.

Albert

Albert felt like someone was banging a mallet against his temple, methodically trying to pound his brain out the side of his head. He tried to swallow, but his mouth was too dry, his tongue felt like a bolt of raw wool. He lifted his head to get his bearings. He saw his dresser, poster of the Chicago Cubs on the wall. Good, he was in his room, even if it was spinning. What had happened last night? He remembered being out at Airport Road, but then the evening was blank.

His brother Steve strode into the bedroom, a stupid grin on his face, his eyes twinkling. Albert groaned and put his pillow over his head.

"Boy, are you in trouble!" Steve laughed, flopping on the bed and making it jump under his weight. Albert's stomach jerked.

"Get off the bed," Albert grumbled, kicking him. "Why am I in trouble?"

"You don't remember? You were blitzed last night and ran over a power line. You got Da's car stuck on it and walked home. He had to go and pick the car up. When he tried to back off the power line, the entire transmission was ripped out. You are in so much trouble!" Steve chortled, enjoying his brother's mischief. Usually, it was Steve who was causing some sort of trouble around the house.

Albert groaned. Bits of the evening twinkled through the black hole of his memory. Albert remembered struggling to keep the car on the road. He then remembered driving through the ditch, banging his forehead against the steering wheel as the car lodged itself on the power line. He threw it in reverse and gunned it, spinning the wheels. Had he walked home? He couldn't remember.

His father was going to kill him. Literally, string him up by his shoelaces and lynch him. Albert had been warned not to let anything happen to that car. He winced as he lifted his head, winced at the thought of facing his father. But the sooner he did it, the sooner it would be over with. He pushed past his laughing brother, who padded behind Albert, excited to see someone else get in trouble.

His mother was in the kitchen, scrubbing the floor on her hands and knees. She shook her head, as she spied him out of the corner of her eye.

"Where's Da?" he asked. She motioned towards the barn at the back of the property where they kept the pigs.

At the entrance of the barn, Albert watched his father digging into the soiled hay. His shirt sleeves were rolled up and his back was drenched in sweat, even though the air was not particularly warm. He looked angry. Albert kicked at the ground, trying to get his father's attention without actually speaking. His father looked over his shoulder and turned back to his labor, a deliberate snub. Albert shifted, waiting for his father to say something.

"You will pay for the repairs," his father said after what seemed an eternity, never looking up.

"I know, Da." Albert stood frozen to the door jam, wishing to melt into the wood. He knew he should apologize, but his mouth would not form the words. His father stopped mucking with the hay, leaned on the wooden handle of the pitchfork and wiped his brow with a blue handkerchief from his back pocket. He folded and replaced the handkerchief before he spoke again.

"You've got to pull yourself out of this, Albert," he said, his voice firm.

"I know, Da."

"It's been four years since you've come back. You need to live your life. The past is the past, you need to move on. I don't know what happened over there, but you've got to put it behind you."

Albert walked back to the house, his head hung low. How could he let go of Rosemary? How could he forget the horrors of Germany? How? If someone could tell him, he would do it.

Rosemary

Beulah threw the door open as she saw them approaching the house. She waited for Kathleen to run and throw herself into her ample bosom. Her face was tired, but happy. She worked hard, struggled to make ends meet. She loved Georgie and Kathleen, was always glad to see them and spend time with them. Rosemary plodded towards Beulah in defeat. To Rosemary, it was another day that she needed help to deal with her own children.

The newspaper was lying in the grass where the paperboy had tossed it. Rosemary picked it up as she pushed the stroller towards the house.

"How are you, honey?" Beulah asked Rosemary. Rosemary shrugged, trying to smile, but she didn't have the energy to try to put on a show that everything was fine at home. She was tired, she needed help, and she knew that Beulah was willing to help. Beulah lifted Georgie out of the stroller. He lit up, smiling and cooing at his grandmother. Another wave of guilt flooded Rosemary. Why couldn't he do that with her?

"Beulah, can you watch the kids for a few hours? I need to go to the doctor. My stomach has been acting up. I can't keep anything down."

"Of course, honey! You need to take care of yourself. I'm sure these two little angels wear you out. You look like you've lost more weight," she said, moving Georgie to her other hip to get a better look at Rosemary. Rosemary pulled her coat tighter around her frame. She was thin, and she knew it. Anxiety and guilt were eating her from the inside.

"A little. I hope the doctor can give me something for it," she said.

"Well, you take as long as you need. We will be here when you get finished."

Rosemary smiled with gratitude and darted from the house. Her spirits lifted as she thought that Doctor Meyer could cure her physically and then she could go to confession and be healed spiritually.

She knocked on the door to her doctor's office. She didn't have an appointment, but she hoped that he could see her. After a moment, the curtain moved and she saw her doctor's narrow, spectacled face.

"Rosie," he said as he opened the door, "How can I help you?"

"I… I can't keep anything down, doctor. I feel like I've lost more weight," she said, looking away. If she looked at him, he would see the reason why she was unwell.

"Come on in," he sighed. "Let's see what's going on."

She followed him into his examining room. He motioned to the scale. She stepped on, leaving her coat and shoes on. He moved the weights lower, lower, lower.

"Rosie, you've lost ten more pounds. You're down to 96 pounds," he looked at her, not accusing, but quizzical.

"I… well, it's just that I can't seem to eat," she stammered.

"Uh huh. And is Harry helping you at all?" he asked. Rosemary's hand flew up to her hair.

"Of course he is! He's a very good husband," Rosemary said, but the lies sounded hollow in her ears.

"There is nothing physically wrong with you, Rosie. I've told you that before. I've known Harry since he was a little boy. He is too much like his father. None of your ailments are physical. I'm afraid it is a nervous breakdown. The only cure for that is rest and a break from whatever is causing the anxiety. And I'm certain that is Harry."

Rosemary bristled. She had *had* that person to take care of her, and he left her to go to war. Harry was a good man, even if he was absent. She had to believe that he would change; he would live up to his promises. Dr. Meyer wasn't going to blame Harry for her shortcomings.

"No, no. That's not it. I... something must be wrong with my stomach!" she protested. He shook his head.

"Fine, let me examine you," he said. He felt her throat, pushed on her stomach, looked in her ears and throat. "You do look a little pale. I'm going to give you some iron pills. I hope you are right, Rosie. I hope that I am wrong."

He gave her a bottle of pills and sent her on her way. Rosemary was rattled. A nervous breakdown? That's what happened to crazy people. She wasn't crazy, was she? She needed to talk to someone who knew her. She needed her mother, but she was a hundred miles away. So she decided to ask the next best thing.

———

Beulah was bustling around the kitchen when Rosemary let herself in. She sank into one of the wooden chairs, her bones clanking against each other like iron anvils. She watched in amazement as Beulah moved from sink to stove and back again. She made the domestic chores look so easy, effortless. It was all laborious for Rosemary, but she knew that she should at least try to help Beulah.

She pushed herself up with her arms, but Beulah waved Rosemary away.

"Sit down, Rosie. Relax," she said. Rosemary sunk into the chair once again, replaying the doctor's words in her mind. Nervous breakdown. Her hands shook as she lit a cigarette, the smoke hypnotizing her, lulling her into a calmer state of mind.

Rosemary opened the newspaper as she tried to think of a way to ask Beulah if she, Rosemary, were crazy and if the problems in her marriage were of her own making. Beulah was Harry's mother, but she also was fair and not blind to Harry's faults.

"Bess and Fred are on their way over. Said they wanted to talk to you about something," Beulah said over her shoulder. Rosemary nodded, lost in her own thoughts. Bess was Beulah's sister. She was a lively woman, and Rosemary had taken to her. They had fun nights playing bridge together.

"Beulah, how did you get taken by Harry's father?" Rosemary asked.

"Psh… Same way you fell for Harry—his charm. He is just like his father. You know that. He poured it on and I was hooked. From the first note I heard him play on his clarinet at that little gin joint. He just had to reel me in," she laughed. It was a bitter little laugh, but not full of the regret that Rosemary felt.

"Sounds familiar," Rosemary said, as she flipped through the pages, not reading a word written. The pages were crisp and made a clean crumpling noise as she turned them. Rosemary took another drag off her cigarette, her nerves unwinding from their tense knot.

"How were you able to raise Harry by yourself? I feel like I never can get caught up," Rosemary asked.

"Well, my ma, Grandma Weston, helped. Harry was the apple of her eye. She spoiled him, gave him everything and anything that he wanted. He was the only person who could please her," she said. "Did you know that when he was fifteen he talked her into buying him a car instead of building an indoor bathroom? That's why we still have the outhouse," she chuckled. "He could talk her into anything."

"Am I a bad mother?" Rosemary whispered, afraid of the answer.

"Oh, God no!" Beulah said, wiping her hands on her apron and coming over to Rosemary. She put her arms around her. "Honey, I know you've got it rough. I love my son, but he is his father—selfish, self-absorbed, interested only in his cars. I know he loves his children, but he is old-fashioned. He grew up that way. He believes that the woman's job is to take care of house and home. I know it is hard on you. You just come over here and let me and Grandma Weston help you with these lovely children. Harry is never going to be much help with that, but he is a good provider. Isn't he?"

Rosemary nodded, she knew Harry was a good financial provider, but she needed more than that. She needed emotional support, even just to keep a grip on her sanity.

The screen door banged open. "Hell-oooo!" Bess called out, her easy laugh filling the house. The air seemed to lighten as she swept into the kitchen. "Hey there, Rosie," she said and wrapped her arms around Rosemary's shoulders. "Oh, honey, you are getting down right bony! You need to eat, girl." Her tone was concerned, not malicious.

"I know. It's this anemia," Rosemary said, relaxing in Bess's presence. "I stopped by the doctor's this morning. He gave me some iron pills. I'll be right as rain soon." She wanted to believe what she was saying, but the doctor's warning flashed. Nervous breakdown. No, Rosemary wasn't crazy.

Bess spotted the paper in front of Rosemary and scooped it up, hiding it behind her back.

"Oh good. I can see I got here just in time," she said, twisting the paper.

"Bessie, it's good to see you. How are you?" Beulah hugged her sister.

"Fine, fine Beulah, but you're not going to be happy when I break the news to you. It seems Harry is following in his father's footsteps," she replied. Rosemary's ears perked up, the tension clutching her shoulders.

"What do you mean, Bess?" she asked before Beulah could.

"I don't know how to tell you this, so I'm just going to show you," Bess opened and smoothed the newspaper onto the table. She stood back and nodded. A photo caught Rosemary's eye. The quality was poor, it was very grainy, but she could see the lankiness, the long arms and legs, the shock of white-blond hair. It was Harry, on roller skates. When had he gone roller skating? Next to him was a buxom girl, the apples of her cheeks shiny, her dark hair rolled away from her face.

She read the caption, "Harry Connor and his girl, Nancy Grey, had a great time at the roller rink this weekend."

Harry Connor and his girl Nancy Grey? *His girl?* Rosemary tried to decipher the photo's meaning. But she knew. This was where he was going after work, on the weekends. She wanted to find Harry and string him up, sew the scarlet letter on his chest. Adultery. The sixth commandment. But Harry didn't care about the commandments or religion or God. It all made sense now… his Klan membership, his stance against God. Her mind twirled like a maple whirly-gig spinning and spinning as it fell. She felt herself fall into the chasm of her mind, a dark place that edged her consciousness, threatened to pull her in and not let her out.

Something deep within her snapped. The thin thread of sanity which she had been grasping with all of her strength gave out. A single thought replaced it. She realized that Harry was the Devil. He was the Devil himself. That was why he wouldn't let her go to church. He wanted her soul and the souls of her children. It all clicked into place for Rosemary. She wanted to scream her revelation to Bess and Beulah, but her mouth would not move, words could not form. She heard them talking, but they were muffled by the vast ocean in her ears. She felt physically removed from the room.

"What?" Beulah grabbed the paper.

"It was only a matter of time, Beulah. Ma spoilt him rotten and he was too much like his father for this not to happen."

"But…" Beulah let her protest trail off, knowing there was no response. As she had told Rosemary, he was his father's son. He was the charmer, the ladies' man, spawn of Satan. Rosemary couldn't surface. She was having trouble breathing.

"He never was one to think about consequences," Bess said. "I warned you about Harry's father before you got involved with him, but you wouldn't listen."

"Oh Bess," Beulah snapped. "Don't bring Harry's father into this. Harry is not his father! And if I had listened to you, I wouldn't have Harry or these beautiful grandbabies." Rosemary whimpered. Her grandbabies, Rosemary's kids. Were they damned like Rosemary was? This was his ultimate goal. It wasn't to get Rosemary, it was to get her children. He wanted to steal their souls. As the thought formed, a wave of blackness closed around her. Harry was blocking her. He didn't want her close to the truth!

"What are we going to do?" Beulah asked.

"Nothing rash. We don't want to do something silly. We need to keep the family together," Bess patted Rosemary's arm. "We will just tell him that he needs to stop this immediately and be the husband and father that his father couldn't be."

No, no! Rosemary screamed, but no words escaped the thick waters of her mind. She couldn't stay with Harry. Didn't they see he was the Devil? How could they not see that? No, Rosemary couldn't stay with him and risk the souls of her children. She may be doomed, but she would get them away from him. He would not take them down too.

"He's the Devil," she muttered.

"What honey?" Bess asked. Rosemary tried to speak again but the words were drowned out. She couldn't move her head or her arms. Nothing was working in her body. Just her mind planned to save her children.

"Fred will talk to Harry, tell him that he needs to quit seeing this girl and then you two will work everything out. Everything will be fine," Bess continued.

The voices faded, drowned out by the thoughts in Rosemary's brain. While they were planning how to keep her family together, she was plotting how to get out. She knew that Harry was evil incarnate now. This confirmed her suspicions. Maybe he was or wasn't a Klan member, but Rosemary didn't need that confirmation to know Harry was Satan and that he was after her children.

She allowed herself to sink into the recesses of her mind, to let Beulah and Bess fall away. *He is the Devil, he is the Devil*, reverberated off all sides of her skull. She felt herself slip from the chair, crashing onto the linoleum floor. She watched from deep within herself as Bess and Beulah struggled to carry her to the couch and place an ice compress on her head. Bess slapped her, hard, and called her name. Oh I'm here, Rosemary thought, and I'm not coming out until I have a plan to save my kids.

———

Rosemary sat up on the couch. The room had an eerie yellow glow, as if bathed in mustard gas. She stretched her arms overhead, willing the stiffness to leave her body. She heard movement in the kitchen and went to it.

"Rosie!" Beulah cried. "We were so worried about you. You passed out and we couldn't get you to come to. Harry is on his way over right now."

Rosemary smiled. It was a sweet, innocent smile. "Oh I'm fine Beulah. I think I'll be heading back home now."

"No, Rosie, you were unconscious for half an hour. Harry is on his way, just wait for him to get here."

"Okay," Rosemary said, feeling like she was dreaming. "Where are the children?"

"Bess took them outside to play and so Georgie could get some sun."

"I think I'll go see them," Rosemary said, gliding towards the back door. The yellow glow followed her, turning everything into a Salvador Dali painting. Were the trees dripping?

Kathleen was chasing a butterfly around the melting tree and Bess was jiggling Georgie in his pram. Her children. Her responsibility to get away from Harry before he sucked their souls from them.

"How are you feeling?" Bess asked. Rosemary turned to see Bess. Maybe she was in on it too. Rosemary had to get her away from the children. Maybe they were all in on it and were trying to make Rosemary sick so they could take the children away from her.

"Oh, a little faint," Rosemary said, keeping the sweet smile. "Would you be a dear and get me a glass of water?"

"Sure Rosie," Bess said and patted her on the shoulder as she went into the house. Patronizing her. But Rosemary was onto all of them.

"Come on Kathleen, let's go home," she sang, pushing Georgie's pram out of the yard. She walked quickly, hoping to put some distance between herself and Beulah's house. She needed to get the children away. Kathleen ran to keep up.

His family was plotting to get her out of their lives, replace her with this other woman. Nancy was probably a witch. That's why Harry liked her. She was going to save her children if it was the last thing she did. Her legs were weak and rubbery, but she pushed through. She felt her throat constrict, her breath choked off. Bands of color flashed across her eyes, pink, orange, purple. She felt like she was going to pass out, lose consciousness. She willed herself forward. She had to make it home.

As she neared her house, she slowed down a little. Kathleen pumped her little legs without a complaint. She seemed to sense something was not right.

Rosemary was lost in her own mind again. The darkness dropped and words formed in stark white. Cleanse the children. Yes, she would go home and wash the sin of their father off them.

She plunged into the kitchen and turned the faucet on full blast. She grabbed Georgie from his pram and held his head under water.

"God, remove the sin of his father. Do not abandon them as you abandoned me. Save them from their father, the Devil," Rosemary chanted over and over. Georgie wailed as the water flowed over his head. Her heart ached, but she knew she must cleanse him to save him. She blocked out his cries and repeated her prayer, louder this time.

Kathleen stared with wide eyes. "Maybe we should call Grandma," she said, her voice not rising above a whisper.

Rosemary pulled Georgie from beneath the water. Kathleen was an angel sent from God. Here was her solution, her way to save her children.

"Yes, why don't we call your grandma in Streator?" she said, laughing. Kathleen shook her head, confused at the sudden change in their mother's mood.

Yes, Rosemary thought, *I'll call my mother. She'll understand. She'll help me to save the children's souls.* Her heart settled back into her chest.

She wrapped Georgie in a towel and dragged the children down the block to the post office to use the phone. It rang once, twice. Rosemary's heart sank with each unanswered ring. Her hope of being saved was diminishing. She looked at her children. Kathleen was holding onto Georgie, her arms wrapped around him, her eyes cautious.

As she was giving up hope that her mother would save her, the receiver was picked up. There was a shuffling at the other end.

"Hello?" her mother's annoyed voice came over the line. Rosemary sank against the wall in relief. Oh, thank God! She's there. She will know exactly what to do, how to make this right.

"Hello?" her mother said again, anger mixing with her annoyance.

"Mother?" Rosemary whispered, her body not able to produce more sound. Her heart thudding against her ribs.

"Rosie?" her mother yelled into the phone, as if they had a bad connection.

Rosemary straightened up, cleared her throat. "Yes, Ma, it's me. I need your help. I need you to help me. Harry, well, I… Well… I found a photo of Harry and another girl. It was in the paper. I think they are planning on having me committed, they want to take the children! They are trying to make me crazy. I can't take this, Ma! I can't do it! I can't!" Rosemary wailed. She felt cleansed, like she did after confession.

Her mother sighed on the other end of the line, "Oh Rosie.

Just come home, girl. Get on a train, bring the children and just come home. We'll sort out everything here."

Yes, home. Rosemary would go home, get some rest and support from her mother and then decide what to do. Yes, she could do that. She got off the phone, and walked to the train station. She wanted to go home and pack suitcase for them, but she couldn't risk Harry being there and capturing her. She just wanted to get out of there, out of that town. Away from Harry and his family and their evil plans.

They boarded the last train out of the town for the evening. Georgie placed his head in her lap and fell into a slumber, too frightened to cry. Kathleen sat quietly next to her. Rosemary looked out the window as the train's brake was released and they began to ease forward. She was escaping, she was saving her children from the Devil. He would not corrupt them. She had saved them. She closed her eyes and leaned her forehead against the window, the glass cooling her, the rhythmic movement of the train lulling her into a deep sleep.

Albert

Albert needed to forget Rosemary. Maybe if he found someone who could take his mind off her, then he could begin to forget about the war too. If he found love, everything else would fall into place. After a few weeks of moping and looking for the right girl, he asked a nice looking young woman out. Evelyn was as different from Rosemary as she could be. She had dark, straight hair with short pin-curled bangs. Her hips were ample and she was plump all around, not angular like Rosemary. Albert picked her up, noticing her full skirt and tight sweater. He forced a smile as he opened the car door for her.

"Oh, did you see the new Frank Sinatra movie? We should go see that," she said. Albert nodded his head. Whatever she wanted, he would try to give it to her. He turned the car towards the Majestic Theater.

Evelyn sat up straight, hands folded on her lap. Albert smiled to himself, realizing she was nervous. He had forgotten what it was like to be on a date.

"So you like Frank Sinatra?" Albert asked to break the silence. Evelyn smiled.

"Yes, he's aces!" she replied. Aces? Albert thought. He hadn't heard that term in a long time. Who had he last heard say that? Where was he? Was it Frank Thomas over in Luxemburg? It was as if he had turned into an old man, the war sucked his youth out of him.

"What's so great about him?" Albert asked. He didn't get the appeal. He thought Frank was a scrawny weakling.

"He sings like a canary!" she said. He threw a sidelong glance at her. Was she trying too hard? He just nodded and they fell back into silence. He pulled up to the Majestic and leapt out of the car. He guided her into the theater.

"You want some popcorn?" he asked, remembering the electricity when he and Rosemary's fingers connected as they reached for the popcorn together. He bought the popcorn without waiting for her answer. He held it out to her and stuffed his hand in as she reached in. Popcorn spilled everywhere. Evelyn jumped back.

"Sorry," Albert mumbled, disappointed that there were no sparks, no energy between them.

The movie was silly and predictable, even had a happy ending. Rosemary would have hated it. It was fluff—mindless drivel to make people forget reality. Albert understood why Rosemary hated these movies. After seeing the awfulness of the world, these movies seemed rote and trivial. He guessed they allowed some people to take their minds off their real lives. But Rosemary ruined them forever.

Evelyn gushed after the movie.

"Oh man, that was bonkers!" she said, clapping her hands together. "Did you love the dancing? Gene Kelley is a hoofer!"

"You liked it?" Albert asked. "You didn't think it was all wet?" He thought he would throw some slang back at her to show her how ridiculous she sounded.

"What do you mean?" She didn't even notice.

"Well, you know, too not like real life? I mean, I never knew guys who were that shallow when I was in the service."

"I never thought about it like that. I just like the singing and dancing. Why you gotta ball it up?" she asked.

Why indeed, Albert thought. *Maybe because I've seen real battle,*

I know what war really is like. And it's not that easy to tune it out.
But Albert couldn't say that to Evelyn, couldn't talk about it
because then she might ask him real questions about what had
happened over there. And he swore he would not talk about
it with anyone who had not been there themselves. It was too
horrible, but yet, words could not express what it had been like.
Only someone who had been there could understand. People
who stayed home romanticized the war, thought it was brave
and honorable. Albert knew the truth.

She chatted as Albert drove her home. He nodded at times
that he hoped were appropriate, but he really wasn't interested in what she was saying. If this is the way women acted, he
would rather be alone.

———

Albert went to the Paddock Club a few nights later, resolute
that he would be alone. He tried to tell himself that it was okay,
it would be okay. He would be the fun uncle to all of his nieces
and nephews. That would have to be enough for him.

Albert ordered a beer as Raymond Dudak waved him over.
He surveyed the club as he walked to the other end of the bar.
The smoke hung in the air like a heavy fog, blurring features
and faces. Rosemary's brother, Junie, was with Raymond. He
leaned against a wooden cane. Albert had heard that he lost his
leg in Italy. He shivered as he thought of his own wound and
how lucky he was that it was not worse. Junie's face was long
and worn, the corners of his eyes drooping. Albert wondered
if he was having a hard time adjusting as well.

"Whaddya say, Al?" Raymond said. "You know Junie, right?"

Albert nodded, his eyes connecting with Junie's. The same
sadness peered out that he saw in Rosemary's eyes.

"How're you doing?" Albert asked, tilting his head towards
Junie's leg.

"With old wooden head?" Junie laughed, knocking on his leg.

"It beats the alternative. The tough part was learning to drive with the left foot. A lot harder than you'd think." Albert heard the false bravado in his voice that all servicemen employed to minimize their injuries.

He took a swig of beer. There were so many things he wanted to ask Junie. About the war, about Rosemary... but he couldn't bring himself to. Not in front of Raymond anyway. Raymond had volunteered for the war, but didn't see combat. All three took large swigs of beer.

"Say, there's my girl," Junie said, hopping on his good leg. "See you boys later!"

Albert watched as he approached a slender girl with cat's eye glasses. She had a kind, open face that lit up as Junie approached her. A stab of envy sliced Albert's gut. It was going to be harder than he thought to turn off his longing for Rosemary.

"You heard about his sister, right?" Raymond said, his eyes sparkling.

"Which sister?"

"Rosie... your old gal," Raymond leaned in. Albert's stomach flipped with apprehension. "She's back in town. Said she went crazy."

"What? Who said that?" Anger flared in Albert. Who was talking about Rosemary? They didn't know what she had been through. Even though she had left him, he felt compelled to protect her.

"Come on, Albert. Don't get sore. I figured you'd be happy to hear this, what with that shitty Dear John letter she sent you."

"How did you hear about that?" Albert balled his fists. Gossip. He hated people being in his business.

"It's all around town. Anyway, serves her right for dropping you while you were fighting for our country," Raymond replied.

Albert couldn't take anymore. He raised his fist and plowed it into Raymond's face. He heard a crack from his nose and blood began to spurt out of it.

"Hey man, whadya do that for?" Raymond said through cupped hands.

"Don't you ever talk about her again. I'll break more than your nose if you do," Albert said through clenched teeth.

"Maybe you two are meant for each other. You're both crazy!" Raymond said. Albert cocked his arm back and Raymond flinched. He turned on his heal and walked out of the club.

He wondered if it were true. Had Rosemary gone crazy? This would add to her sadness. Why couldn't she have waited for him? He could have taken it all away for her, restored her—and his—belief that humans were good and life could be happy. He felt destined to remain in his black cloud of misery.

Rosemary

The sun was well into the sky before Rosemary opened her eyes. Where was she? The room looked familiar, smelled familiar. Her hand gripped the eyelet covering that weighed her down onto a bed. She was deep inside herself, looking out from a tunnel.

The door opened and her mother came in. Mother! She tried to say, but the words couldn't escape the black tunnel. A man in a dark suit followed her mother into the room.

"She's been like this for three days, just lying here. I can't get a word out of her," her mother said, motioning to Rosemary. Three days? Rosemary tried to move her arms and found they were pinned under the blanket.

"What happened before this?" the man said.

"She took the train up here from Taylorville. When she got here, she was mumbling that her husband, Harry, was trying to replace her and that she needed to cleanse the children to save their souls. She tried to take them out at midnight. Said she was taking them to the church so she could save their souls from her husband," her mother replied.

"He's the devil!" Rosemary's voice shouted. The man and her mother both snapped their heads towards her.

"That's the only thing she will say. Keeps repeating it over and over," her mother said and pursed her lips.

"I've seen this before. Catatonia from a nervous breakdown. She's retreated into herself. I'll give her a sedative and she needs to rest." This man must be a doctor.

"Will she be okay?" her mother asked, hands on hips. Rosemary didn't want to be a burden to her mother.

"In time. In time, she should make a full recovery, but she should not have any contact with her husband as he seems to be the stressor."

Her mother snorted, "He put her in a whole heap of trouble, keeping her from church, not helping with the kids. Not that she didn't go willingly."

"Well," the doctor said, "We will take care of her from here, but if she gets worse, she will need to go to the hospital." The hospital! She couldn't. She needed to save her children.

They left, and Rosemary let the tunnel close over her.

In the darkness, she saw Albert. He was trudging through a muddy pit, rifle clutched to his chest. She tried to call out to him, but once again, no words were formed. Several men in khaki coats followed him. They crouched low and bullets zinged over their heads. The sky was black, dark clouds blocking the stars, the moon. Albert rose up to assess their position. A bullet moved through the air as if floating in gelatin, right for Albert's face.

"Albert!" Rosemary screamed. Albert turned to look at her. The bullet suspended.

"I only wanted to be with you," he reached out to her, into her black cave. She could almost touch his hand. But a red clawed hand swiped Albert away, dragged him into the sky and disappeared in the darkness.

"You're the evil one," Harry's face swam in front of hers. She jerked back. "You're the devil, not me." He laughed and laughed, like a hyena. And then his face vanished. Was it real?

She couldn't see anything except darkness.

After a succession of similar dreams, Rosemary slowly began to regain consciousness. She first became aware of her surroundings, this room, her old house, the sounds of the household running. She lifted her arms. They were stiff, joints rusty. She dragged herself to a sitting position and looked around. No yellow haze on anything. The room looked normal.

She heard Kathleen's voice, little Georgie's high giggling seep through the closed oak door. A wave of guilt washed over her. She had children to take care of, their souls to save. Didn't she? In the sunlight of her old room, the ideas that ran through her head seemed ridiculous. Harry wasn't the devil, not in the way she had imagined. Still, she wanted to take the children to church and get them blessed just in case.

With a heavy sigh, she pulled herself out of bed and walked over to the dresser. The reflection staring back at her did not look like the young, vivacious Rosemary that she used to be. The face staring back was skeletal, with sharp, angular cheekbones. Her eyes were recessed deep into wide sockets, huge holes in her skull. Her lips were dry and cracked. She licked them to try to get some color into them. Her hair was listless and dry. The life had leaked out of her. How long had she been there? Time was suspended. She turned and walked into the living room, pulling her cotton robe around her narrow body, the warmth escaping her.

"Mommy!" Kathleen yelled and threw her arms around Rosemary's legs. She lost her balance, feeling like a newborn colt. She grabbed the coffee table to steady herself. Georgie toddled over to her too. She wrapped her arms around them, inhaling their baby smell.

Her mother came in from the kitchen.

"Well, well, looks who's arisen from the dead," she said and pried Georgie off her legs. Rosemary's face reddened, her memory blank. "You feeling better?"

Rosemary nodded and buried her hands in Kathleen's curls. She felt connected to her life again.

"Well good, because we've got a lot to figure out. You've been here over two weeks. I thought we were going to have to have you committed!"

Rosemary was shocked. It seemed like yesterday that she brought the children here. The black cave was a vacuum. She was so glad to be free of it.

"I want to take the children to church," she said, the only coherent thought she could process.

"I know, I know. We've been taking them every day since you got here. The priest even said a special blessing over them."

"Oh thank God," Rosemary breathed. "I was so worried... and then I thought Harry was the devil..."

"You had some crazy ideas. The doctor said it was catatonia, whatever that is. But you're getting better. That's the important thing. Now we need to decide what to do next. Beulah called after you got here. She was mighty worried. She told me about Harry and his affair," she snorted. "I knew he was trouble when he walked in. But you wouldn't hear a thing against him and he turned you into his little puppet. Yes, Harry, no Harry. I couldn't watch that."

"I know, Mom. I just was so afraid... everyone was leaving me. Dad got sick, Junie joined up, then Albert joined up. I thought I would be alone forever," Rosemary said.

"You weren't abandoned!" her mother narrowed her eyes, tilting her head at Rosemary. "Your father getting sick had nothing to do with you. And Junie and Albert, well, they did what they had to protect us. No one abandoned you." Disdain crept into her mother's voice. "It's time you looked at your part in all of this, Rosie."

"I know, I know. So what do I do now?" she asked, defeated.

"You can't go back to him," her mother said. Rosemary

nodded, she knew she could not go back.

"He's ruining you. You need to move back in here and get your job back at Owens again," her mother was staring past Rosemary, the wheels in her mind turning.

Her mother was right, he was ruining her—her health. She couldn't eat, was no more than bones, had been in a black hole, unresponsive, for over two weeks. Her hands shook. No, there was no going back to him now. She placed them in her lap to stop them from trembling.

"Now," her mother continued. "What about the children?"

Rosemary's head snapped up. The children? She looked at Georgie curled up on her mother's lap, his feathery blond hair twisting in all direction. How could she take care of them if she hadn't even been able to take care of herself?

"I don't know," she mumbled, tears forming, "I don't know what to do." Her lower lip trembled as she sat paralyzed in fear and anxiety.

"Oh don't start crying. You need to be practical. I have an idea," her mother pushed her hair back off her forehead. "You just can't take care of them right now. And I can't either. Since Harry thinks it is so easy to raise children, that it takes no work, let him raise them and see how stressful it really is."

Rosemary tilted her head, trying to understand what her mother was saying. The words were just sounds, not coalescing into complete thoughts.

"No, no. I rescued them from him," she said, wringing her skirt in her hands.

"You ran away from him in the middle of the day. You didn't rescue nobody. Get that crazy notion out of your head. Harry can take care of his own kids for a while."

"Harry take the kids…." Rosemary trailed off.

"Yes, high time he learnt some responsibility. He's too spoilt."

"You mean for a few days?" Rosemary asked, not liking the look on her mother's face. It reminded her of the other time her mother had pushed her to do something that she wasn't sure she wanted to do. Like writing that horrible letter to Albert.

"Well, I don't know. For as long as it takes. You have a lot you need to do, Rosie. You need to get a lawyer, get a job, get your health back. If you don't take care of yourself, you might as well go back to him. Here's my plan: let him take the kids while you take care of your business and you can stay here. If you don't want to take care of yourself, then take the kids and go back to him."

Rosemary blanched. Her mother was so cold at times, calculated. But maybe this was what Rosemary needed, someone to tell her the right thing to do while she was regaining her sanity.

Maybe, Rosemary thought, *I could do this. I can let Harry and his new girlfriend take care of the children until I get back on my feet. I'll get my health back, my job at Owen's back and then I will take my kids back. I'll raise them Catholic. A few weeks with Harry can't be that bad. Beulah will probably take care of them anyway. Yes, this could work.*

"But what if he won't let me have the children back?" she asked her mother, praying that she would have the answer.

"He will. He will, Rosie. He won't be able to take care of them. It's just temporary, to let him see how much work it is and to make him do the work. He won't be able to take them forever. You'll get them back once the divorce is final," her mother said. She nodded her head in agreement. Her mother patted her hand, but Rosemary's stomach gurgled with dread.

———

A few days later, with her mother's prodding, they borrowed Junie's car to take the children to Taylorville. Her mother arranged it all. Rosemary's confidence in the plan faltered. She didn't want to see her children leave her, but her mother insisted.

"We're going to see your daddy," her mother said to Georgie and Kathleen. The children whooped with glee, glad to be going back to what they thought was normal. Guilt shot through

Rosemary's heart. This didn't feel right, wasn't what a mother did to her children. But it was her mother's ultimatum—let Harry have the kids and she could stay. Otherwise, go back to him. She shuddered at that thought.

The sun warmed the interior of the car as they drove south. Kathleen sang in the back seat, her angelic voice filling the car. The rhythmic movement of the car over the road lulled Georgie into sleep, his cheeks puffed out as he breathed. Rosemary felt hot, sweaty. These were her babies, could she really just hand them over? Her heart thundered in protest, not wanting to be separated from her children. They were the reason she had gone crazy in the first place! But then she heard her mother's voice of reasoning—it's only temporary, until Rosemary could care for them. She knew she was not thinking clearly yet.

She knew she needed to do this, so she could be a better mother. Once she got on her feet and her emotions stabilized, then she would get her children back and be the mother that they deserved.

———————

Her mother pulled up in front of Harry's shop. Rosemary took a ragged breath, her nerves pulled to the point of snapping. Her mother smiled at Kathleen and said, "We're here!" Kathleen looked out the window, her brow furrowed in confusion—this wasn't their house. Rosemary looked straight ahead to avoid Kathleen's expression. *This is the right thing to do*, she told herself.

Harry leaned against the door jam, a lazy smile on his face. The red bull raged inside her, indignant that he should be smiling at them after what he'd done. He had no shame, no conscious. Kathleen ran into her father's open arms and he twirled her around, laughing. Rosemary pulled a sleepy Georgie out of the car. He whimpered but did not wake up. She wobbled over to Harry, her mind whirling in confusion. She inhaled Georgie's hair, the downy fluff. It might be the last time she held him for a while. Fear held her frozen. She didn't want to give up her children, but she knew she couldn't take care of them. Before she had a chance to explain, her mother raged.

She grabbed Georgie from Rosemary's arms and shoved him towards Harry.

"Here! Take your children! You think you are a man, running around on my daughter, leaving your children home alone. You have responsibilities. It's time you stop acting like a playboy and acknowledge them!" Her face was red with anger. All of the pent up feelings that she never voiced before Rosemary married him came pouring out.

Harry turned to Rosemary and put on the charmer smile. Rosemary felt her knees weakening. "What is this all about? You left without even telling me … and now this?" The smile never faded from his face. "I want to work this out, Rosemary. I want you to move back to your home, our home."

Rosemary wavered. This was her family.

"You're killing her, Harry. Do you know that?" her mother stepped between them, providing a shield for Rosemary. "Her doctor said she had a nervous breakdown because of you—you!" She jabbed him with her finger.

"Clara," Harry said, stepping into her. "This does not concern you. This is between me and my wife." The charming mask dropped as he glared at Rosemary's mother.

"Wife? Ha! Is that what you thought when you were running around with that floozy?" her mother screamed.

Harry tried to step around her mother, the smile slid back into place, eyes twinkled. Rosemary stepped back. She wasn't ready for this, couldn't face Harry.

"Rosemary, is this what you want? You want to abandon your children? Your responsibilities?" he said, holding Georgie out to her. Georgie's head swiveled in confusion from mother to father. Then he burst out crying.

"You need to learn what the word responsibility means. Leave her alone and take care of your kids for a while, the kids who you left her with while you were with that home wrecker!" her mother responded for her.

Harry turned to Clara, anger spewing from his eyes, mouth.

"Stay out of it! You're the reason that Rosemary can't take care of her own kids! You coddled and spoiled her, brainwashing her with religion!"

"Don't talk about my mother that way!" Rosemary sprang to life, lunging towards him, her fingernails sinking into the flesh of his cheeks. Georgie yowled in fear, but Rosemary couldn't stop. Four years of pent-up aggression poured out.

Harry stumbled backward. Clara yanked on Rosemary's arm, dragging her away from him.

"You are crazy," Harry said, voice full of rage; the mask was gone. The charming façade dropped and the condemnation betrayed his true feelings. "I wouldn't let you raise our children. You've been an unfit mother from the beginning! Go back to your priest and beg for forgiveness. He'll never give it to you because there is no God!"

Clara raised herself to her full height. "You disgust me. You almost ruined my daughter and I said nothing. I won't let it happen again. I was wrong to bring my grandchildren here." She reached for Georgie, but Harry reeled away from her, laughing,

"Oh no, my children are not leaving with two crazy women. I see where Rosemary got it from," he sneered.

"Mommy!" Kathleen ran to Rosemary and clung to her leg. Rosemary sobbed and buried her face in Kathleen's hair. Harry yanked Kathleen by the arm and pushed her behind him. Rosemary lunged for her, but he side stepped, pulling Kathleen with him. She staggered into the void as he backed away, holding onto both children.

"Get off my property. You'll hear from my lawyer," he hissed. He turned to walk away, pulling Kathleen behind him. Rosemary panicked and saw the futility of her mother's plans. She sprang towards them, wanting to take Georgie and Kathleen back. She'd find a way to take care of them.

Her mother's hand was like a vie-grip on her arm. "Let them go," she said. "It is better this way. You'll get them back. No judge in his right mind would give that madman custody."

She let her mother lead her back to the car. It is only temporary, she thought as her mother sped out of town, her family becoming smaller and smaller. She will get her children back when the divorce is final. A shiver of fear went over her, and she felt like she had just seen her children for the last time.

Albert

Everything was frozen. Albert's stiff hands clenched his rifle. He couldn't move his fingers if he wanted to, they were frozen in place. His knees ached as he walked, one foot after the other, along a narrow path flanked by snow covered brush. He looked up, but the sky was the same color as the ground—a grey blanket covering everything. He was leading his men; he felt them moving behind him. Ahead, in the distance, he could see the orange machine gun fire and hear the screaming meamies through muffled ears. The river surging on his right was inky black with an ice shelf along the bank, glittering water rushing past.

He crouched, his frozen knees protested, and he motioned his men forward. From across the river, machine gun bullets peppered their line. Where had they come from? Albert dove behind a snowy bush for cover. He watched his men falling, clutching legs, chests, stomachs. Their faces were blurry, black holes where eyes should be, a straight plane where the nose should be and a gaping abyss where their mouths should be. Albert ducked his head to not see these creatures writhing in agony. They were some sort of demons. And the screams, the screams! They sounded like they were rising straight from the depths of Hell. Albert covered his ears with his bare hands, but he could still hear, still feel the agony of these men-creatures. He opened his mouth to scream as he saw the blood cover the ground, turning the grey blanket a bright crimson.

———————

He awoke, drenched in sweat, his hair sticking up in all directions. He smoothed it back with a shaky hand. These dreams were so real. He knew he hadn't seen demon-men in battle, but everything else—the setting, the machine gun, the screams—were exactly what he experiences in those bloody days in Germany. Would his memories ever fade? He pulled off his soaked nightshirt and put on a fresh white undershirt. This was his life now, he had to accept it.

He walked into the kitchen, his mother at the stove, frying bacon for breakfast. The fat sizzled and popped as his mother flipped the slices with a double-pronged fork. "*Dobré ráns*," she said as Albert kissed her cheek. "More bad dreams, *zlatko?*" She could read Albert without him saying a word. He nodded and bit into a slice of crispy bacon. "It will pass. *Všetko zlé je na niečo dobré*," she said, raising her chin. *Everything bad is good for something*. Albert hoped so, but the dreams had gotten no less vivid since he'd returned home and he couldn't see any way in which they would be good. He sighed and walked into the dining room. Sitting at the table were his grandma and grandfather.

"Babka and Dedko!" he exclaimed. His grandma held her arms out to him. "Albert, let us see the medals again," Dedko said, his watery eyes pleading with Albert to indulge an old soldier like himself. Dedko had fought for Austro-Hungary in World War I. He had been drafted by the Austrian Emperor near the end, when they were using old men and boys to fight the French and British. Secretly, he had fought with the resistance to overthrow the emperor and set up a republic in Slovakia. The final breaking point for him had come when the emperor's troops had taken the bronze bell from St. Stephen's Church and melted it down to make a cannon. He was glad Austro-Hungary was defeated and Slovakia set up its own country with the Czech Republic.

Albert brought out his Purple Heart and bronze star. The medals looked so small, compared to what he had seen. He had been awarded both of them for his service at Helenenberg. Babka and Dedko fussed over them. They were so proud that he had fought for America, that he was an American hero. Albert had trouble keeping up with their quick Slovak. It was so fast and garbled.

"Slow down!" Albert laughed.

"I'm sorry, *zlatko*. Your mother should speak more Slovak," Babka said. His mother rolled her eyes.

"These children want to be American. They don't want Slovak!" she said. Even though she loved her heritage, she was proud that her children were considered American, even if that meant they lost their mother's language.

"Hmpf! They should never lose their culture," Babka said, glowering at his mother. His mother rolled her eyes and headed back into the kitchen. She was not going to fight with her mother-in-law in front of Albert.

"Albert, you are so brave," Babka gushed over Albert, thumping him on the back.

"But it is a pity that the Soviets took over Slovakia," Dedko replied. "We should be free, not forced into communism."

Albert half smiled. Free... but what good is freedom if he can't have the things he wanted?

―――――

Albert walked into the factory as he had done for the past four years, as he had before the war. His waking life was a set routine. He knew what to expect when he came to Owens, he knew what he had to do. There was a normalcy and safety in that routine. It allowed Albert to return to his pre-war self, to the time when he had his innocence intact and Rosemary was his girl. For as long as he was there, the war was suspended in his mental limbo.

He changed into his uniform and lumbered past the lady's locker room. A head of curling blonde hair caught his eye. His head snapped around to catch a glimpse of the woman. Rosemary! Her back was to him, but Albert knew it was her narrow waist, her slender, muscular legs. She turned and Albert caught her profile, the high cheekbones, small mouth and deep-set eyes.

He poked his neighbor, Wally Simcock, in the back, "What's Rosemary doing here?"

"Don't you know?" Wally said. "She's getting a divorce. Moved back into her mother's house. Just started back at work here."

Albert's heart hammered in his chest.

After work at the Paddock Club he saw her brother-in-law, Merle, playing poker.

"Al! Join us in a game!" Merle said jovially, but coming from Merle, it sounded like a growl. Albert nodded and sat down, biding his time to pump Merle for information.

The cards were dealt, more drinks ordered and Albert settled into the game. He loved playing cards of all types, but especially poker where he could bluff. He was good at bluffing. He looked into his hand—three kings. The other players were studying their cards. The guy to Albert's left folded, throwing in his cards. The next guy scratched his head and raised, but Albert knew from the twitch of his left eye that he really didn't have anything. Merle called the pot. Albert called too. Another player folded, then another, leaving just Merle and Albert. Merle held his cards close to the table, bending forward to see them. He looked over the top of his cards, sizing Albert up. Albert raised his eyebrow to appear innocent and nervous. Merle fell for it and raised Albert again. Albert called; there was a lot of money in the pot.

"Ah ha! Two pair!" Merle fanned his cards out. Albert rolled his eyes as if he'd been beaten. Merle reached out to pull the money out of the center of the table and Albert laid his cards on top of the money, spreading them out slowly. The three kings smiled up from the table.

"You son of a bitch, Al!" Merle cursed, but good-naturedly so. It was the chance one took when playing poker. Albert had lost many a hand by thinking he had won too early. Albert grinned.

"Let me buy you a drink, Merle, since I took all your money," he laughed. Merle agreed and the two of them went to the bar. Albert ordered two Schlitzs and handed one to Merle. He fidgeted with the label.

"So how's the adjustment back to civilian life?" Merle asked. Albert shrugged. Even though Merle had been in the Navy, he hadn't seen fighting like Albert had.

"Heard you were in Germany, in Hitler's backyard, the bastard!" Merle growled, envy curling around his words.

Albert just nodded, that wasn't what he wanted to talk about. His brain was scheming a way to bring up Rosemary. He wasn't sure how open Merle would be able airing his sister-in-law's dirty laundry.

"Let's do a shot!" he said, slapping Merle on the back.

"No, no! I can't do a shot," Merle protested, but Albert set the whiskey in front of him.

He picked up his shot glass and said, "To peace."

He clinked his glass against Merle's. Merle scooped it up and threw it down his throat, shaking his head as he swallowed.

"Whooo-eey! That was good," Merle said, leaning back in his chair. He looked relaxed, so Albert decided the time was right.

"So Merle," Albert began his fishing. "What's going on with Rosemary?" There. He had asked. He held his breath as Merle looked at him with watery red eyes, the alcohol affecting him.

He swayed, grinning, "I knew you were going to ask about her, you dirty dog!" Albert tried to protest, but Merle waved him off and continued talking. "She and her old man had problems.

That's what the wife said. She never should have married him, but she tried to make the best of it. Then she found out he had another girl. Saw a picture in the paper! The paper! What a way to find out your old man is cheating on you!"

Merle laughed, but Albert was sad, sad for Rosemary, sad for himself. He never would have cheated on her, never would have given her that heartache. She must have been heartbroken, Albert thought. She was so afraid of people leaving her and this man did just that to her.

"She kind of lost it after that happened. Came to Streator to get away from him and figure things out," Merle said. "I guess she's got a lawyer and is getting a divorce. She goes to court in a few weeks."

A divorce! Albert groaned. He knew what the Catholic Church thought of divorce. She must be feeling awful about herself and life in general. Albert wanted to make her feel better, wanted to see her.

"I saw her at Owens," he said. "She's back on the line?"

Merle nodded, sipping his beer.

"I want to talk to her. I'm going to see her," Albert said, pushing away from the bar. Merle put his hand on Albert's arm.

"Al, I like you. I think you would be good for Rosie, but she's had a real hard time of it. This wouldn't be the best time. Let her get over her issues first. You don't want to make a bigger mess. I hear the divorce is gonna get ugly."

Albert wanted to comfort her, not make her life harder. She couldn't be seen with her old fiancé before she was divorced. He knew that would be a problem and could be used against Rosemary. But still, he wanted her to know that he supported her. When she was ready, she would come to him. He knew what he would do until then.

———

The next day, Albert brought in licorice for Rosemary. He

went to her work station before she arrived and set it on her bench. Then he stole up to the catwalk to watch her reaction. She walked over to the sorting station and stopped short, seeing the package of licorice. She picked it up, flipping it over in her slim hand. Her head swiveled from right to left, trying to see who had left this. Albert crouched down on the catwalk, so he would not be discovered, but Rosemary never looked up. A small smile spread across her weary face as she slipped the package into the pocket of her overalls, hand lingering.

Albert exhaled, smiling, knowing he had made her happy for just that one day. That was enough for him.

Rosemary

Rosemary changed into her blue jumpsuit. She'd been getting the licorice every day. She'd asked around and no one seemed to know who they came from. They were a small relief, a reprieve from everything else that was going on. She looked forward to seeing them at her station.

Junie crowed, "Rosie's got an admirer!"

She slapped him for teasing her. He was the same, still teasing, still joking. She thought the war would change him. And it did—but his character had come back intact. Rosemary was glad to have him back, she missed his joking while he was away, while she was with Harry. Her life had been missing that fun that she got from Junie. She didn't know how his wife, Claire, could put up with him for too long. He was never serious. But he was attentive and loving towards her. He had met her when he returned from the war. She was sweet and quiet and balanced Junie's loud, rowdy behavior. Rosemary was happy for him, that he had found someone who accepted him as he was and loved him unconditionally.

She and Junie had fallen back into their routine of riding to work in the mornings. He still drove like a maniac—even worse now that he lost his leg. The government had given him a special car with the gas pedal on the left side. He had to learn to drive all over again, but it didn't slow him down. He sped and still rolled through the stop sign by the Majestic Theater. Rosemary made an exaggerated showing and cringed every day, but she loved it, loved having him back.

"So I know who your admirer is," he said one morning as they drove. He didn't slow down for the tracks and Rosemary bumped her head.

"Junie!" she protested. "Who is my admirer?" she narrowed her eyes at him. Did he know or was he teasing her? She never could tell.

He laughed, "You'll never guess!"

"Why don't you just tell me then," she grumbled.

"That would take all the fun out of it!"

Rosemary slumped against her seat and folded her arms, pouting. She wanted to know who her admirer was, who it was that knew everything she liked. She didn't like surprises. Junie grinned at her as her mind raced to think of who it could be.

"Gotta guess yet?" he laughed. She shot him a scowl. No, she didn't have a guess yet. She watched the budding trees whiz past as they sped down the road, trying to take her mind off it. She just wouldn't think about who it could be. The lilacs were blooming, their delicate purple blossoms filling the air with fragrance.

But Junie would not be dissuaded. "Come on! I'll give you a hint. He works in the mold shop." Rosemary was perplexed. The only person she knew who used to work in the mold shop was Albert, but she didn't know if he worked there anymore. She didn't know what he was doing now. Albert—could it be him? Her heart quickened at the possibility. She'd thought of him often since she'd recovered from her breakdown. She had wanted to talk to him, to tell him that her marriage had been an impulsive mistake, that she never wanted to send that letter to him in Germany, that she was getting a divorce. But was that fair to him? She didn't want to drag him into her problems. And he probably hated her for the letter, that she hadn't waited. I would hate me, she thought. He'd probably found someone already, Rosemary thought.

"I don't know, Junie. I don't want to play your stupid game anymore," she said, tired of his verbal banter.

"Fine, Sourpuss. I won't tell you then," he lifted his chin, trying to hide his smile and pushed the accelerator down, propelling the car forward. She narrowed her eyes and crossed her arms, signaling the end of discussion.

———

Another packet of licorice was waiting for her at her station. Now her curiosity was getting the better of her. Was it Albert? Could he work here again? She turned to her partner on the line, Ed Norton. Betty had quit once the war was over. Her beau had come home and they had gotten married. She had two children and stayed at home. Rosemary hadn't seen her since she'd returned to Streator. She didn't feel right calling on her, her situation was exactly acceptable to most people.

"Does Albert Jedoga work here?" she asked Ed.

He didn't even blink. "Works in the Mold Shop." Then he turned back to sorting, very serious about the job at hand.

———

Rosemary met with her lawyer, a small, balding man with wire-rimmed glasses. Thin strands of hair were combed over his bald dome. *Who did he think he was fooling?* she thought. He explained the proceedings to her, what would happen when they went to court. All Rosemary cared about was being finished with all of this and getting her children back.

Her lawyer pushed his glasses back up the bridge of his nose and cleared his throat, "Now, Mrs. Connor, we will need to show fault in our petition to ask for the divorce."

Rosemary stared at him. She did not understand the legal vocabulary; she just wanted to be divorced. Her lawyer continued, "The only cause for divorce in Illinois is if there was physical abuse. We can say that your husband was physically abusive to you and caused extreme duress…"

Rosemary interrupted, "But Harry didn't beat me."

Her lawyer smiled patronizingly, "Of course he didn't, but this is what we will need to argue for you to get custody. We will plead extreme cruelty and fault by your husband for the dissolution of the marriage."

"What about adultery? What about him going out with Nancy?" Rosemary was floundering. She wanted to be divorced from Harry, but she didn't want to slander his name.

"Unfortunately, that does not make him an unfit father."

"That is crazy! How can that not make him an unfit father? He broke his vows! To be faithful!"

"Now, now," her lawyer held up his hands, treating her as a child. He knew her fragile mental state. "I know this is very emotional for you, but we need to work inside the constraints of the law."

Rosemary chewed the inside of her cheek. Could she accuse Harry of cruelty? He was absent and mentally cruel, but never physically abusive to her. He would never fight with her, let alone raise a hand to her.

"No, I can't do that. It will have to be adultery and then I'll leave it to the judge to decide."

Her lawyer sighed, "It's your case."

"When can I get my children back?"

He snapped his briefcase closed and stood. "I'll take our plea and recommend custody be granted to you. Once I meet with your husband's lawyer, I'll let you know their response and hopefully, we will agree and file the paperwork."

"And what if he doesn't agree?"

"We'll cross that bridge when we get to it."

Rosemary left the meeting with no more serenity than before. She had wanted reassurances from her lawyer, answers. Why did the government make it so difficult? She shook her head, not wanting to think about it.

Instead she focused on the blooming happening all around her. The lilies of the valley were blooming, their delicate white bell flowers opening, releasing their fragrance. And in her backyard, the tulips were just opening their inverted bells, erupting into a rainbow of colors—the pink with the white edging were her favorites. She loved sticking her nose into the bell and breathing in their scents. The trees were budding, little bright green buds fighting to break out of the end of the branches. New life was erupting all around her. She wanted to be a part of it, but she was incomplete without her children.

She noticed a blue Nash coming down the road towards her. The car looked like it was smiling at her, the headlights like wide eyeballs, the grill a toothy grin. Her heart skipped and the fluttering started in her stomach. She saw the widow's peak and long nose. She raised her hand in a half wave, her heart thundering, the blood pounding through her ears. The Nash came closer and passed, the driver was one of Albert's brothers. He stared at her outstretched hand and gave a confused wave in return.

Her heart sank, plummeted to the pit of her stomach and pushed the bile up. She swallowed hard, tasting her disappointment. She found that she wanted to see Albert. It still didn't seem right with everything else going on in her life, but Rosemary found herself yearning for him anyway, a magnetic force she could not fight. She sighed and continued on toward home.

Albert

Albert hurried into the building, early for his shift. It was pouring, the skies squeezing water from ominous green-grey clouds as if wringing sopping blankets. He shook the raindrops from his coat and smoothed back his hair. He reached into his coat pocket. The licorice was still dry, hadn't gotten wet in the deluge. He smiled and hurried to Rosemary's station, to place the surprise before she got there.

"So it is you."

Albert froze as he heard the familiar lilting voice. He smelled her before he saw her. Rosemary. Her arms were folded across her chest, a small smile playing on her lips. Her hair was covered with a blue bandana, framing her heart-shaped face. His breath caught, he'd forgotten how beautiful she was, even though she was frightfully thin. He shrugged his shoulders. There was so much to say, but he couldn't even say hello.

"Why?" she asked. He could see her chest rising and falling, the pulsing in the depression between her collar bones. He wanted to be debonair and suave, a worldly man. Instead, he felt like an awkward teenager on his first date. He looked down at his shoes and shrugged again. She studied him, her blue eyes scanning over his face. What did she see? A man crushed by a war he had been naïve about? A man whose heart she had shattered, but still possessed? He felt completely vulnerable, his feelings naked to her.

"I heard about your marriage," he said, choking on the words. Rosemary shrank back, blushing. Albert held up his hands. "I didn't mean to embarrass you. I.. just… Well, hell Rosie. There's so much I want to say to you, to ask you. But I know this is not a good time. I know you're going through a divorce and probably shouldn't talk to me right now. I just… I still care… you know? I know it probably doesn't even matter…"

"No, Albert. I love the licorice. I was wondering… hoping it was you bringing it. But you're right. This isn't a good time for me. And if you keep bringing it, you'll make me fat!" she forced a laugh, trying to lighten the tension. Albert looked at her. Her wrists were so narrow, nothing but skin covering her white bones. Her cheeks were gaunt, sunk in under her dominating cheek bones. Her chest was sunken, collarbones exposed, hip bones jutting out.

"I don't think you have to worry about that," Albert said, letting his eyes travel over her. "I think you look great."

She looked up at him, gratitude in her steel eyes, starved for a compliment. Albert flushed with pleasure, glad he could make her feel good.

"Thank you, but I know I look horrible. I'm sure you heard about my … everything. Everyone in this damn town talks. The divorce is probably going to get worse before it gets better," her eyes saddened again, the momentary happiness evaporated like a morning mist. Albert noticed how worn her face looked, the droop of her shoulders. He wanted to smooth it all over for her, to make everything easier for her. But he knew he needed to step back and let her work it out herself, so he simply said, "Let me know if there is anything I can do to help."

"Just knowing you care enough to bring me licorice is enough," she said, a true smile spreading across her face. Albert's heart thundered and he floated on happiness to the mold shop. Even with the unasked questions, there was a glimmer of what should have been. And Albert hung on to that tighter than he had clutched his rifle in Germany.

———————

He dropped his bowling bag onto the molded plastic chairs and sat to put on his bowling shoes. The thundering of the pins and the swoosh of the balls rolling down the lane mingled with the smoke in the air. Albert looked at his brothers putting on their shoes too.

"We got a good shot of winning the league this year," Steve said, grinning. He was always grinning, always happy. Albert was glad he hadn't seen action to jade him.

"Only if Al gets his head out of the clouds," Ed said, doffing Albert in the back of his head. Albert swatted at him and smoothed his hair back. His brothers Larry and Jim laughed.

"I could bowl without my head and still beat all of you," Albert grumbled, but he was happy to be joking with his brothers, his spirits lifted from his conversation with Rosemary. He rosined up his hands and took a practice throw. The ball barreled down the lane, breaking to the left. It banged the head pin and sent it spiraling into the other nine. All ten fell down. Albert pumped his fist. "See? What did I tell you's?"

"Yeah, yeah, yeah. Just do it when it counts!" Ed teased.

Albert settled back into his chair and watched his brothers practice. His mind was still on Rosemary, her slender waist, the veil of sadness lifting. Could there still be a chance for them? Could she still love him as she said she did before he left for the war? He shook his head, knowing the fantasy of them living in a cottage in the German countryside was just that—a fantasy from an innocent time before they had both experienced loss and pain. They could never return, were too changed by their circumstances.

Ed sat down next to him and patted his back.

"It's nice to get us all out here again," he said, looking down the lanes. Albert nodded.

"You doin' alright?" he asked.

"Yeah, yeah," Albert said, brushing Ed off. "It's hard getting back into the routine, but I'm good."

"I hear ya. Wasn't it weird to come back and not have the discipline and order?" he said. Albert snorted. What he thought was weird was not having the constant threat of death prickling his neck, not worrying if the next 88 was going to hit him. Ed had a different experience, he was on a battle ship. He didn't get to see death up close. Sure, there was a risk of the Japs hitting his ship, but at least when he fired the mortars, all he had to see was the explosion, not the charred flesh and devastation.

"You ever think about it still?" Albert asked. He didn't have anyone else to talk about this with.

"How can I not?" Ed said, taking a drag off a cigarette. "I don't know anyone who came back and doesn't think about it. The key is to put it in a box, lock that box up tight and don't let it open now that we're back here. This is our time. Over there... well, that was a diversion, something that needed to be done. And it's done and now we just get to live our lives, marry a great girl, have a whole bunch of kids. Life is pretty simple after what we've been through, huh?"

Albert nodded. Yes, it was simple for most. But for him, the promise of marriage and children had vanished when he found out about Rosemary. Even now that she was getting a divorce didn't guarantee that she would come back to him. Maybe he would just lock himself up with his memories of the war and throw away the key.

"Let's beat the tar out of these guys," Albert said, changing focus to just the game at hand. He would just live in the moment and let everything take care of itself.

Rosemary

Every day, Rosemary looked forward to the licorice waiting for her at her work station. It was a diversion from the events in her life which she had no control over. The days ran into each other, the monotony of the factory exactly as it had been before the war. She had not spoken to her lawyer in a few weeks and she was getting anxious to get on with the proceedings. She couldn't stand the unknowing, she just wanted it to be over, to get her children back.

Junie was waiting for her after work, leaning against the car, his face tilted towards the June sun. Rosemary slapped him in the stomach as she walked past, jolting him out of his day dream.

"I found out who my secret admirer is, no thanks to you," she said as she climbed into the car. Junie rubbed his stomach and gunned the engine, accelerating the car out of the parking lot.

"Junie! Slow down!" Rosemary said as they narrowly missed side-swiping a red Chrysler. Junie grinned at Rosemary.

"Yea, who's your admirer?"

"Albert, who else?" Rosemary said, angry that Junie didn't tell her himself. "I caught him leaving the licorice."

"Yeah, you caught him, huh? I don't know why he's bringing you licorice. After what you did, you should be begging him to talk to you—you should be bringing him gifts!" Junie joked, but his barbed words cut into Rosemary's heart. She flushed in embarrassment. She didn't want to be reminded of her betrayal, especially from Junie. She pulled her arms against herself and looked out the window, trying not to cry.

"Oh, Rosie, I was just fooling!" Junie shook her, trying to get her to laugh. She jerked her shoulder away from him and he raised his hands in mock-surrender. His words stung, the truth in them too close to home. Rosemary knew that she did not deserve gifts from Albert. Was she worthy of his love after all that she had done to him? That was the question that plagued her day and night.

When they arrived at home, Rosemary leapt from the car and ran into the yard, the tears still welling in her eyes. She rubbed at them, pushing the tears back. She did not want to cry, she would not cry. The late afternoon sun lit the house in an orange glow. Inside the kitchen, she saw Norma's outline. Her heart lifted, her sister had come for dinner!

She rushed in and threw her arms around her sister.

"It's nice to see you too, Rosie!" Norma laughed as she untangled herself from Rosemary's embrace. Rosemary was just happy to have company for dinner. Marsha, Sandy and Carol were running around the kitchen, weaving between her mother and her sister.

"You kids go play somewhere else!" her mother yelled at them. Their laughter filled the room. The house was full of bustling activity, the children, the cooking, her sisters conversing. Rosemary sank into one of the kitchen chairs, snapping the green beans on the table.

"Where's Merle?" Rosemary asked as she snapped green beans for dinner.

"Oh he's at poker night at the Paddock Club," Norma said, whipping potatoes in a metal bowl balanced on her hip.

Rosemary nodded, concentrating on the beans. They broke with a crisp snap before she dropped them into the bowl. It was a clean sound that reminded her of summer. When was she going to hear news from her lawyer?

"I haven't been there since…" she trailed off. *Since I've been home*, she thought and was awash in shame. She hadn't done anything since she returned home. All she could focus on was regaining her mental health and her strength so she could get her children back. Carol came over and stole a bean, munching down on it. Rosemary chased her away with her waving hand. Carol gave her a toothy grin before darting into the living room. Rosemary missed her children so much, she missed Kathleen's inquisitive eyes, Georgie's toothy smile. She felt like she was getting her life back on track, that her emotions were stabilizing. Her routine at the factory was giving her stability and security. She felt she was ready to be their mother again and was impatient that she hadn't heard back from her lawyer in so long. What could the delay mean?

"What's with the glum face?" her mother asked, taking the bowl of snapped beans.

"I'm just nervous that's all."

"Have you been taking your pills? The doctor told you that you needed to keep stress away or you could fall back into, well… you know," her mother said.

"Yes, mother," Rosemary said, annoyed. "I'm worried because I haven't heard from my lawyer and I miss my children. Will I ever see them again?"

"Only the Lord can answer that question," her mother replied. But Rosemary still felt that God had abandoned her, and the knot tightened in her stomach.

———

Her lawyer called her a few days later. She rushed to his office on Main Street. She smoothed the front of her skirt and knocked on his door.

"Rosemary," her lawyer motioned towards his office. "Come in."

She walked past him, her stomach flopping as he closed the

door behind her. She sat on the edge of the chair and waited for him to round his desk and take his seat. The office had a smell of old papers, musty and brittle. It tickled Rosemary's nose.

Her lawyer sat and opened the folder in front of him. "We have a completed petition and if you agree to everything in it, we'll sign it and the divorce will be final and you'll be a free woman."

"What about the children?" Rosemary asked. She clenched her hands together, the sweat making them slick. That was all she cared about, getting her children back.

"Well, there is an issue with that. Mr. Connor did not agree to give you custody," her lawyer shuffled his pages, not making eye contact with her.

"What does that mean?" Rosemary asked, her voice unnaturally high. She rubbed her hands over her skirt, leaving streaks on both legs.

"He said you abandoned them," he looked at Rosemary over the top of his silver rimmed glasses, the light glinting off them and striking Rosemary in her eye. She blinked rapidly, not comprehending. "Mr. Connor claims you dropped them off while he was working and never contacted him again until he got the divorce summons."

Rosemary licked her dry lips, trying to form the words. Her mouth twitched as she spoke, "Well, yes. I… My mother thought it best for the children. But it was only until the divorce. Then I would take them back."

"In Illinois, the law says that if you relinquish control of your dependence for more than twenty-four hours with no communication, you have abandoned your children."

"What?!?" Rosemary's heart ached as if her rib cage were crashing in on it. She clutched her throat, trying to push her heart back down. "But I needed a break. It was never a permanent situation."

"Unfortunately, that's not how the courts see it. Harry will not file for abandonment if you agree to give him custody. He'll plead guilty to adultery and you'll be divorced. Isn't that what you want?" her lawyer said, a note of impatience creeping into his voice.

He pushed the papers to Rosemary to sign. She shook her head. No, no, this was not supposed to happen this way. He was supposed to take the children until she could get on her feet. That is what her mother said would happen, that is what she promised her. Rosemary saw white stars and felt the earth tilting off its axis. She gripped the arm of her chair, fearful that she would fall into the black chasm again. Abandonment. That was not what she had done. She had not abandoned her children, had she? She only wanted Harry to watch them for a while, until she could regain her health. Her mother said he would give them back.

"What happens if I don't sign this?" Rosemary asked. The light glared off the white papers, taunting her to sign away her rights to her children. She shrank away from it.

"Well, then we will go to court. Harry will file for abandonment and then we'll have to prove that you did not abandon them. Do you have proof that you were coming back for the children?" her lawyer said, not hiding his impatience. Rosemary shook her head.

"Did you tell him that you would be back for the children? Maybe send a letter or make a phone call?" He was grasping for anything, but Rosemary had nothing to give, no evidence other than what was in her heart to show that she intended to get her children back. She shook her head, the reality of her situation sinking in. She had no proof because she had been in no state of mind to make arrangements like that. Her mother had said this was the right thing to do, and Rosemary believed her. Now, she was at the mercy of the court, and Harry had all the cards.

"With no proof, he will win and you'll lose your children." Her lawyer pushed the papers once again towards her, holding out a pen. "I suggest you sign and agree to this, even if it isn't true. This way, you'll get generous visitation with your children and we won't have to go to court and fight."

Rosemary tried to swallow, but her mouth was too dry. She coughed, gagging at the hopelessness of her situation. Shakily, she took the pen and signed her name. It was little more than a scribble, but it was enough in the eyes of the court. With that scribble, she signed away her children.

———————

She held back the tears until she had left her lawyer's office. As soon as the door shut, Rosemary felt the tears, tears of rage, tears of disappointment. Her chest was tight, like she was wearing a corset, her breath uneven. The dark cave appeared at the edges of her vision, pressing against her consciousness. She fought against it, determined not to fall into it again. She stumbled down the sidewalk, guiding herself with her hand as she knocked into hard brick buildings. Her stomach was heaving, churning like waves during an ocean storm. She had lost her children. Oh God! She looked to the sky, hoping that He would appear to her and bring her children back. The azure blue gaped in return. Her heart hurt, was being squeezed into a tight ball in her chest. What had she done? She was only supposed to be getting a break, a chance to gain her sanity back, to be stable for her children. And Harry had used that against her, he said she abandoned them. She heaved at that thought.

The tears blurred her vision, melding everything together in a bright smudge. She heard a car slowing behind her, but she didn't have the energy to wipe the tears from her face. She didn't care who was seeing her cry, her only care the loss of her children.

"Rosie?" she heard Albert's voice, the deep baritone. She tried to walk faster, to escape, but she tripped over her feet, falling onto the concrete. She felt the footsteps behind her and Albert's thick hands wrapping around her thin arms, steadying her. Her chest collapsed, the weight of holding herself up was too overwhelming.

"Whoa, I've got you. I've got you," Albert soothed her, lifting her limp body into his arms. She gripped the front of his shirt, balled it into her fists.

"What's the matter?" he asked.

She looked into his eyes through her tear-soaked lashes. He sparkled in the refracted sunlight against the edging blackness.

"I lost them," she croaked, her voice hoarse. With that declaration, a new wave of sadness crashed against her. She would never see Georgie rousing from sleep, his eyes still heavy as he took his breakfast. She would never see Kathleen crawling into bed, to hear a bedtime story, and become so enraptured with the fairy tale that she would forget wasn't real. She would get stolen moments, a day here, a weekend there, but she would never again be their full-time mother.

"Who? What happened?" Albert said, not releasing his tight grip on her. It gave her strength.

"My children. I lost them," Rosemary gulped through her tears, "My lawyer said that to get a divorce, I had to give up custody."

Albert froze at the mention of divorce. Rosemary felt that she'd offended him by bringing up her failed marriage. Maybe he was finally realizing that she was damaged and that he couldn't be her dark angel.

"I... I don't know what to say, Rosie," Albert said, his voice heavy with emotion. "I can't imagine losing your children."

Rosemary sniffled, "My lawyer said that to get a divorce, I had to say that my hus... that Harry beat me." Albert gasped when he heard this. "He didn't... He was having an affair. That's why I left. But Harry told my lawyer that he was going to say that I abandoned my children to get custody. So I agreed. I just gave them away without a fight." She should be more composed, but she couldn't hold it in anymore, couldn't pretend she was alright. Heavy sobs came from deep within her, full of her pain and frustration.

Albert

Albert stood motionless, just holding Rosemary, feeling the rage against this man build inside of him. He wanted to rip him apart, beat him with his fists until he was unrecognizable. How could he take Rosemary's children away from her? How could he have added to her sadness? Albert knew when he had first met her that she was fragile and needed protecting. He could never have hurt Rosemary as this man had done. Perhaps he put some sort of spell on Rosemary to get her to marry him. He must have had charms that Albert only dreamt about. What had this guy told Rosemary to get her to forget him?

He pushed the thoughts away and rocked her back and forth. Her thin shoulders jerked with every sob. She laid her head on his shoulder and he smelled her hair, closing his eyes as he breathed her in. He wished this were a happier occasion for her to be in his arms, but he was there to be her comfort.

A car slowed as it drove by, the occupants staring at this couple in a close embrace on Main Street. Albert became aware of how they must look.

"Let me drive you home. You're in no condition to walk," Albert said.

"No, I…" Rosemary tried to protest.

"Honey, please. I want to do this for you," he said. She gave in and let him guide her to the car.

Albert eased the car down the street. He stole a glance at Rosemary from the corner of his eye. Her head was lowered into her chest, but she was not sobbing anymore. His heart hurt for her, wanting to take away her pain.

"Why did you do it, Rosie?" he asked, dreading the answer.

"Do what?" her forehead scrunched up, either in pain or confusion. Maybe both. Albert wasn't sure.

"You know…. Marry him." There. He asked the one questions he had longed to ask since 1945 in the hospital in England.

"Marry him? Oh Albert….I was… I just… I was so afraid that you weren't coming back. We got a telegram about Junie, I had this dream that you died in Germany… Everything was twisted. Maybe that was when I started to lose my mind. I think that was the beginning. I got your letter that you were alive, but then it was too late," she started crying again.

"I understand. I really do," Albert said, gripping the steering wheel as he let his own memories flood over him. The charred landscape, gutted bodies, Eddy. "I thought the war was going to be different and I was going to be a hero. I guess we both were naïve about life."

They lapsed into silence as they rolled down Vermillion Street, the trees providing a canopy of shade to break the sunshine. Albert put his hand out the window to feel the coolness float over his hand. Rosemary stopped crying and looked out at the trees.

"I'm sorry to cry like this on you," she said, throwing him a small smile. "You don't deserve this, especially after what I've done to you. And I'm sure the last thing you want is to deal with a hysterical woman." She tossed her head to cover her embarrassment. Albert wondered why she did this, why she wouldn't just let him see her.

"I have lots of practice at home," he lied. His mother was not hysterical, never cried. She was stoic and held her emotions in check. But he wanted to make Rosemary feel better so she could open up to him. The color returned to her cheeks as she smiled. Albert grinned. Her smile had always felt like a prize.

She cocked her head and said, "What?" She narrowed her eyes in a mock suspicion, her lips still smirking.

"Nothing!" Albert shook his head.

"That's the look my brother gets when he is up to no good!" she laughed, a high tense laugh, but a laugh nonetheless.

"I know. You told me that the night we went to the Paddock Club," Albert said, remembering the night, holding her wrist and tracing the Big Dipper.

"Yes, I did," she said, her eyes glazed over as she remembered her own moments, before complications had changed both of their lives.

"Rosie, I know it doesn't seem like it now, but things will get better for you," Albert said, a sudden seriousness coming over him. He didn't know why, but he needed her to know this.

She sighed, "I know. I know they will, but I feel like I've made many mistakes that I can't ever correct."

"Mistakes happen, but they are in the past. You need to move forward with your life and learn from your mistakes." Albert was thinking of the conversation he'd had with his father after he crashed the car. He didn't want Rosemary to live in remorse as he had been. He wanted her to be happy, whether that was with him or without him. She deserved that happiness, she deserved not to live in regret.

Albert stopped the car in front of her house. Rosemary glanced at the house, her hand twitching. It probably wouldn't look very good for her to be getting a ride home from him, but Albert didn't care what anyone thought, he just wanted Rosemary to be comfortable.

"Thank you, Al. For the ride home, for the licorice…. For everything," she said as she climbed out of the car, her grey-blue eyes misting up once again. Albert reached over and took her hand, not willing to release her just yet.

"If there is anything you need, just let me know and I'll be here for you," he said and let her go. She flashed a grateful smile before she walked up the sidewalk.

He couldn't say what he wanted to her in her fragile state of mind. He wanted to tell her that he needed her in his life to make the horrors of war seem justified, that all of that suffering wasn't for nothing. He needed to take care of her to prove to himself that he had a purpose in life, that he survived the war for a reason, to restore both of their faith in God and in life itself. But he could say none of these things to her, not today when she was at her lowest. So he said the barest of words, words that didn't even scratch the surface of what he meant to say. She glanced backward as she opened the front door, gratitude in her small smile, and disappeared into the house. He sighed and swallowed all of those unspoken words, hoping one day he would speak them to her.

Albert parked the Nash in front of his house and walked in. The house was a flurry of activity as always. His father was at work, but his younger brothers, Jim and Ray, were listening to the Cubs on the radio. "Al, the Cubs are winning!" Jim called from his stretched out position on the floor, in front of the radio. Albert nodded and flopped into a chair. Steve looked over at him, worried at his brother's lack of enthusiasm for the Cubs. Usually, he was on the floor with the boys to listen to the game. Albert fiddled with the button on his shirt.

"You get into a fight or something?" Steve said, nodding towards Albert's shirt. Albert looked at the wrinkled fist impressions. He shook his head, pressing his lips together.

"What's eating you?" Steve said.

Albert shrugged and started to talk but stopped. What could he say that his family would approve of? Nothing, but he didn't want to hide anything from them.

"I saw Rosemary today," he said, bracing for the verbal barrage his brother was sure to launch.

"Oh yeah? What was she doing?" Steve said, trying to keep a light tone in his voice.

"Getting a divorce," Albert said, staring into space. "She just got out of her lawyer's office and found out that she lost custody of her children," Albert paused and shook his head. "I can't imagine how that must feel."

"Wow. So what are you going to do?" Albert heard the hesitation in his voice. He knew his brother loved him and did not want him to get hurt yet again. But once Albert made his mind up about something, there was no changing it, no matter what anyone else thought.

"I don't know yet," was all Albert said.

Rosemary

The summer passed as the spring had, days running into days. The only bright moments were weekends when Kathleen and Georgie came up on the train with Beulah. Rosemary knew that Beulah was worried that Rosemary would fall back into her depression. She never told Rosemary what her son Harry was doing, and Rosemary never asked. She wanted that chapter of her life to be closed, locked, and thrown down a deep well. She wanted to get on with her own life, whatever that meant. She wanted to find happiness, but wasn't sure exactly how to find it or if she deserved to find it. She thought of Albert. He was a constant, still bringing her licorice and treats. She had seen him at the Paddock Club the night of Japan's surrender. He held up his beer and toasted her from across the club, but didn't approach her, dared not talk to her. She was glad, disappointed, fearful—a jumble of emotions. She knew she didn't deserve him after what she had already put him through.

Sighing, she walked across the yard to the house next door which Virginia and her new husband, Ed, had bought it. When it had come up for sale, Virginia said they had to buy it, not wanting to be far from her mother. Ed had spent weeks painting the inside and outside of the house, making it their home. Rosemary opened the screen door and saw Carol and

Sandy playing on the floor in the kitchen.

"Where's your mom?" Rosemary asked.

"Downstairs," they replied in unison, not lifting their heads from their game of pick-up-sticks, Sandy reaching for a thin, garishly painted stick from the tangled pile. They were getting so big, so grown up. The tendrils of guilt surrounded her. Those stolen moments with her own children did not compare to knowing and seeing their development every day. The guilt strangled her, like ivy tangling her insides.

She rushed downstairs to avoid her own thoughts. Virginia, clad in a thin summer dress, was bending into the washer, emptying the wet clothing into a wicker basket at her feet.

"Hey Ginny," Rosemary said, startling Virginia. She jumped and bumped her head on the washer tub.

"Rosie, don't sneak up on people like that!" she said crossly, rubbing the back of her head. Rosemary giggled but didn't apologize. Virginia knitted her brows together and finished emptying the clothing. She hefted the basket onto her hip and walked up the stairs. Rosemary followed her. They began hanging the clothing, Virginia shaking out damp, white sheets, and Rosemary taking the opposite end and fastening it to the clothesline with a wooden clothes pin.

Rosemary studied Virginia as she pinned the sheets. They fluttered in the slight summer breeze, reflecting the sunlight into Virginia's face. She glowed pink in the brightness. Virginia, pessimistic by nature, had a calmness to her that she had never had while she was married to her first husband. Rosemary knew this aliveness in Virginia was due to her new husband, Ed. She wondered if she would have been feeling the same had she waited for Albert. Would this same happiness have been hers?

"Are you happy, Ginny?" Rosemary asked.

"Of course I'm happy," Ginny snapped. Rosemary always asked questions which she knew the answers to instead of what she really wanted to know. Virginia looked over the clothesline sagging with the weight of the wet sheets. She sighed, paused to say something, but then thought better of it. She took another sheet from the wicker basket and handed one end to Rosemary. They stretched the sheet between them and began pinning it.

"Why wouldn't I be happy?" Virginia asked as they reached each other in the middle of the sheet. Rosemary shrugged. She wanted reassurance from Virginia that her life, once bleaker than Rosemary's appeared now, was content. She needed that hope.

"Were you afraid that Ed wouldn't want to marry you because you were divorced?' she asked, staring off into the cornflower blue sky, watching the cotton clouds glide by, pushed by the invisible current.

"Why would you ask me a question like that?" Virginia replied, anger mounting with each word. "Of course I didn't think that! Ernie was a loser. I picked wrong. Shame on me, but that didn't make me a bad person!"

Virginia focused her gaze on Rosemary. "You need to stop living in the past. Get your head out of the clouds and face facts. Your life is your life. You need to live it, not feel sorry for yourself. You chose the life you had, and now you've chosen a different life. You need to decide what to make of it."

Rosemary shrugged. She knew what Virginia was saying was true, but could she ever be truly happy again?

"Rosie," Virginia said, obviously annoyed, "what is it that you really want to ask me?"

"I don't know, I—I feel like damaged goods. I need to know that my life will go on, that everything will be okay," she said in a small, constricted voice. Her lowered lip trembled as she spoke, overcome by the unspoken need, the need to be worthy of love again.

"Rosie, you are not damaged goods," Virginia said, her eyes softening. "No one knows if everything is going to be okay. But life does go on. If you're lucky, you will find someone other than Harry to spend your life with."

She ducked under the sheets and stood facing Rosemary, placing her hands on Rosemary's shoulders. "But you'll never know if you don't take a chance. If you stay stuck in this pity party you're throwing for yourself, you'll never give yourself a chance for a better life."

Rosemary tucked her chin into her chest and rubbed the tears from her eyes before they fell. "I know you're right, Virginia. I just need to accept what has happened. My kids are lost. My marriage was a mistake"

Virginia hugged her. "Just open your eyes and see the good around you."

Rosemary nodded. Virginia had gotten a second chance at a happy life with Ed. She wasn't a broken woman to him, damaged goods. She was a wonderful woman with a huge capacity for love, if one was patient enough to glean it from her.

Could Rosemary have that too? Could she see herself as a complete woman, a woman who had taken a few detours, but was wiser and empathetic for the experiences? There was someone who already did see her as a complete woman—Albert. He never wavered in his affections for her. His love for her had never abandoned her, even when she doubted and abandoned him. And she had never lost her feelings for him. She loved him, had always loved him. Her love for him had been a constant through it all.

"When you say the good around me," Rosemary began, realizing what Virginia was trying to tell her, "were you talking about Albert?"

Virginia raised her hands in thanksgiving, "Yes! Rosie, you've shut yourself off from him, but he has always been there."

"*Should* he still care about me? I'm a divorced woman without her children. He deserves someone clean and pure, not damaged like me," Rosemary said. Even though she felt his love for her, was it possible that he would want to marry her still and be the step-father of two children? He was Catholic, like her, and although she had not been married in the church, she still had been married.

"Rosie, you made some bad decisions. We all agree about

that. But the past is the past. Albert is a grown man, and he knows your past. Obviously, he still cares about you and doesn't care about your past or he wouldn't be asking after you and bringing you presents," Virginia said. "Maybe it's time to look into your heart and find what you really want and let Albert know if it is him."

Rosemary looked off, her mind spinning. What was in her heart? She'd closed it so long ago, when she had thought he had died. And then it was too late when she realized he was still alive. She had never thought about a second chance. A second chance at love and happiness. She was prepared to live with the choices she had made, but she couldn't remain wallowing in her unhappiness.

Virginia was right. It was time to get what was in her heart, what she really wanted from her life. And if she was honest with herself, she wanted a life with Albert. She wanted to be with him and to love him, if he would have her. If he could agree to take her and her children and forgive her transgressions against him, she could have a happy life with him.

Rosemary dropped her clothespin and broke into a run. She knew what she had to do before she lost her nerve.

"Where are you going?" Virginia hollered after Rosemary, shaking her head. Rosemary felt as if she were always running. This time, it was towards her future.

Albert

Albert was pulling ripe tomatoes off the vines in the garden when he noticed a flash of color, a skirt flapping as the wearer sprinted towards him. Her blonde hair bounced with each of her footfalls, the curls shining in the sunlight. His heart hammered against his breast bone. Rosemary. Her arms flailed as she came towards him, swinging in wild circles. She stopped short, leaning against the garden fence. Her chest heaved as she struggled to catch her breath. Albert couldn't help but smile. She was always over-exerting herself, pushing herself to her physical limits.

"Hi there, are you okay?" he asked, laughing as her cheeks puffed in and out. She nodded, holding up her finger to say wait a minute. Her face was flushed, red splotches on her cheeks, drops of sweat forming on her brow. She rubbed her forehead with the back of her wrist, her delicate white wrist. Albert felt the quivering in his abdomen that he always felt when he observed Rosemary, that tense excitement that her presence made him feel.

She tried to regulate her breathing so she could speak. Albert wiped his hand on his trousers and walked to the other side of the fence.

"To what do I owe this honor?" he stood near her, feeling the heat radiate off her body, smelling her fragrant sweat. It was intoxicating to him, like a moth to a flame.

"Albert, I…" she began. His pulse quickened, pounding in his ears. She took another deep breath before speaking again. "I know I've hurt you. I made a huge mistake in not believing that you would come back. And I have to live with that." She looked pained. "I'm sorry I hurt you. But I don't regret having my children. I would not undo the past, because if I did, I wouldn't have my children. I love them so much."

She fidgeted, her fingers running over the top of the wire fencing, twisting a piece of loose wire.

"I know, Rosemary," he said. "It's the past and we can't change it."

"You're right," she interrupted him. "It is the past. And I've been living in regret for my past actions. Today, my sister told me to see the good before me. And, Al, you are the good."

Albert felt the heat rise to his face, blushing. He'd waited for her to come to him, to say these words, and they felt even better than he could have imaged they would. His ears vibrated, ringing as the words traveled through him.

"You've been there for me the whole time—bringing licorice for me at work, taking me home when I found out I'd lost my children. Always there. Albert, my love for you has never changed. It's just that my fear was stronger. I didn't want to be alone, so I did something foolish. But I still love you. I always will. I just wanted, no *needed*, to tell you how I felt. And if you think I'm damaged or a ruined woman because I'm divorced and have two children who I've lost, I won't hold it against you…"

Albert interrupted her with a kiss. He took her in his arms, the back of her dress warm and wet. Her lips were open, surprised by his sudden movement, of his lips on hers. He breathed into her, all of his disappointments and fears melting from him, dissolving into the ground around them. This is what he had been waiting for, this is what he went to war to come back to, her open arms, her lips returning his kiss.

She broke away, pushing off his chest. Her eyes were full

of fear, the sadness threatening to return. "Do you think I'm damaged?" she asked, trepidation shaking her voice. He wilted, powerless against her enormous fear. He pulled her to him, just holding her thin frame against his, feeling her heart hammering, like his was, the thundering between them.

"No, Rosie. No. I don't think you are damaged. I wish you had waited for me. But you didn't. My feelings for you never changed either. I love you. You kept me alive while I was over there. Even when I got the letter. I was crushed, but even that didn't change my feelings. When I came back and heard about your troubles, I was sad for you. I never wanted any pain or sadness for you. I only want you to be happy. And I hope that you will be happy with me, that we can make a life together."

He took her face in his hands, his brown skin against her smooth white face. The steel gray eyes were blurred with tears, but Albert could still see. The fear was gone, the sadness faded.

"What do you want, Rosie?" he asked.

"I want you!" she cried, throwing her arms around his neck, clinging to him. "I want to make a life together."

Albert swayed with her in his arms. He never thought he could feel like this—this complete, this *alive*. His future flashed—drives in the country together, making a family, Sunday masses together, big family holidays. He wanted to fuse their lives together, to love her for the rest of his life.

"Then that's what we'll do, Rosie. That's what we'll do," he said, sealing his promise, his future with a deep, passionate kiss. Rosemary returned his kiss with equal passion and love. That is what they would do—they would build a life together, one that they had both dreamed of, one that was better than they had dreamed of. *This was worth the wait*, Albert thought. Worth the heartache and disappointments, because he knew that Rosemary was the only woman for him. And he knew they would have a wonderful life together. He couldn't wait for it to begin.

1950

Rosemary

Rosemary pulled at her white lace, elbow-length gloves. She looked to her mother, who fussed with her veil. This was the day that Rosemary had been dreaming about her entire life. They stood in one of the side rooms of St. Anthony's Church, preparing for Rosemary's wedding to Albert. Albert, her rock, her dark angel. He had been there through a second custody case, standing at her side as she fought for the children, only to lose once again to Harry. Albert had comforted her, had held her and told her everything would work out.

Now she smoothed the front of her wedding dress. It was light blue, as she didn't feel that white would be appropriate since it was her second marriage. The dress fell to the floor, chiffon tulle floating over the skirt, flaring from her satin waistband. The bodice was simple blue taffeta with cap sleeves.

Her mother lifted the rounded light blue fabric tiara with attached white veil. She placed it on Rosemary's head. Rosemary stared into the mirror, noticing their reflections. They had the same cheekbones, straight nose, small mouths. Rosemary had never realized how much she looked like her mother before. She may look like her mother, but Rosemary was much more emotional.

"You look beautiful, Rosie," she said. Rosemary swelled with pride, drinking in the rare compliment.

"Ready, Rosie?" her father stuck his head into the tiny dressing room. He looked dashing, the color back in his face. He had made a recovery, the tuberculosis fading once he took the penicillin, a new medicine that had been created during the war. Rosemary's heart swelled to see her father healthy again. The doctor warned that it may not last, but Rosemary didn't care. He was here for her special day. She took her father's arm—it was slender, but strong and solid. Rosemary glanced up in her father's face and nodded that she was ready to go.

They moved to the rear of the church as the organ filled the nave with the Wedding March. Rosemary peered out from under the veil, everything fuzzy. She could see Wilma, her attendant, standing to the left of the altar, looking regal in her yellow chiffon dress and wide brimmed hat. She wore yellow elbow length gloves and a smile that swept across her entire face. On the other side of the altar was Larry, Albert's brother and attendant. And next to him was Albert. Albert looked dashing in his gray suit, the yellow carnation pinned to his lapel. His hair was slicked back off his face, his brown eyes shining, the cleft in his chin appearing deeper. He shifted as he watched Rosemary's father lead her down the aisle to him.

Rosemary's heart rushed out in front of her to meet Albert at the altar. She had to hold herself back from running after it and throwing herself into Albert's arms. Rosemary squeezed her father's arm, urging him to walk faster, but he maintained his even pace. She couldn't believe that the day was here, that she was walking down the aisle to marry the man who had loved her, still loved her, in spite of all the false steps she'd taken.

This was how it was supposed to be, married in the eyes of God, joined together as man and wife. *Thank you, God*, Rosemary looked upward, *for bringing me back to Albert*. Rosemary thought of their first meeting at the Paddock Club, she was so nervous, she couldn't speak to him. The night he told her he loved her, she went from being so angry to realizing that she loved him too. And then breaking his heart... and he had still wanted her, he had never waivered in his love for her. The butterflies stirred inside her, fluttering up and down her spine, her arms and legs. She floated to her place before the altar, the candles flickering and the veil creating a dream-like state. Her father lifted the gauzy veil, and the dream lifted. This was really happening. He bent forward and kissed her cheek, placing her hand into Albert's.

Albert—he took her hand, his strong hand cradling hers, urging her to trust that he would take care of her, always and forever. She looked in his intense brown eyes and saw what she had been searching for, what she was trying to find—security, comfort, and love. Love radiated from him, bathing her in warmth and devotion. Her face broke into a smile, a true smile, knowing that this was her purpose in life, this was where she was meant to be—as Albert's wife and partner.

Albert

The palms of Albert's hands were clammy. He tried to wipe them on his pants, but then thought better of it since he didn't want a mark on them. His brother Larry thumped him on the back. Albert waited, as he had been doing for a long time. This moment had gotten him through his combat experience in Germany. All along, Albert had never doubted that he and Rosemary would be together. It had seemed hopeless at times, but Albert never lost his resolve.

The organ started to play, the pipes vibrating, and Albert looked to the rear of the church. And there she was, her face covered by the white gossamer veil. Her father looked proud, his head lifted high as he walked down the long marble aisle. Rosemary's chiffon netting swirled back and forth as she walked in time with her father. Albert wanted to see her face, to see if she was smiling. He strained to look through the veil, but he could not make out her features. He just wanted to know that she wanted this as much as he did, that it was worth all the trials and tribulations that had to go through to get to this place.

"Who gives away this woman in holy matrimony?" the priest's voice boomed into the cavernous church. Rosemary's father assented and lifted the veil. Albert's heart rose as the veil rose, climbing up his throat, lodging there, choking off his breath. Rosemary turned to face him. Her lips were drawn into a smile, small crimson lips stretching against her skin. Her cheeks were flush, rosy. But Albert had to see her eyes. And he looked into the steely blue eyes, holding his breath. Rosemary's eyes shone, the sadness and anxiety melted away. All Albert could see was love, love filled her entire face. Albert took her hand. It was clammy—like his. He smiled at her, reassuring her that this was what they were meant to be doing. He felt her shoulders relax as they turned and faced the priest.

The ceremony was a blur, words, readings of love. All Albert wanted was to be man and wife.

"Repeat after me," the priest turned to Albert.

"I, Albert Jedoga, take thee, Rosemary Connor, to be my lawfully-wedded wife. I promise to be true to thee in good times and in bad, in sickness and in health. I will love thee and honor thee all the days of my life." Albert thought his heart would explode, the happiness he felt was overflowing from him, like a flooded river breaking its levee. He wanted to swim in this happiness.

Now, Rosemary repeated, "I, Rosemary Connor, take thee, Albert Jedoga, to be my lawfully-wedded husband. I promise to be true to thee in good times and in bad, in sickness and in health. I will love thee and honor thee all the days of my life." She blushed under Albert's intense gaze, flushing with pleasure. She looked up at Albert, causing his stomach to flip over.

They exchanged the rings, Albert finally being able to put the ring on her finger which he had been holding since he left for Europe. It sparkled on her slender finger, giving weight to her frail hand, but not caging her and chaining her to him. Rosemary beamed, shining brighter than the golden ring.

Finally, the priest said the final blessing, concluding the ceremony. Albert and Rosemary turned to the congregation as the priest said, "I now introduce to you Mr. and Mrs. Albert Jedoga. What God has joined together, let no man put asunder."

Let no man put asunder. Albert looked at Rosemary, his heart full, beating heavily, the blood pounding through his ears. He squeezed her hand, felt the flesh and bones move. She was real, she was standing next to him—his wife. Rosemary looked up at him at the pressure in her hand, smiling, finally smiling through her eyes. Albert leaned over and put his lips on hers, sealed their marriage with a sign of their love, a physical showing of how many disappointments they both had overcome in their lives before they were able to stand here, together, and finally join their lives together as one.

Epilogue

Rosemary and Albert had been married for twenty-three years when I was born. My mom was the second of their children. As a child, there were many things that I didn't realize. I didn't realize that Aunt Kathleen had a different father than my grandpa or that my grandma had been married before. That came later.

I used to ride my bike over to my grandparents' house, a little white bungalow on a shady street in Streator. Even as a child, the house seemed tiny, too small to contain all of the lives that it nurtured. My grandma planted lots of flowers all over the yard—a lily of the valley patch up front, a tulip bed in the back. My grandfather kept a garden in back as well, but it was difficult to grow much there. He managed to coax tomatoes, green beans, and cucumbers from the coal-covered earth. The green beans were the sweetest I'd ever tasted, crisp and juicy.

Albert died in 1985 when I was twelve. I was just beginning to learn about World War II. I remember when I was smaller, maybe five or six, he was sitting in his easy chair in the living room in just an undershirt. I crawled onto his lap and saw the scar, still purple all those years later, and asked him what happened. He smiled and said it happened in the war. My mother scolded me later, "Don't ever ask him about the war! He doesn't like to talk about it." He never did tell any of his children or my grandma what happened in the war. My grandma told me that he and Junie would sit at the picnic table on the side patio and talk in hushed voices about what they saw in Europe, the things that happened during the war. My cousin inherited his Bronze Star and Purple Heart. There was no information about where he had been injured, and I was left to speculate.

Rosemary and Albert remained close to their siblings. I remember picnics at my Aunt Norma and Uncle Merle's house. They moved into Rosemary's childhood home, and Virginia still lived next door. All of us kids would run around in the shade of the oak trees while the adults played poker at the picnic tables.

I remember my Great Uncle Junie as a joker. His wooden leg fascinated me as a child. Whenever I saw him, I would ask, "Which leg's your wooden leg, Uncle Bill?"

He would extend both of his legs and say, "See if you can figure it out!"

I'd reach my tiny hand around his left leg, and it was strong, muscular, but flesh. I'd wrap my hand around his right leg and his pant would slide over the wood, no flesh resisting. My face would light up with the realization.

"It's this one, Uncle Bill!"

"Right again," he'd say and rumple my hair.

My grandfather introduced me to the majesty and pageantry of the Catholic faith. Right before he died, when I was twelve, he took me to Easter Vigil mass, the mass the night before Easter. We held slim, tapered white candles and sang hymns. His deep brown eyes sparkled in the candle light. It felt like a secret society that we were being inducted into. I remember going into the courtyard to throw the candles into a big bonfire, to symbolize Jesus dispelling the darkness from our hearts. It was so mystical and wondrous to me as a child.

When I was older, years after my grandfather died, I went

to my grandma's house and drank beers with her, sitting at the kitchen table, the winter sun low in the sky. She would play Hank Williams' music and polkas. She loved to dance polkas at weddings. By this time, I knew she had been married before my grandfather, and I was curious about it. She seemed like such an enigma to me, full of secrets and a secret life of which I knew nothing. I wanted to know more about her relationship with Harry and what made her marry him. I had met him once, spending the weekend with my cousin, Kathleen's daughter, in Taylorville with him.

"So what happened between you and Grandpa?" I asked. I had figured out the timeline, knew that she had met my grandfather before he left for the war, but didn't marry him until 1950. I wanted to know how she could marry Harry when Grandpa was fighting in Europe. Was she really frightened that Albert wouldn't come back as I had imagined? She waved her hand, trying to brush me off.

"Oh, I don't remember," she said, taking a long drag from her cigarette. Not remembering, that was her alibi when she didn't want to talk about something.

"Well, what happened? Were you engaged to Grandpa before he left for the war? What did you tell Grandpa when you married Harry?" I pressed her, fascinated and curious as to her motivations.

"I wrote him a Dear John letter," she said, her voice dropping an octave.

"Grandma!" I said, shocked to hear that my grandma was one of those women.

She looked past me, lost in her memories that were tightly locked in her mind.

"I only kept one letter from him," she said. "I was afraid Harry would find them."

"Can I see it?" I asked, my heart thundering at the possibility of reading my grandfather's words to my grandma when he was in the middle of the war.

She got up and went into her room. She came out with a box full of memories—pictures, news clippings, Christmas cards, wedding invitations, laminated prayer cards. After rifling through the box, she produced a yellowed envelope. My grandma's name and address were written in my grandfather's tight script. An airmail stamp was smudged in the corner. I opened the envelope and took out the letter carefully, as if it were a holy relic. The pages were yellowed and brittle. The Red Cross logo was at the top. I read the letter, the emotion of my grandfather coming forth. This was not the man I remembered. My grandfather was never this open with his feelings. This letter also helped me to pinpoint when he had been injured.

"Here's a picture from when we were dating," my grandma handed a small black and white photo to me. She sat in the lower left corner, around the table were my grandpa, his brothers and sister and Grandma Jedoga, as I knew her. Their faces radiated happiness.

"Oh, and here's our wedding album," my grandma said, pulling a book out of the box. She had several 8x10 black and white photos. There was one of her and my grandfather kneeling in front of the priest, my grandmother's dress fanning out around her legs. The picture was taken from the balcony.

"The photographer wasn't allowed down in the church," my grandma explained. I picked up one photo of my grandpa lifting a piece of cake to my grandma. Her mouth was open and her eyes sparkled with joy. My grandpa was looking at the camera, a huge grin on his face, the cleft in his chin deepened.

"He was so handsome," my grandma said, sighing.

I decided to write their love story, the good, the bad and the ugly. I didn't want to shy away from the unpleasantness of Rosemary's actions or of what Albert saw in Europe. I wanted to show them as flawed, *human* characters. Harry may seem like a villain in this story, but he was not. He was just a human being with his own set of flaws just like my grandma, and all of us, have.

I mined my grandma for whatever information I could get out

of her. I pried the story out of her, bit by bit. She told me about throwing my grandpa's keys into the cornfield after he got fresh with her on Airport Road and how upset he was because it was his father's car. I marveled at my grandma's nerve. She wouldn't or couldn't remember much about her marriage to Harry, other than they had fun and she wondered if Harry was in the KKK. Sometimes she wouldn't answer my questions, claiming she forgot or it happened too long ago to remember. But more often than not, she answered my questions. Those answers gleaned from my grandmother became her side of the story.

Albert's story was harder to develop. No one in my family knew what he had experienced in Europe, where he fought, what happened to him. Through the wonders of the internet, I found a book written by the 304th Infantry. My heart dropped and then swelled with pride when I saw my grandpa's name listed under Purple Heart and Bronze Star lists. I discovered he was a staff sergeant. With the letter my grandma had saved and knowing which company he was in, I deduced where he had seen action and the likeliest location of his injury. I felt guided while writing his chapters and flooded by images, maybe my grandpa's memories that made the scenes authentic, I hope. I believe my grandpa helped me to write those chapters.

The rosemary plant, Rosmarinus officinalis, is a symbol of remembrance. That is what this story is, my way to keep my grandparent's story alive for generations to come. Much of the thoughts of Rosemary and Albert are entirely my imagination, what I thought they would have said to each other and done during the war years. I never met my grandma's first husband Harry, so his character is entirely my imagination and probably bears no resemblance to Harry the real man. My grandma did have a nervous breakdown while she was living there, but as with many other questions, she provided no logical explanation and tried to deny that it happened. My grandma had faults, but so does every human being. She never gave me an answer on why she married Harry when Albert was in Europe; I had to

277

infer from what I know of her and fill in the blanks to create the person I wanted her to be. She read the first two parts of the story before she passed away. She said with a wry smile, "I don't know about that Rosie character."

My grandma's name is appropriate. When I was writing this story, I would see the fragrant, evergreen hedges of rosemary in my Las Vegas neighborhood. It does what it needs to do to survive the harsh, desert climate. Rosemary also did what she had to in order to survive. She got a divorce in a time when not many women were getting divorces; she worked at Owens after the war when many women returned to their domestic duties. According to Greek mythology, Aphrodite, the goddess of love, was draped in a cloak of rosemary when she rose from the sea. Albert bathed Rosemary in love like the plant of her namesake. Even after the false start, they were able to put their trust in each other and heal all the hurt caused by World War II.